The Illuminator's Gift

The Voyages of the *Legend*, Book 1

By Alina Sayre

The Illuminator's Gift

The cover illustration was painted on cold press illustration board with watercolor and acrylic paints and detailed in pen and ink.

ISBN: 1494226227

ISBN-13: 978-1494226220

Dedication

This book is dedicated to Mama, Daniel, Michael, and Whitney:
the tent pegs who hold me up.

And to Papa, who was the storyteller in the first place.

Contents

Acknowledgments

Making this book has been a bit like raising a child—it has taught me that nothing big happens as a result of one person alone. Though I can't possibly recognize everyone who has helped or encouraged me on this page, here are a few without whom this book might never have seen the light of day.

First thanks go to God, the first Author and Artist. His call is the reason I am a storyteller, and this book came from Him and is for Him.

To Mama: Without you, I really might have ended up writing this book in a cardboard box! Thank you for believing in this dream of mine enough to house me, feed me, and listen to random spurts of book information, even at weird hours. Thank you for doing psychoanalysis on my characters (and recommending therapy for some of them). Thank you for the beautiful VR logo, for helping me name chapters, and for crying over that first story when I was eleven—without that, I might still think I hated writing.

To Daniel: Thanks for rolling your eyes over my rejection of natural laws and helping me devise new ones! Your ship designs, creative brainstorms, and diplomatic nods have been great.

To Michael: Neither this book nor I would be what we are without you. Thank you for being my action scene consultant, for listening to my dreams for this book, for your Photoshop wizardry, for building an amazing website, and for believing I could do this.

To Whitney: Sister, you've read drafts, cried over these characters, and talked me out of giving up on this book. You are my Jariel. Who could have imagined this in our Story Weavers days?

Thank you to my test readers: Amy and Sarah B., Bekah G., Bob F., Marlee B., Michael D., Paty G., Peter S., and Rod and Braden T. Your comments and ideas transformed the final draft!

Thank you to Bekah, friend and editor, for promptly and professionally dotting my I's and crossing my T's.

Thanks to Angela for blazing the writing and publishing trails ahead of me. Thank you also for doing the e-book format!

Thanks to Audry for the creative meets over coffee, your words of encouragement, and your insights into art and typography.

And last but by no means least: thank you to Mollie, a real-life illuminator, for the AMAZING cover art! A few months ago, I couldn't even have imagined this beauty you've created. Thank you for your enthusiasm for this story, your visionary ideas, and your willingness to learn about book publishing with me.

Chapter 1
The Orphan

Ellie pulled the shreds of her sketchbook closer as the carriage jolted to a stop. Just outside, a tall, narrow building stood at attention like a tired old soldier. The chipping white shutters hung crookedly on their hinges, and a weathered sign read *Sketpoole Home for Boys and Girls.* Aunt Loretha yanked open the carriage door and shoved Ellie out.

"Not one word from you, miss," Aunt Loretha hissed, stepping out and straightening her hat. "You so much as open your mouth in there, and I'll whip your backside till the hide comes off."

Ellie pressed her lips together tightly. She'd already tried arguing and pleading, to no avail. Uncle Horaffe and Ewart followed them to the front door, where Aunt Loretha let the tarnished iron knocker strike with a deep *boom.*

After a moment, a maid with frizzled gray-brown hair answered the door.

"Welcome to the Home for Girls an' Boys, mum. Have you come to adopt an orphan?"

Aunt Loretha forced a tight smile. "No. Actually, I'm afraid we've come to return one."

The maid's forehead puckered. "We're awful full, mum. But I'll let Miss Sylvia know you've arrived."

Uncle Horaffe's hat brushed the dim entryway ceiling. The walls were dingy with fingerprints, and a basket of mending sat on a crooked side table. The sound of many children screaming and playing came from a back room.

"This place smells like fish," remarked Ewart.

Aunt Loretha sniffed disdainfully. "Why yes, it does. I do hope this business doesn't take long."

Ellie fingered the fraying handle of her carpetbag. She already knew that it wouldn't take long. They would argue. The orphanage keeper would reluctantly agree to take her. And another family would walk out of her life before the smell of orphanage could stick to them.

She and Ewart had been with Aunt Loretha in the marketplace only that morning. Aunt Loretha was shopping for a new hat before they all set out on the ship for Bramborough. Ellie had never been on a ship before. While Aunt Loretha was busy in front of a booth, Ewart leaned toward Ellie, lowering his voice to a whisper.

"Puddle-eyes."

Ellie didn't look at him, letting the insult roll off her back.

"Maybe that's why you can't read. You can't see through all the water."

She glanced up at the sky, wondering if it would rain.

"Oh, but the real reason you can't read is because you're so thickheaded," said Ewart with a smirk. "I forgot."

Ellie turned her back to him. She watched a vendor slice open a smooth-skinned yellow *blethea* fruit, exposing the hundreds of tiny purple seeds within. Ellie's fingers drummed against her leg, tingling to draw the textures, the colors. As the vendor pushed his sleeve out of the juice, Ellie caught a glimpse of a silver tattoo in the crook of his elbow.

It looked like intertwined letters, perhaps a V and an R, but he tugged the sleeve back over it before Ellie could get a really good look.

"You read like a three-year-old." Ewart popped back up in front of her. "I can read a whole book in the time it takes you to read one page."

"Ewart! I think your mother's calling you," Ellie said. As he turned to look, Ellie ducked behind a barrel. She quickly pulled her sketchbook from under her coat and glanced from the piece of cut fruit to the paper, her pencil stub darting quickly back and forth.

Without warning, Ewart snatched the book out of her hands, his leering face inches from hers. "You're so worthless. No wonder your parents didn't want you."

Ellie jumped to her feet.

"Ewart, you give that back!"

"Make me!" His eyes glittered as he danced backward.

She lunged for him. "Give it *back,* I said!"

"Worthless little orphan." With a glint in his eyes, Ewart dangled the book over a puddle filled with mud and horse droppings.

Ellie's eyes widened.

"Ewart, please don't. That's my sketchbook."

He loosened his grip on the book, now suspending it by just one page.

"Please!" she begged. "I'll give you whatever you want. You can have my special red pencil."

"I don't care about your pencil." His smile was slow, but his hands moved quickly. Ellie saw the rip before she heard it. Shreds of paper, beloved pictures of things both real and imagined, fluttered down into the manure like torn butterfly wings.

With a scream of pain, Ellie jumped at him. He dodged and ripped out another fistful of pages, the sound raking jaggedly over her ears. She reached for his throat, but he grabbed her wrist, dropping what remained of the book into the mud puddle. Blind with desperation and fury, Ellie used the only weapon left to her. She bit down on Ewart's soft-skinned hand. Shrieking like a little girl, he let Ellie go. She pulled her sketchbook, dripping, from the mud puddle and wiped it carefully on her coat.

But Aunt Loretha heard Ewart's scream. One look at the red marks on Ewart's fleshy thumb, and she shot Ellie a glare that meant doom. With Ellie's ear firmly pinched between her fingers, Aunt Loretha marched them home and ordered Ellie to start packing.

Through a door at the opposite end of the orphanage hallway, a woman appeared, wiping her hands on a faded apron. Though she had silver hair, which was wound into a bun at the nape of her neck, her back was straight and her gray eyes clear.

"Good afternoon," she said. "I am Sylvia Galen, keeper of the Sketpoole Home for Boys and Girls. How may I help you?"

Aunt Loretha spoke in the syrupy voice she only used when she was bargaining for something in the marketplace.

"Good day. My name is Loretha Cooley, and I'm here to return an orphan."

Miss Sylvia looked from Ewart, dressed in a new black wool coat, to Ellie, wearing the brown tweed the Cooleys had adopted her in. "One of these children?"

Aunt Loretha's smile grew strained. Her plump hands took Ewart by the shoulders and pulled him toward her.

"*This* is my son, Ewart Horaffe Theodemir Cooley. This," she prodded Ellie forward, "is the orphan."

"Ah. And what is your name, young lady?"

"I'm Ellie . . . ma'am."

"I'm very pleased to meet you, Ellie. Come into my office, all of you." Miss Sylvia gestured toward a side door.

A desk piled with papers and three mismatched chairs were the only pieces of furniture in the small room. "I apologize for the mess," said Miss Sylvia, sweeping papers to the side of the desk. "We've had so many new children come in this month that I've hardly had a moment to think. Please, sit down. So you want to return this young lady to us? Did you adopt her from here?"

One of the fragile stick chairs groaned loudly under Aunt Loretha as Uncle Horaffe took the other. Ewart shifted uncomfortably from foot to foot. Ellie looked out the window. The sky, blackening like a bruise, threatened rain. A little girl was trying to untangle her feet from a skipping rope in the yard, and two small boys tugged a cloth horse back and forth. Ellie wondered if there were any children her age here.

"No," Aunt Loretha answered Miss Sylvia. "We brought her from . . . from another part of the island three years ago."

"Three and a half," said Ewart.

She silenced him with an acid smile. "We thought we'd find a better life here in Sketpoole, but living here is simply too costly. We're moving to Bramborough, taking a ferry this very evening, because we simply can't afford to live here anymore. Why, we can barely keep our Ewart in shoes, let alone give him the education his fine mind deserves. And feeding and sheltering an orphan on top of it all! We'll be ruined." She gave a theatrical sigh. "So we simply can't keep Ellie, you see. You do understand, don't you? We only want to do what's best for the child, since we can't care for her properly."

Ellie couldn't suppress a smile. Aunt Loretha could have made it as a stage actress.

"Isn't there a way you could—rearrange your finances to include Ellie in your plans?" asked Miss Sylvia, leaning forward on the desk. "Perhaps—take out a line of credit until times improve?"

Aunt Loretha dramatically waved her handkerchief in the air. "Oh! You have no idea what creditors are like these days. Wolves. Simply animals. That would be impossible."

"I understand it would require some sacrifices, Mrs. Cooley," said Miss Sylvia, her gaze traveling over Aunt Loretha's ostentatious purple hat, adorned with a real *drunyl* feather. "But you did make the commitment to adopt Ellie, and it is your responsibility to fulfill that commitment. Only in the very direst of circumstances would we allow you to return her."

"Well," Aunt Loretha lowered her voice confidentially. "I don't like to bring this up, especially with the child here, but . . . well, you see, she has *fits.*"

Ellie raised her eyebrows.

"Fits?" said Miss Sylvia. "Are you saying that the child is insane, Mrs. Cooley?"

"Oh, I would hardly call it that," said Aunt Loretha with a nervous laugh. "There are simply—moments when she can't control herself. Why, this very morning, she *bit* my son Ewart. Come here, Ewart; show the lady your hand. The girl is good help around the house, and I know she'll do you good service, but I simply cannot have her around my son."

Miss Sylvia inspected the red marks on Ewart's hand dispassionately. She shook her head. "I am sorry for your difficulties, Mrs. Cooley, but I cannot help you. We are very full, and we simply cannot accept a child with an existing family."

Aunt Loretha stood up, banging her hand on the desktop. Her lips trembled with rage. "We are not her family! She's returned our hospitality with violence. She's an ungrateful little leech, and I'll leave her here if I have to drop her on your doorstep!"

Miss Sylvia rose as well, looking coolly from Aunt Loretha to Ellie, who was trying to melt into the wall.

"Well, if that's the case, we may just have room after all," she said, her voice low and tight. Her eyes blazing pale fire, she slapped a stack of papers down on the desk. "Sign this. By doing so, you relinquish all claims on the child. Permanently."

Aunt Loretha grabbed a pen from the desk with equal vigor. "With pleasure." She scribbled off her signature and thrust the pen at Uncle Horaffe, who did the same.

"Well," said Aunt Loretha, straightening her drunyl-feather hat ferociously. "That's the last we see of *you,* Ellie. Goodbye and good riddance. Come along, Ewart, Horaffe."

Miss Sylvia saw the Cooleys out, but Ellie stayed in the office, watching through the window as their carriage pulled away, taking her last hopes of family with it. Maybe some people just weren't good enough to belong.

Chapter 2
The One Kingdom

"Ellie?"

Miss Sylvia stepped back into the office, closing the door behind her. She looked at Ellie a long time. "Well, it seems you have come to join us here," she said.

"I'm sorry to add to your crowding, Miss Sylvia. I know how it is. This is the fourth orphanage I've lived at."

"The fourth?" Miss Sylvia's voice softened. "Well. You are welcome here. Let me show you to the dormitory."

Ellie followed Miss Sylvia back into the hallway. Turning the corner to go up the stairs, they nearly ran into a girl sitting on the third step. Ellie blinked when she saw the girl's hair—a tangled, outrageous orange shock, deep as a sunset, bright as a wild poppy. She'd only seen hair that color on one other person in her whole life. The girl watched Ellie with an intense pair of dark eyes, huge in her freckled face.

"So, have you come to stay?" she demanded, her bony arms wrapped around her knees.

Ellie glanced at Miss Sylvia. "I . . . think so."

"Hooray!" The girl launched herself off the stairs, tackling Ellie with a squeeze so tight that Ellie thought her ribs might crack.

"I'm so glad there's finally someone else my age here!" The red-haired girl grinned, a huge grin that showed all her teeth, even the crooked ones. "And you're a girl, too. We're going to be friends." Suddenly, as if remembering a formality, she jumped back and stuck out her hand.

"I'm Jariel. Jariel Kirke. Who are you?"

Ellie kept hold of her carpetbag, declining the handshake. "Ellie Altess."

Jariel kept talking. "Pretty bad scene you had there. Those people sounded like beasts. I'm sure we have it better than that here. Sure, we have chores, and lessons, and have to help with the littler kids, but when they're all in bed, you get to sneak downstairs and beg cookies off of Chinelle in the kitchen—oops, sorry, Miss Sylvia." She grinned at the orphanage keeper. "Anyway, orphanages aren't so bad if you have someone who knows the ins and outs. I'll be your guide."

"Thanks, but you don't have to," Ellie said. "I already know how orphanages work."

There was a pause. Jariel shifted from foot to foot. Suddenly a chorus of screams erupted from the back room, and Miss Sylvia looked over her shoulder. "That sounds like trouble. Jariel, would you please show Ellie to the girls' dormitory?"

"Sure!" Jariel brightened and bounded up the stairs, two at a time. Ellie climbed more slowly, listening to the hollow, echoing sound her footfalls made in the cold stairwell.

Jariel's voice bubbled down from above her. "We'll have to drag in a cot for you from the storage room. You can put it next to mine, if you like. Then we can whisper after the lamps are out."

At the top of the stairs, Jariel turned the knob on a door to the left. It was a small room cluttered with old furniture.

"Here, help me out with this," said Jariel. Ellie set down her carpetbag and the two girls wrestled a squeaky metal bedframe and a thin mattress from the room. Huffing and puffing, they carried it down the hall and stopped in front of a doorway to the right.

"Home sweet home," panted Jariel. At the end of a long, dingy room, one window illuminated a dozen beds marching along each wall. The bare plaster walls were scarred with nail marks and strokes of dried glue, as if they had been stripped for painting but never finished. Some of the beds had a colorful blanket or a rag doll peeking from under their rough brown covers, and a few pieces of scribbled artwork were tacked to the walls. Ellie's eyes took it all in. It looked so familiar.

"We've been in this building nearly four years, but you can't tell," said Jariel, walking backward as they carried the new bed into the dormitory. "Miss Sylvia wants to get it all fixed up and painted, but she's so busy looking after the kids and keeping the daily things running that nothing else ever gets done. This bed's mine." Jariel kicked the bedstead on her right, the one closest to the window. The wall above her pillow was a swirl of dried red and orange leaves, leftovers from a colorful autumn.

They squeezed Ellie's bed between Jariel's and the wall and set it down, panting. Jariel pulled down a big *meriaten* leaf from the wall.

"Here." She tacked the leaf above Ellie's bed and grinned. "Your first decoration. Maybe it'll make this feel more like home."

Ellie sat down on the edge of her new bed, listening as it creaked loudly. It was just a few metal bars and a mattress, probably one that dozens of kids had used before her. Even the floor space it sat on was borrowed. How could this feel like home?

"Do you want some help unpacking?" Jariel asked.

Ellie shook her head, her eyes wandering to the cold white window.

Jariel bit her lip. "I'll leave you alone, then. The bell will ring when it's time for supper."

The door closed behind her, and Ellie was glad for the quiet. This place wasn't nearly as military as the Liaflora County Orphanage, but it was an orphanage nonetheless. Ellie would have known it just by the smells: the cheap, harsh soap used to scrub dozens of pairs of stockings, the cold plaster of the walls, the mildew growing on the damp windowsill.

Ellie walked to the window, touching her nose to the cold glass. From here, she could see the closely clumped buildings of Sketpoole stretching away in a suffocating expanse of city. But just past the edge of the buildings, she could catch a tiny glimpse of the silver ocean, and she heard the distant bellow of a steamship's horn. In a few hours, the Cooleys would be leaving on just such a ship, forever turning their backs on this island—and on her.

Ellie vividly remembered the day the Cooleys entered her life. She had been sweeping in the orphanage entryway when they came in—a plump woman in a faded calico dress, a rail-thin man with sharp cheekbones, and a boy, about her own age, with a nose that turned up slightly at the end. One of his shoes had a hole in the toe. He glanced at her over his shoulder as Mr. Howditch, the orphanage keeper, ushered them into his office and shut the door.

Ellie stood a moment, her broom poised above the floor. She knew it wasn't right to eavesdrop—but was it her fault if sound carried through the door? She took a step closer, slowly sweeping the floor by the office wall.

". . . perhaps one about our son's age?" she heard the woman saying in a wheedling voice. "You see, Ewart's all we have, though we always wanted more children."

There were low murmurs Ellie couldn't catch. Then the woman again:

"Oh, boy or girl, it doesn't matter. We just want one *now,* today—we can't wait another minute." She gave a shrill giggle.

More low murmurs. Wood groaned as Mr. Howditch opened the big drawer in his desk.

"By the by"—the man was speaking now—"isn't there a new law in effect, something about . . . stipends for orphan adoption?" Ellie didn't know what a stipend was. She leaned closer to the door.

"Indeed," Mr. Howditch said. "Due to the current problems with overcrowding, the regent has offered a hundred *cillas* a year to any family who adopts an orphan, to help with the cost of raising the child."

"And how soon would the first payment come?"

"Most likely within a month of the adoption, but it depends on how long it takes the government to process the paperwork."

"Can't we have it now?" The woman's voice piped up again, now sounding a bit strained. She gave another artificial giggle. "I mean, there's school enrollment coming up so soon, and we want to get the child some proper clothes, and—as you can see—times haven't exactly been kind to us . . . "

"Well, that's not exactly in my control," said Mr. Howditch. "It's the government that sends me the money to pass on to you." A pause.

"Although, if it's really so urgent, it would be possible for me to write you an advance . . . "

"Done," said the man. "What do we sign?"

There was no more conversation, and Ellie jumped away from the door as it opened suddenly. She tried to look busy sweeping as Mr. Howditch stepped into the entryway, followed by the family.

"Ah." Mr. Howditch looked from her to the round-faced boy. "How old are you, Ellie?"

She tried her best to curtsy, but her legs wobbled. "Nine, sir." She nodded politely to the newcomers.

"Perfect!" exclaimed the woman, her eyes almost disappearing into the folds of her plump cheeks. "Just the same as our Ewart. We'll take her."

"Me?" Ellie gasped, clutching the broom handle for support.

"I don't see why not," said Mr. Howditch. "One free bed in the dormitory is as good as another. Pack your things quickly, Ellie. The Cooleys want to take you with them at once."

"Come here, Ellie, and give me a hug," sniffed the woman, dabbing her eyes with the corner of her smudged apron. "Call me Aunt Loretha, will you, dear? I do love the sound of that."

Half an hour later, Ellie was sitting in the back of a small wagon. It was dim under the oilcloth cover, and it smelled like smoke and grease inside, but Ellie didn't care. She could hardly believe her good fortune. After six months at the Liaflora County Orphanage and a few of Mr. Howditch's famous whippings, she hadn't much to show except a few more protruding ribs and a little less skin on her backside. At least at her last orphanage, Harwell House, there had always been enough to eat, even if the grassless yard had turned to a lake of mud every time it rained.

As Aunt Loretha climbed into the cart, her weight making it creak, Ellie closed her eyes and resolved to do whatever it took to make this family keep her. No matter what the Cooleys were like, she never wanted to go back to another orphanage. Maybe she really would be the daughter they'd never had. She opened her eyes and looked at Ewart, who was sitting across from her.

"Hello," she said, trying to sound friendly.

He leaned toward her, his small black eyes narrowing. He had soft skin like a baby's and greasy, dark brown hair that stuck to his forehead.

"You have funny eyes. Why are your eyes like that?"

"My eyes?" Ellie had never thought about them before. "Like what?"

"They're not even blue. More like . . . clear." He shuddered. "Ugh. It's like you can see through me. Gives me the creeps."

"I . . . I'm sorry?"

"Well, just try not to look at me, okay? Turn around."

"Oh . . . okay." Ellie moved to face the back of the wagon.

"Everything packed, Loretha?" The man's face appeared through a slit in the oilcloth wagon cover. He tossed a leather pouch to his wife. "These hundred cillas should set us up wherever we settle. But we'd better get a move on. If our creditors from Arbuck catch up to us, even this money won't be enough to pay them off."

"Yes, yes; everything's ready," she answered impatiently.

"Let's go, then." His face disappeared, and a moment later, the cart lurched forward.

"Don't mind Uncle Horaffe—he's a bit flustered at the moment," said Aunt Loretha to Ellie. "You've come to us at a bit of a difficult time, you see. We'll need your help getting settled in our new home, wherever it is. But once we get situated, I'm sure we'll be a happy family." She pulled Ellie in for a smothering squeeze.

"I'll do whatever you want me to, Aunt Loretha," said Ellie when she could breathe. "I'm just happy to be going with you. I hope you keep me forever."

"Well," said Aunt Loretha, surveying her. "You're not exactly the comeliest thing." She fingered a lock of Ellie's wispy, mouse-brown hair. "And zooks! Ewart, you were right about those eyes. Downright unnatural. But a little fattening up might help your looks, and if you do your work and don't complain, we might have cause to keep you for quite a long time." She smoothed the leather pouch flat and tucked it inside her bodice. "Quite a long time indeed."

Ellie sighed, her breath fogging out the vision as a bell clanged loudly. Downstairs, children began to run and shout, causing the upstairs windowpanes to rattle slightly. Ellie stepped in front of the mirror behind the door, her reflection split nearly in half by a long crack, torn in two like the pages of her sketchbook. She smoothed her hair and tried to brush the wrinkles out of her coat. On her first night in a new orphanage, she always tried to make a good impression. Were her eyes really that strange? They *were* very light blue, almost clear, like a cold winter sky, with black rings around the blue. But they weren't . . . *puddle-eyes.*

The dining room doorway was clogged with children fighting over a bucket of water where they were all trying to wash their hands.

Ellie took one look at the murky water and decided her own hands were clean enough. Inside the dining room, children were running around, tugging bowls back and forth, and racing each other to seats around the long table. The room stank of sweaty bodies and oil from the several guttering lamps around the room. Miss Sylvia sat at the head of the table, trying to feed three crying babies, while Jariel sat on the far bench, pinched between bookends of squirming little girls. She waved when Ellie came in.

"Oh Ellie, I'm so glad you're here," said Miss Sylvia. "Would you look after the other side of the table, please? I've already told Niara she can't be excused until she finishes her supper. Jardon, ask Ellie to help you button your cuffs."

"Look what I found!" A leggy girl with tangled brown pigtails thrust her hand into Ellie's face, revealing a very dead frog. Ellie's stomach lurched.

"Um . . . how about you go put that outside," she said faintly. "And . . . please wash your hands." She picked up a bowl for her own supper, but suddenly she didn't feel very hungry.

Miss Sylvia stood up and clapped her hands. "It is time to sing the blessing!"

The mob of children stood up noisily and grabbed hands. In the process, someone got pinched, someone's foot got stepped on, someone didn't want someone else's hand, and there was more crying. Ellie sighed and folded her own hands behind her back.

Miss Sylvia began to sing and some of the children joined in, warbling along tunelessly. Ellie listened to the words:

To you, our Father King

Our voices do we bring

For this food our thanks we give

Teach us how to truly live.

It was a strange moment, a bubble of time that was almost peaceful in the midst of so much chaos. But it did not last long. The echoes were soon drowned in the rumble and clatter of everyone scrambling for a seat. The maid, Chinelle, came in carrying a huge basket of whole potatoes, still in their skins. She hurried around the table, dropping one potato in each bowl. Moments later, she returned with a deep pot and poured a spoonful of thin gravy over the top. Before she'd even gone all the way around the table, three children had already spilled hot gravy on themselves and were crying, and one little boy had dropped his fork and couldn't find it. By the time Ellie got to her own potato, it was cold and gluey.

By the fireside after supper, Ellie bounced a screaming baby on her legs while Miss Sylvia told a story. At first she nearly had to yell to be heard over the din.

"Children, how many archipelagos are there?" Miss Sylvia asked. "Yes, Jardon?"

"Can I have a cookie?"

"Not now, Jardon. Someone else. How many archipelagos are in the ocean?"

"Fwee!" shouted a tiny girl, jumping to her feet.

"No, *four*," said a girl with brown pigtails, pulling her back to her seat.

"Very good, Adabel. There are four archipelagos in the ocean. But did you know that once upon a time, there were five?"

A chorus of *noes* resounded.

"Well," said Miss Sylvia, leaning forward. "Once upon a time, there was only one kingdom, and one king."

"Was he a bwave king?" asked a little boy.

"Yes," Miss Sylvia smiled. "He was immortal and powerful, yet he was also kind. He took time to listen to even the poorest people, and was not too busy to talk to children. It was his Song that bound the islands together in the One Kingdom, and all the islanders, from the Orkent Isles to the Numed Archipelago, called him Adona Roi, the Good King. There were so many islands in his kingdom, however, that Adona Roi could not personally give justice to all his subjects. So he appointed regents for all the islands. They governed on behalf of Adona Roi and kept peace for all the people. This went on for many years. But after several generations had passed, some regents forgot the Good King. They had never seen him for themselves, so they wondered if he was just a story made up by their ancestors. One of these was a young regent called Thelipsa. She administered justice on the island of Vansuil in the Elbarra Cluster."

"What is the Elbarra Cluster?" asked a little girl in front.

"It was a group of islands in the Southeast Quarter," said Miss Sylvia. "Now it is called the Lost Archipelago."

"Why?"

"Listen and I will tell you. Thelipsa was beautiful and very clever. But though Vansuil was the largest island in the Elbarra Cluster and she held much power, merely governing the island was not enough for her. She wanted to be its queen.

"She began to seek advisers, first from the other islands in the cluster, then from farther away. One of these was a man called Kaspar. Scales clung to his face instead of a beard, and webs grew between his long fingers. He was a servant of the evil monster Draaken and an enemy of the One Kingdom. Yet he was fair-spoken, and his advice Thelipsa preferred above all. He counseled her to make her own decisions instead of acting for a king she had never seen. She obeyed. She became too busy to listen to the poor, and she taxed the people heavily to beautify her own palace. Justice began to falter. But the web-fingered adviser counseled her to give away bread in the streets and throw festivals to keep the people quiet. She continued to obey. At last, he gave her a small vial that glittered as bright as diamonds.

"'This is the key to our liberty,' he said. 'Go down to the core of the island and pour this into the water. It will set us free from this imaginary king.'

"That night, under cloak of darkness, Thelipsa stole down to the center of the island. She went down, down, down a winding staircase until she reached the water level. There she saw the strand of pink coral, thick as a tree branch, which bound her island to the Elbarra Cluster. It glowed faintly in the dark, as all healthy coral does. Thelipsa took a deep breath and poured the contents of the vial into the water."

"Then what happened?" a little boy almost shouted. The baby in Ellie's lap started to cry at the noise, and Ellie bounced her knees up and down to calm it.

"The water went dark," said Miss Sylvia softly. "The glow of the coral was extinguished. For the vial had been full of the terrible poison called *asthmenos,* which is deadly to coral. The next morning, Vansuil shook with an earthquake as its coral broke, severing the island from the Elbarra Cluster. People screamed and held tight to one another during the shaking, but soon the shocks passed. Kaspar told Thelipsa to throw a celebration and announce their independence to the people. Her entertainments were lavish, and the people cheered when she introduced herself as Queen Thelipsa. But there was something even she did not know.

"Children, the ocean flows with an outward current. The current flows harmlessly past islands anchored down by healthy coral, but when Vansuil broke free, it began to drift outwards. Now, our ocean is wide, but it is not endless. Ultimately it comes to an Edge, where it is said the waterfall turns on its head and flows upward."

"What's on the other side?" Ellie asked, almost surprised to hear her own voice.

Miss Sylvia paused. "That, no living soul can tell. Perhaps it is an airless, sightless void where nothing can exist. Or perhaps the legendary city of Adona Roi is there—a city that floats above the clouds, a city which darkness and storm cannot touch. Our only certainty is that the Edge is the boundary of what we know—and that none who cross it ever return."

"So what happened to Vansuil?" said Jariel.

Miss Sylvia shook her head. "Kaspar never warned Thelipsa of the island's peril. In fact, he disappeared soon after she announced their independence. Thelipsa ruled for only a few weeks before her island reached the Edge. There it teetered for one moment before slipping into oblivion—taking her and all her deceived people with it.

"But there were consequences still more disastrous. The asthmenos did not disappear after it had killed Vansuil's branch of coral. It dissolved into the water, and the ocean spread it far and wide. It was not long before the other coral branches of the Elbarra Cluster began to die, severing first one island, then another. In time the entire archipelago's coral tree withered to a stump and all the islands of the cluster drifted away. And still the toxin continued to spread."

"So did all those people die?" asked Jariel.

"Many did," Miss Sylvia said. "But that is not the end of the story." She glanced up at the clock. "However, the rest must wait for another night. Now it is time for sleep."

Chapter 3
Sketches

The next morning after breakfast, Jariel handed Ellie a scrub brush and a pail of water.

"Chinelle does the cooking, dishes, and laundry, and Kyuler comes twice a week to run errands and deliver packages," she explained. "The rest is our job. Today's the floor." She grinned. "I pretend I'm a stowaway on a pirate ship. Ahoy there! Swab the deck, mate!" She tossed Ellie a quick salute, then headed for the dining room. Ellie got down on her hands and knees in the hallway. At least she'd rather scrub floors than deal with dead frogs.

After lunch, Miss Sylvia gave Ellie a faded brown book of sums and readings, along with a stub of charcoal pencil.

"Jariel already has a book of lessons," she said. "You two go in the dining room, where it's quiet, and work on these for a while. I have some things to do in the office, but I want you two to keep up on your education." She smiled, tired lines crinkling beside her eyes, and shut the door.

An hour later, Ellie's mind felt crushed with exhaustion and defeat. She'd already fought through two whole pages, not remembering much of what they said, and tried to answer the questions at the bottom. But then she turned the page, and there was yet another regiment of letters rising up to meet her in battle. Ellie's shoulders slumped and she leaned her forehead on her arms.

"Ugh! These sums are impossible," Jariel groaned, dropping her pencil to the tabletop with a clatter. "Why should I care if eighteen and fourteen make thirty-two? They could make a hundred for all I care."

Ellie sat up, nodding emphatically. "The letters, too. They always seem like they're trying to scramble themselves up instead of make words." She leaned her chin on the tabletop, her eyes level with the book.

"What are you doing?" Jariel asked.

"It looks more interesting this way. You can see the roughness of the paper and the way the ink stands up off the page. It makes the letters look like they're going to jump into the air and fly." She inhaled through her nose. "They smell good, too."

"Really?" Jariel lifted her own book to her nose and breathed in. "I never knew books had a smell! Reminds me of . . . " she breathed in again. "Dust!"

"Mine smells like cinnamon."

"I want to smell yours!" Jariel switched the books and breathed deeply. "Yep. I like yours better. What's this?" She turned the book sideways, looking at the margin.

Ellie snatched the book back. "Nothing."

Jariel cocked an eyebrow. "Then why are you hiding it?"

"I'm not. I'm just . . . done with my lesson."

Jariel put her hands on her hips. "Ellie. I'm not a fool. You don't have to show it to me if you don't want to, but I know it's something."

Ellie chewed on her bottom lip. "Promise you won't tell anyone?"

Jariel's eyes sparkled and she scooted closer. "Not a word."

Ellie hesitated, then passed the book back to Jariel.

In the bottom margin of the page was a border of fluffy clouds. At the corner, they transformed into the quick lines of a whirlwind that became strands of hair, and ultimately a face. The profile was unmistakable: the sharp nose and chin, the liberal sprinkling of freckles, the wide mouth turned upward in a smile.

Ellie squirmed. "Sorry."

Jariel beamed. "I think it's neat. Especially the way those clouds are tied to my hair. It'd be like having pet clouds on a leash." She climbed up on the bench and pulled her wild red hair into a tail. "Heeere, little cloud, follow me!"

Ellie laughed. "Watch out, Miss Sylvia will hear you. Do you think she'll be mad at me for drawing in her book?"

Jariel shook her head. "I don't think she even checks these things. She's too busy changing all the diapers and hankies around here. And anyway, she'd probably think your drawing was too good to be mad at you."

"You really think so?" Ellie looked down at the page.

"Would I say it if I didn't mean it? I wish I could draw like that."

"I'd rather draw than read any day," said Ellie. "When I read, sometimes it's like the letters scramble up on purpose to confuse me. But when I draw, that doesn't matter. You can change the shape of a window or turn a tree upside down and make something that no one's ever seen before. Even the most ordinary things can be beautiful if you look at them differently. You might be better at drawing than you think. But you might like it more if you used colored pencils."

Jariel shrugged. "I don't have any."

"I have some in my satchel. You can borrow them if you like."

Jariel smiled. "Thanks." The clock on the wall began to strike. "Whoops!" She scrambled to her feet. "I forgot what time it was. We'd better bring the kids inside for their naps."

That night, Miss Sylvia continued her story. The children were quieter than usual.

"Now, the news of Thelipsa's Rebellion came by messenger bird to the city of Adona Roi, ruler of the One Kingdom, and to his son, named Ishua. Ishua was the commander of the winged armies, a fearless warrior who rode out to battle in armor that glittered like a thousand stars. Yet Ishua wept when he heard the news of the Rebellion.

"'Father, let me go to them,' he begged. 'They have been deceived by Draaken and his followers to rebel against the One Kingdom. Now their islands are diseased, but the leaves of our *stellaria* tree could heal their coral. I must teach them your Song and offer them a way to return home.'

"'You cannot take the winged armies, my son,' warned Adona Roi. 'The people would see you from miles away and think you had come for battle. They would defend themselves against you and never give you a chance to speak.'

"'Then let me go alone,' said Ishua.

"'You cannot wear your armor, my son,' warned Adona Roi a second time. 'The people would be afraid and run from you before you had a chance to speak.'

"'Then I will go in disguise,' said Ishua. 'I will walk among them, unarmed and sailing a lone ship. Then I might persuade some to listen and be rescued.'

"To this Adona Roi at last agreed, though there were tears in his eyes as he watched his son sail away in a ship that rode the air instead of the water. Ishua sailed for many months. His hair grew long and his cloak wore to tatters. The drifting islands were hard to track, but he found them all, one by one. Letting down a ladder from his ship, he walked quietly among the people, listening to their sorrows and telling them of the one true Kingdom. Many scoffed at him and said he was talking nonsense. Some became angry, and one mob beat Ishua so badly that one of his legs was crippled and he could walk only with crutches. But some believed, and he offered them *caris*: the powdered leaves of the stellaria tree, which could rebuild their coral and anchor them to another archipelago. Some islands were too far gone to rebuild their coral, and from these Ishua rescued any who were willing, bringing them aboard his own ship. Some of these begged to join Ishua in his mission, in spite of the danger. They sailed with him from island to island, telling people about caris and the One Kingdom. In time, Ishua's followers grew too numerous for one ship. Then Ishua taught them to build flying ships like his, and they formed a fleet of rescue. In time, Ishua had to return to his father's city. But his comrades stayed in Aletheia, sailing the skies and calling themselves the Vestigia Roi."

The children had listened so carefully that they were not at all sleepy by the time they got upstairs. Jariel tried to calm the girls by making up a story of her own about a bunny rabbit in a field of candy, but it was interrupted by the boys' rowdy yells from across the hall. When at last everything was dark and quiet, Ellie lay awake in her bed, picturing the people from the story. They were so vivid they almost seemed real: the beautiful, terrible Queen Thelipsa; the web-fingered adviser with scales on his face; and Ishua, the man who walked with crutches and carried rescue in his beggar's cloak. She wanted to try drawing them, but it would have to wait until tomorrow. She rolled over and tried to sleep.

The next day Ellie and Jariel sat on a bench, watching the children play in the yard. Ellie was using one of her precious remaining sketchbook pages to sketch the characters from last night's story. She was giving Ishua a wild, curly mop of hair and kind, dark eyes.

"So . . . are you ever going to tell me about that family who returned you?" Jariel asked. "Why did they bring you back?"

Ellie pressed her lips together, keeping her eyes on her page. "I'd rather not talk about it."

"Please? I promise I won't tell anyone."

Ellie shook her head, her fingers jerking in short strokes as she began to outline Thelipsa's royal gown.

Jariel shrugged. "They just seemed like a mean bunch. The boy especially. I can't believe you had to live with him. The lady too, ordering everyone around like her servants."

Niara limped up to the girls, wailing. She lifted her hem to show a red scrape on her knee. Blood was dribbling down her shin. Ellie's stomach lurched.

"Come on," said Jariel, gripping the little girl's hand and hauling her inside to Miss Sylvia.

Meanwhile, Adabel marched up to Ellie and handed her a knotted skipping rope to untangle. Ellie set her sketchbook to the side and tried to work out the snag, but she still hadn't managed to pry it loose by the time Jariel got back. The knot was pulled so tightly that she couldn't even get a finger inside it.

"Here, let me try," said Jariel.

"Usually I'm pretty good at untying knots, but this one's just too big," said Ellie, handing it over. As Jariel's strong, blunt-tipped fingers worked the rope, Ellie picked up her book and started sketching again.

"It must be pretty bad, getting returned," said Jariel after a pause.

"I said I'd rather not talk about it."

Jariel continued as if she hadn't heard. "It's not the end of things, though. At least you don't have to live with *those* people anymore. Next time maybe you'll get adopted by a nicer family."

Ellie's pencil went still. She looked Jariel in the face. "This isn't the first time I've been returned, Jariel. I've had three families, and they've all brought me back. All of them. And I'm going to be thirteen this spring. I know I'm not going to get another family."

"How do you know? You're nice, and pretty, and smart. You've got as good a chance as anybody."

"And what would happen even if I did? They'd just return me again. I'm just not the kind of kid people want to keep."

"That's not true. You just haven't found the right family yet." Jariel put her arm around Ellie's shoulders.

Ellie didn't say anything. Jariel was one of the friendliest people she'd ever met. Certainly no one else had called her smart or pretty in a long time. But Jariel, with her long, tangled hair that flew wherever it pleased and her wide mouth always ready to crack a smile, just didn't understand. Ellie looked at the mangled skipping rope that had rolled to the ground. Some knots were just too hard to untangle.

That night, Ellie dreamed that she was outside the Sketpoole Home for Boys and Girls. She tried the doorknob, but it was locked and wouldn't turn. She pounded on the door, hearing the *thud* of her fist on the wood, but no one answered. She looked up and saw faces in the windows. They belonged to her former families: Aunt Loretha, Ewart, Uncle Horaffe, the long-gone Alston family, and the Beswicks from before them.

"Let me in! Please!" Ellie shouted. But the faces did not move. They just stared down from the upper windows.

Suddenly she had the prickling feeling that someone was behind her. She pounded harder on the door, but it remained shut. *Better to see the danger face-on,* she told herself. She swallowed hard, and turned slowly.

At the fence stood a man with curly dark hair that fell into his eyes. He wore a stained, worn coat with holes at the elbows. Ellie shrank back, jiggling the doorknob in desperation.

"Ellie," the stranger said. His voice was softer than she'd expected.

He held out one hand, and she glimpsed a rough wooden crutch under his coat. She cocked her head. "Do I . . . know you?"

He gave a half-smile, his cheek rough with stubble. "Not yet."

Suddenly she recognized him, though she didn't know how. "Ishua?"

He nodded, his shaggy hair bobbing. "Come with me."

Ellie shook her head. "I can't. I'm waiting for them to open the door."

"What if they do not?" Ishua asked.

"Then I'll just . . . sit here, and . . . wait, I guess."

Ishua stretched out his hand again. "Come."

Ellie glanced up at the windows. The faces were still there, but the door wasn't opening. She took a step toward Ishua.

"Where—where do you want to take me?"

"Come, and you will see," he said.

Ellie gave one last glance at the windows, then reached out and took Ishua's hand. His palm had a row of calluses right below his fingers.

Suddenly they were sitting on a grassy hilltop, dotted with tiny white daisies. Twilight was deepening, and the first stars appeared in the sky.

Ishua looked at her. Now his shaggy hair was out of his face, and she could see his eyes. They were dark and rich, twinkling in the weak gleams of starlight.

"Do you see the music?" he asked eagerly.

"*See* music? Don't you mean hear?"

"No, do you *see* it?"

Ellie looked around, puzzled. "No."

"Oh, that's right. You don't have your Sight yet," Ishua sighed. "Then you'll just have to listen." He tipped his face up and opened his mouth in a round *O*. Out came one rich note, so deep that Ellie felt it rumble in the ground. Then, from somewhere inside the hill, another voice matched the note, and from the distant ocean came another. The same note in a higher key came from the tiny white flowers in the grass, their voices clean and delicate as flower petals. Above them, the brightening stars sang the highest note of all in voices like glass wind chimes. All the voices blended together into one many-layered sound, the first harmony of a magnificent song. And still Ishua sustained the first note, the sound that had started it all.

Ellie opened her eyes and found herself on the edge of her mattress, her blanket kicked to the floor. She pulled it up to her chin and lay still, listening to the sound of the other girls breathing.

What a strange dream. She could still hear the one note resounding with many voices. She closed her eyes, and the music carried her back to sleep.

Chapter 4
The Gift

One afternoon Ellie was in the kitchen, cleaning out the stove. It was a dirty job, but Chinelle was doing laundry today, so the task fell to Ellie. She had to crawl almost halfway inside the cold, dark stove to scoop out the ash collected at the back. The insides of her elbows and knees were slick with sweat, and the gray-black flakes of ash stuck to her skin. Her back ached from kneeling in this position. She coughed, sending even more coal dust swirling into her mouth and nose.

"Ellie?"

Ellie jerked backward, banging her head on the stove. She yelped and rubbed her head, squeezing her eyes shut in pain. When she opened them, Chinelle was standing in the doorway, balancing a huge basket of dirty pinafores and socks on her hip.

"Miss Sylvia wants you in the dining room right away," she said.

Ellie looked down. She was black all over with soot. "Right now? Don't I have time to wash up first?"

Chinelle shook her head. "She said it's urgent."

"All right." Ellie wiped her hands on her apron. The cloth instantly turned black, but her hands didn't look any cleaner.

Miss Sylvia was sitting at the head of the dining room table, with Jariel on her left. Jariel raised her eyebrows when she saw Ellie.

"You're a sight."

Ellie slid in next to her with a shrug. "Chinelle said it was urgent."

"It is," said Miss Sylvia. "Girls, there is something I need to talk with you about."

Ellie swallowed. Were they in trouble?

Miss Sylvia looked from one of them to the other. She sighed. "Dear girls, if it were my choice, I would place you with wonderful families or keep you here forever. You're such a help to me, and the other children look up to you so much. But the laws of Freith do not allow me to keep you here past your thirteenth birthdays. Ellie, yours is coming up in just a few months, and yours, Jariel, is this summer. Have you given any thought to what you would like to do once you leave the orphanage?"

Ellie sat motionless, looking down at her sooty hands. She'd tried to avoid thinking about what would happen when she turned thirteen and lost all chance of finding a family.

"Well, I've found an opportunity for you," Miss Sylvia continued. "Mr. Silas Matshoff is the owner of a wool mill just outside of Sketpoole, and he is looking for young people to do light work in his mill. I've invited him here this afternoon to talk with you about it. I want you girls to have a chance at a good future. The mill sounds like a place where you could earn an honest wage and make a living after you leave the orphanage."

Just then, there was a knock at the door.

Chinelle bustled in and curtsied. "Mr. Silas Matshoff, mum." She stepped aside to reveal a square-looking man, as broad as he was tall. He had thick hands and a thick neck with a wart on it.

"Mr. Matshoff," said Miss Sylvia. "Thank you for coming. These are the two girls I wrote to you about: Ellie and Jariel."

"Pleased to meet you," Ellie stammered in unison with Jariel, embarrassed to be looking like a chimneysweep.

Mr. Matshoff dropped onto the bench opposite them. He wore a thick coat with a fleece-lined collar. He removed his cap, revealing a shiny, bald head like an egg.

"Mr. Matshoff, in your letter, you mentioned you were looking for able-bodied children to work in your mill," Miss Sylvia prompted politely.

"Aye, that's true," he said in a gruff voice. "Back to back, girls. How tall are the both o' ye?"

Ellie turned her back to Jariel. She already knew she was shorter by half a head.

"Hm. Show me your hands."

Ellie reluctantly put her hands on the table. Her fingers, blackened with soot, looked small and spindly next to Jariel's, which were long and thick with short nails. When he saw how much taller and stronger Jariel was, surely Mr. Matshoff would take her away, leaving Ellie behind.

Mr. Matshoff pointed to Ellie's hands. "Narrow fingers. You quick with those hands, girl?"

Ellie thought about the swift strokes she used when she drew raindrops.

"I think so, sir."

"How's your eyesight?"

She blinked. "Good, sir."

"Fine, then. All right, ma'am, I'll take this one."

"What about me?" said Jariel.

"Mr. Matshoff, these girls must go together," said Miss Sylvia. "Both deserve a chance at a future."

"Sorry, ma'am. I'm only lookin' for a certain type o' worker."

"But these girls are the same age! What difference could there be?"

"The fingers," he pointed at Ellie's. "Thin, quick. Good for mending broken threads. She's smaller, too. The smaller ones have less . . . trouble with the looms."

"What do you mean?"

"More room to move; less likely to get snagged in the machines."

"Snagged in the machines?" Miss Sylvia's eyebrows rose. "Exactly what kind of work do you have in mind for them?"

"Takes grown men an' women to work the weaving machines, ma'am. But it's only children can crawl underneath, mend threads, fetch lost pieces, keep dust out o' the machines while they're runnin'. Saves us having to stop an' fix 'em."

"But the risk to the children . . . !"

Mr. Matshoff shrugged. "We house 'em, feed 'em, put coins in their pockets. Most don't lose more'n a finger. Anyhow, it's better 'n begging on the streets or falling in with them troublemakin' Basileans."

Miss Sylvia stood up quickly. Her voice was taut like a string about to break.

"We will discuss it. Good day, Mr. Matshoff."

The man scraped the bench backward as he got up. "All right, ma'am. Just don't discuss too long. Those fingers are just what I want for my mill." He winked at Ellie and went out. Miss Sylvia showed him to the door.

When she returned, her lips were pressed tightly together. "Well," she said. "That was an opportunity I liked less and less the more I heard about it." The clock struck two and she looked up.

"Ah, girls—I have an adoption appointment for one of the babies just now. But . . . come to my room after story time tonight. There is something I would like to show you." She hurried out into the hall.

"Phew," said Jariel when she was gone. "What did you think of all that?"

Ellie stared blankly at the far wall.

Jariel propped her elbows on the table. "I know, me too. At first I was mad that he didn't want me. But after he started talking about crawling under machines and losing fingers, I was glad he didn't. At least now you don't have to think very hard about your choice, Ellie."

Ellie spoke in a daze, half surprised at the words that came out of her mouth. "I think I'm going to accept."

"What? Why?"

Ellie looked down at her hands. "I don't think I have much choice. I'm turning thirteen, and I'm not going to get adopted again. I can't read well, or cook well, or do anything else that might help me get a job."

"But you can *draw*! And if you lost your fingers at the mill, you'd never be able to draw again!"

"But drawing isn't a job, Jariel." Ellie sighed and leaned her cheek on one hand. "I've got to do something, and this might be my only chance."

Jariel shook her head. "I don't think it will be. Will you at least wait to see what Miss Sylvia wants to show us before deciding? Maybe that will help."

Ellie tried to smile. "It would take a lot to help me out of this one. But I'll wait to decide until tomorrow, if you want me to."

Jariel hugged her, bringing her arms away covered with soot. She laughed. "You never know. But first, I think we both need a bath."

That night, after all the children were in bed, Ellie followed Jariel down the cold hallway to Miss Sylvia's room. Ellie had kept her stockings on underneath her nightgown, but the floorboards still chilled her feet. In front of her, Jariel's bare feet strode confidently ahead, her hair illuminated in a fiery halo by the candle she carried. When they reached the door at the end of the hall, Jariel knocked and Miss Sylvia opened, her long silver hair in a braid over her shoulder.

"Come in, girls," she whispered. Miss Sylvia's room was small, with gray plaster walls like those in the dormitories. It was brightened by the glow of a yellow oil lamp standing on a dark wooden trunk beside the low bed. In one corner stood two chairs and a table ringed with water spots; in another, a birdcage hung from a narrow wardrobe. A lean white bird bobbed its head back and forth on a spindly neck.

"Please sit down," said Miss Sylvia, gesturing toward the table. "Be careful, though; the far chair has a mended leg. You'll have to sit gently."

Ellie gingerly lowered herself into it. The chair squeaked, but held.

"Well, then. What did you think of the offer Mr. Matshoff made this afternoon?"

Ellie bowed her head. "I'm thinking of accepting, Miss Sylvia."

"Accepting?" Miss Sylvia said with a face as if she'd eaten sawdust. "Why?"

Ellie looked at the white bird poking its beak between the bars of its cage. "I'm going to be thirteen soon, and I don't want to end up a beggar."

"And you think this is your only other choice?"

"Well, except for falling in with those Basileans Mr. Matshoff talked about, whatever those are."

Miss Sylvia let out a breath as she sat down on the bed. "That option may not be as evil as you think. What I am about to show you will change everything. But first you must promise to keep what you see an absolute secret as long as you are in Sketpoole. If Governor Hirx found out about this, I could go to prison and lose all the children in my care. Do you promise?"

"I promise," Jariel breathed. Ellie noticed how the lamplight stoked her deep chocolate-brown eyes to amber.

"I promise too," Ellie said.

"Good. Jariel, will you hold this lamp, please?"

As Jariel lifted the oil lamp off the trunk, Miss Sylvia drew a small brass key from around her neck. She knelt beside the trunk and Ellie heard the lock click. The lid groaned as Miss Sylvia lifted it.

"All still safe and sound," she murmured, gathering up an armful of scrolls that rustled like the leaves of another century's trees. She laid them on the table and unrolled the first scroll, her wrinkled hands gently smoothing the old parchment.

Ellie's first glimpse was of pure color. An ocean, painted in solid cobalt blue, was dotted with green and brown islands and the names of places in red letters that curled and waved like banners. Whatever paint had been used here, she wished she had some for her sketchbook.

"This is a map of all Aletheia," said Miss Sylvia. "Here we are on Freith"—she tapped a spot in the familiar, star-shaped archipelago of Newdonia—"and here are the other three archipelagos: Numed, Arjun Mador, and the Orkent Isles. But right about here," she touched an empty blue space near the center of the map, "is another island, an island so secret that it is never drawn on maps. It is a flying island called Rhynlyr, where the sky-ships of the Vestigia Roi make berth. Rhynlyr was founded by Ishua himself, and is invisible from underneath. I could be arrested if the governor knew I was telling you this. But on Rhynlyr, there is an Academy where you could train for service in the fleet of the Vestigia Roi. You could study to be navigators, cooks, physicians; there's a special program for captains . . . "

"But . . . " Ellie looked at Miss Sylvia. "The Vestigia Roi is just a story—you just made it up to get the children to sleep!"

Miss Sylvia smiled secretively. "Most stories contain some truth, if you look far enough back." She raised her eyebrows. "Even you, both of you, are part of a story, if you think about it. You have a part to play in determining the ending. We all do."

"So Ishua and the Vestigia Roi are . . . real?" said Jariel, fingering the edge of the map.

"More real than this floor we're standing on. If anything, life on Freith is the illusion, and the work of Vestigia Roi is the reality—or, at least, a glimpse of it.

"Now at the Academy on Rhynlyr, there are courses of study to train new members. Some actually become sailors in the fleet, while others take positions in the city. With that kind of training, you could become much more than a mill worker. The Vestigia Roi works to bring Ishua's hope and rescue to the islands."

"You keep talking about . . . about Jariel and me," said Ellie. "Do you mean *we* could actually go there?"

Miss Sylvia smiled. "This *eyret* bird just brought me a message this evening." She drew a tiny piece of paper from the pocket of her blue dressing gown. "Tomorrow night, a Vestigian ship will be directly above Freith, headed for Rhynlyr. The question is: do you want to be on it?"

Ellie watched the bird in the cage. It made a deep burbling sound in its throat and fluffed its white wings. Its gleaming black eyes reminded her of Ishua's in the dream, twinkling with music.

"What is it like, Miss Sylvia?" Ellie asked, still looking at the eyret. "I mean, have you ever been to Rhynlyr?"

"I spent two years at the Academy before I joined my first crew, many years ago," Miss Sylvia said. "It is a bustling city with a beautiful stellaria tree at its center. The people there produce almost everything the city needs. I sailed with the fleet for a number of years, but when Freith became my mission, I disembarked to bring Ishua's work here."

"So *you're* part of the Vestigia Roi?" Jariel asked, her eyes wide.

"Well, yes," Miss Sylvia smiled. "And I am not the only one here—there are other Vestigians on Freith, even in Sketpoole, though here they are called 'troublemaking Basileans.' You have met some of them."

Jariel leaned forward eagerly. "Is Mr. Matshoff one of them? Chinelle? Kyuler?"

"Questions, questions," Miss Sylvia evaded with a smile. "The question for now is, do you want to go to Rhynlyr and train at the

Academy? We must send your response to the transport ship as soon as possible."

"Can we ever come back?" Jariel asked. "What if we don't like it there?"

Miss Sylvia laughed gently. "I think it unlikely that you would be unhappy on Rhynlyr. But Vestigian ships do roam the entire ocean. I should hope you would come back here to visit someday."

Jariel nodded. "I'm in. What about you, Ellie?"

The eyret ruffled its wings and tried to flap them. Ellie watched it crash against the bars of the cage.

"Are you sure they'll want me there, Miss Sylvia? They won't send me back?"

Miss Sylvia knelt down in front of Ellie, taking both her hands. "Ellie, the Vestigia Roi is not like the families who have treated you badly. There is room in Ishua's fleet for all who come. As long as you want to stay, he will never send you away."

Ellie looked away from the birdcage at last. "All right. I'll try it."

"Yippee!" cried Jariel, engulfing Ellie in a tight squeeze.

"But what will we tell the other kids?" said Ellie. "We can't just disappear."

"We could tell them that we're going to work in the mill," said Jariel.

"I'll tell them that you're taking an opportunity—transferring to a school for older children. That's the truth," said Miss Sylvia. "And now it's time we were all in bed. Pack your bags in the morning and leave them in my office. Then, after all the children are in bed, meet me there."

The stars glittered so brightly that they seemed to dangle like cherries within reach. Ellie stood on tiptoe and held up her hand for one, but it lingered just beyond her fingertips. The night sky's dazzling beauty drew her; she wanted nothing more than to hold one star in her hand. She stretched taller, her muscles straining until they hurt, but still the star eluded her. Tears of frustration started in her eyes and she sat down on the ground. She would never be able to reach one.

"Do you really want to touch one?"

Ellie recognized Ishua's voice, deep and calm as honey. She looked up and saw him standing over her, leaning on one of his crutches. She vaguely knew she must be dreaming, but she nodded. "I can't, though. I'll never be able to reach that high."

"Not from here, you won't," Ishua agreed.

Ellie cocked her head. "Can you help me?"

Ishua smiled, softening all the angles of his face. "I thought you'd never ask."

He put his arm around her and they suddenly shot up into the air. Seeing her feet dangling over empty space, Ellie couldn't even find the breath to scream, but the sensation of lightness and the rush of wind through her hair were also exhilarating.

When she opened her eyes, she was standing on a cloud. It was a pearly gray-white color in the moonlight, with misty tendrils that curled around her feet and ankles. She bounced gently and found that it was soft and springy. A thick curtain of stars hung all around, closer than ever.

Ishua looked up and sang the deep note that had started the music last time. It seemed to awaken everything around them. The cloud's wispy tendrils were stirred by a sudden wind, and the stars seemed to glitter even more brightly, their voices adding to the chorus. Ellie felt something within her quiver, like the string of an instrument being tuned. With some sense other than eyesight, she glimpsed a fleeting image of a dark-haired woman bending over a cradle.

Then Ishua began to chant a melody in soft words Ellie could not understand. The voices of the cloud and the stars harmonized with his. At the same time, Ellie saw fine threads materializing in the sky, strands on which the stars hung suspended, like roses in a glittering garden. As if in response to Ishua's voice, the strands began to glow.

Ishua delicately caught one between his fingers. "The Song," he murmured, looking at the glowing line resting in his open palm. "The living light that holds the universe in place." He looked at Ellie, his eyes twinkling. "Do you still want to touch a star?"

Ellie nodded eagerly. Ishua held out the strand to her. Trembling, she grasped one star, and it came free, resting between her fingers like a dandelion puff made of pure light.

But the star quickly began to soften and lose its shape. Horrified, Ellie cupped it in her palms, watching it melt into a lump, then a puddle, of translucent, silvery liquid. Ishua held out a small wooden cup, and Ellie poured the liquid into it. But to her surprise, when she looked into the cup, she did not see her own reflection, but instead saw *through* the bottom of the cup to her feet.

"Drink." Ishua held out the cup to her.

Ellie wrinkled up her nose. "Why?"

"It will give you the gift of Sight," said Ishua.

"But I can already see."

"Not as I see." Ishua held up the glowing strand in his palm. "These threads reveal where Adona Roi is working in the world around you. They are woven of his living Song, which formed it all in the first place. If you can see them, you can follow him even through great darkness. They can be found in anything, even in people, if you have the eyes to see. Do you want to see?"

Ellie frowned. "What if I don't?"

"Then you will never know the difference between illusion and reality."

Ellie looked at the silvery liquid in the cup. In drawing, seeing clearly was everything. What if she lived her whole life without knowing if she possessed clear sight? She squeezed her eyes shut. "All right."

Taking a deep breath, she swallowed the liquid in one draught. To her surprise, it had a faintly sweet, perfumey taste, like eating flowers—not a bit metallic. But the minute she swallowed, it burned like a rush of fire on her insides. She doubled over, clutching her stomach.

"Ishua . . . " she moaned.

She felt his hands on her shoulders. It felt like years before the agony passed, but it did, and Ishua helped her straighten up.

"Why . . . ?" she panted. "That was awful!"

Without speaking, he began to sing once more, never taking his deep eyes off her. This time, his music moved her in a new and different way—it was inside her now, as well as around her. It felt as if it were rushing into her through her nose and mouth and ears, getting in any way it could. Now she could hear not just the voices of the stars and clouds, but the sky itself and the roar of an ocean, and even her own small voice joining in. The music felt like a rush of wind and the lightness of flying, and it made Ellie glad enough to dance. The glowing threads around them brightened and spread, crisscrossing through the cloud beneath their feet, and then began to link many clouds together.

At last, the horizon began to glimmer. It started at the edges, glints of light like sunrise peeking around the bottom of a dark blanket. Then, all of a sudden, the blanket was torn off altogether, and brilliant, diamond-white light poured through the sky as through a glass ceiling. It was so bright that Ellie thought she would be blinded, but when she looked around, squinting, she found she could see everything clearly. The stars sparkled with tiny faces, and the sky around her rippled like ocean waves teeming with brightly colored fish. From the cloud they stood on, strands of light went out like highways in all directions. But Ishua himself was the best to look at. Though everything was beautiful in this bright light, he was the most beautiful of all. He stood with perfect ease, his crutches cast away. He wore a suit of armor that glittered like the stars around them, but his eyes shone still brighter. Their twinkle was at once merry and mysterious, like the radiance of a deep, strong, jubilant secret.

"Welcome, Ellie," he said, smiling broadly. "Welcome to the One Kingdom."

Ellie awoke to find that it was dawn. Wrapping herself in her blanket, she crept to the window and watched the horizon lighten and the stars fade. It wasn't hard to imagine that they were singing.

Chapter 5
Into the Dark

When the other children found out about Ellie and Jariel's impending departure for "school," they fought not just to sit *next* to the girls at dinner and storytime, but to sit *on* them. Tears overflowed at bedtime, and Jariel had to invent no fewer than three stories before the little girls finally settled down and fell asleep. Wearily, Ellie and Jariel snuck out of the dormitory in their stocking feet, trying not to make a single board creak. When they were finally inside Miss Sylvia's office, they breathed a sigh of relief. She was already there waiting for them.

"Well done, girls. Now, put on all your warm clothes—you'll need them before the end of tonight."

Ellie kept putting on layers until she felt like a stuffed chicken, ready to burst. She had on a thick petticoat, two pairs of stockings, her only sweater, and a pair of Ewart's too-big, cast-off gloves, with her worn brown coat over all. Her carpetbag was almost empty. Then she looked at Jariel and barely stifled a laugh. In addition to her old, dark red coat, Jariel had on a pair of bright green stockings riddled with holes, and an enormous, orange-and-blue striped muffler that swallowed her neck and left only her eyes and the top of her head showing. She waddled across the room.

"It's hot in here," she panted.

"You'll be glad for all those layers later tonight, trust me," Miss Sylvia said, her eyes twinkling. "Here, put the rest of your belongings in these." She handed them each a simple cloth knapsack with shoulder straps. "I sewed them up after we talked last night. You're going to need your hands free later. Now, are we ready?"

Ellie and Jariel nodded. Miss Sylvia opened the door of the office and looked both ways. The house was dark and silent. Taking two new candles and a handful of matches from her shelf, she lit one candle from the oil lamp on her desk, put the other supplies in her pocket, and blew out the lamp.

"Quietly, now," she whispered. "Follow me."

They tiptoed through the dark dining room and into the kitchen. Ellie almost jumped when Chinelle greeted them at the door, lamp in hand.

"Ready to go?" she smiled, her eyes creasing. Ellie shot a worried look at Miss Sylvia, who seemed perfectly calm.

"Yes, we are ready, Chinelle. Do you have the key?"

"O' course." Chinelle pulled a heavy pewter key from her apron pocket, along with two small packets wrapped in paper. "These're for you girls," she said, pressing them into their hands. The packets were warm and smelled of melted butter. "Not much, but they'll taste good after a long journey."

Ellie weighed the warm packet in her hand. "So . . . you know about Rhynlyr and the Academy, and all that?"

Chinelle's smile broadened. "Aye," she said, pulling back her left sleeve to reveal an intertwined V and R tattooed in the crease of her elbow. "We all keep our secrets."

"If all goes well, I should be back at least an hour before dawn," said Miss Sylvia, pulling the chain with the tiny key off her neck and handing it to Chinelle.

"Very good, mum. I'll keep an ear out for the children, and Kyuler's watchin' the door. All should be quiet 'til you get back."

Chinelle led them down the stairs to the cellar. The damp, earth-floored room was barely large enough for the four of them to stand inside together. Potato sacks and jars of preserves lined the shelves. Chinelle went straight to the right wall and inserted the pewter key into a hole too dark for Ellie to see. She pushed hard, and the entire wall of shelving swung out. A whiff of cold, musty air blew in from the blackness beyond.

Chinelle hugged both girls. "You take care of yourselves, now." Turning to Miss Sylvia, Chinelle tapped two fingers of her right hand to her left shoulder and then to her forehead.

"To the One Kingdom."

"May it be found," Miss Sylvia answered, returning the gesture, and stepped forward into the darkness.

Her candle illuminated the walls of a narrow dirt tunnel, rough with roots and rocks.

"Stay close," she said. "The ground is uneven. You'll need the light."

She was right. A few yards into the tunnel, the ground dropped away, and a flight of dirt steps led steeply downwards. Ellie could not see the bottom. The air smelled stale. Hesitantly she followed Miss Sylvia and Jariel, careful to plant her feet solidly on each step before attempting the next one. In one place the stairway was so narrow that she had to turn sideways. She felt as if the dirt walls were closing in around her. There was barely room to turn around.

Just keep moving, Ellie. One step at a time.

At last they reached the bottom of the stairs and the tunnel widened a bit. They stopped to catch their breath and Ellie stretched her arms, glad for the space.

"We've much ground to cover," said Miss Sylvia after a moment. "Let's keep up our pace."

Ellie wasn't frightened when she looked forward and saw the tunnel plunging deeper into the earth. It was when she looked back that she froze. She could no longer see the way out. There was no glimpse of Chinelle's lamp or the distant cellar door. Ellie felt her mind collapsing in panic.

We're trapped. I have to get out.

Heart pounding, she lunged back toward the stairs. But arms seized her, pulled her backward into the darkness. Ellie struggled to get away. She had to make it to the stairs, the stairs that led upwards to light and air.

"Let me go!" she yelled. "I don't want to die!"

"Ellie! Calm down!" It was Miss Sylvia's voice, sharp and commanding. Surprised, Ellie went quiet. The candlelight threw sharp shadows on the old woman's face.

"We are not going to die," Miss Sylvia said. "I have led dozens of people to the end of this passage in complete safety." Her expression softened, and she touched Ellie's cheek with a cool, smooth hand. "I know the tunnel is long and dark. But it is taking you to freedom—and protecting us all from the eyes of unfriendly watchers."

"We're going to make it out of here, Ellie," Jariel whispered in Ellie's ear, wrapping her in a hug. "But the way up is down. We have to go forward."

Ellie moaned, burying her face in Jariel's shoulder. "I don't think I can do this. My lungs feel squeezed."

"You *can* do this. I'll walk behind you," said Jariel, moving behind Ellie and putting her hands on her shoulders. "Don't give up."

Miss Sylvia's candle bobbed onward. Forcing herself to breathe, Ellie followed. The walls hovered darkly around the edges of her vision, pressing inwards, crushing her.

"Concentrate on the light," Jariel whispered from behind her, still steering Ellie by the shoulders. "Just watch the candle. Don't look at anything else."

Ellie obeyed, her eyes following the orange-yellow flame jerking and quivering against the darkness. "It looks like your hair," she blurted out.

Jariel laughed. The sound lightened the air for a moment before the dirt walls swallowed it.

The tunnel sloped down until Ellie's feet hurt from being crushed into the toes of her shoes. Once she lost her footing on some loose pebbles, but Jariel caught her before she fell. At last the ground flattened out. They had a brief stop to eat the buttered rolls Chinelle had packed for them, then continued on.

For such an elderly person, Miss Sylvia kept up a surprisingly quick pace. The dirt walls dulled the sound of their footsteps so that they walked in a vacuum of near-silence. It felt as if they'd been underground for hours, days, years.

"Who made this tunnel?" Jariel said at last, cracking the oppressive shell of silence.

"The Vestigia Roi," said Miss Sylvia. "We have had a presence in Sketpoole for over ten years. At first we merely traveled overland to rendezvous with the Vestigian fleet. But when Governor Dorethel Hirx came to power, he termed us Basileans, rebels bent on undermining the government of Freith. Now, anyone found to bear the mark of the Vestigia Roi or to have dealings with us may be arrested and have their property confiscated. That is why I had to show you my map in secret.

"About four years ago, several Vestigians taking a group of emigrants to Rhynlyr were caught by the governor's soldiers as they traveled on the road. They were accused of plotting against the governor, beaten badly, and placed under arrest for months. The native Freithians were eventually released, but those with the V-R tattoo were cut off from their previous employment and banished from Freith forever. Those of us who remained undiscovered realized the need for a secret way to get in and out of Sketpoole. At about the same time, this house was given to me by a wealthy Vestigian as a home for my orphans. It was decided that a tunnel, with one end under my house and the other at the island core, would be a perfect solution. No one would suspect people coming in and out of an orphanage." She glanced over her shoulder, a little smile dancing on her lips. "Since then, scores of new Vestigians have traveled safely to join the fleet."

"Are we . . . are we Vestigians now too?" asked Ellie. "Could we be arrested?"

"Only if the governor catches you," said Miss Sylvia. "And though it may be dangerous to be a part of this fleet, it is far more dangerous not to be."

Ellie glanced fearfully overhead, as if the governor's soldiers might already be hunting them down. They walked on in silence. After a while, Miss Sylvia slowed her pace and began to stoop down.

"Be careful. The tunnel gets smaller here. We had to dig around the city sewer. It gets worse before it gets better."

Worse? Ellie swallowed hard.

"Not far to go," Miss Sylvia called, already a few feet ahead.

The ceiling began to drop. Ellie had to hunch down, then bend her knees, then fold herself nearly in half to fit through. She could touch the walls with her elbows. What if she got stuck and couldn't get out? Her breath came in gasps and she thought she was going to suffocate. All she wanted was a glimpse of open sky and a breath of fresh air. When the tunnel shrank down to a hole just big enough to crawl through, she froze.

"Help," she whimpered, staring at the tiny space.

"Oh, no you don't," said Jariel. "Not after how far we've come." She kept coming up behind Ellie, forcing her forward. Ellie's lungs constricted. She began to cry.

"I can't," she moaned.

"You have to!" Jariel shoved her toward the hole. Ellie stumbled, ducked her head, and squeezed her eyes shut. When she opened them, she found that she was already halfway through the hole. In front of her was a much larger space, where Miss Sylvia was standing upright in front of a wooden door. Ellie quickly wriggled the rest of the way through the hole and stood up, shuddering. Jariel was right behind her.

"Is this it?" Ellie said, looking at the door.

"We have arrived," said Miss Sylvia. She handed Jariel the candle, then slid the heavy wooden bolt aside. The door creaked outwards.

They were standing on a spiral staircase in a deep, narrow well. Far above was a patch of sky studded with stars; below was a small circle of dark ocean. Pink strands of coral glimmered faintly below the surface of the water. Hanging straight down the shaft in front of them was a silken rope ladder that looked like woven starlight. Its threads seemed too fragile to climb, but it trailed up into the sky until Ellie lost sight of it.

"Where are we?" she asked, her voice echoing faintly against the walls.

"This is the center of the island—the core," explained Miss Sylvia. "Best feed the coral while I'm here." She descended the steps to the water's edge and poured the contents of a small envelope into the water.

"Where does this go?" Jariel reached out and tugged gently on the ladder. She had a dirty smudge on her forehead.

"Up to the transport ship," said Miss Sylvia with a smile. She pulled a scrap of paper out of her pocket and read it aloud, squinting in the light of the guttering candle. "The ship is called the *Legend,* and it is commanded by Captain Daevin . . . Blenrudd. Yes, that's what it says. Here, take the paper with you." Jariel put it in her pocket.

"So we're supposed to climb this?" Ellie asked, fingering the threadlike fibers and looking up. The ladder had no end that she could see.

"Yes," said Miss Sylvia. "Don't worry! It will hold you. These ladders are made for much heavier loads than just the two of you. But you must be careful, especially as you get higher. The ropes can sway quite a bit, especially if it is windy. Oh! And I almost forgot. When you reach the top, you must give the Vestigian greeting. Knock first, then say, 'To the One Kingdom.'"

"To the One Kingdom," Jariel practiced.

"And they will answer, 'May it be found.'"

"May it be found."

"The greeting is important. It serves as a password, so the crew will know that you are friends, not enemies."

Ellie swallowed. "What do they do to enemies?"

Miss Sylvia smiled and shook her head. "You can ask them when you get there. Now, it's getting late. You should be on your way, and I must be back before sunrise. Be safe, girls." She hugged each of them.

"Thank you for everything, Miss Sylvia," said Ellie.

"Yes," echoed Jariel. "This will be a great adventure."

Miss Sylvia smiled. "I'll miss you both." She looked from one of them to the other. "May Ishua watch over you. Now, up you go." Miss Sylvia held the ladder steady for them to climb on.

"You go first, Ellie," said Jariel. "If you slip, I'll be right behind you to catch you."

The flimsy ladder made Ellie too nervous to argue. It didn't look strong enough to hold the tiniest child from the orphanage.

"Go, Ellie," laughed Miss Sylvia. "You must trust it to hold you."

Swallowing hard, Ellie grasped the highest rung she could reach and pulled herself up. The ladder wobbled beneath her, and she clung to it for a few moments, swaying back and forth like the pendulum of a clock. But Jariel's weight behind her felt steadying.

They began to climb, and the rocking of the ladder grew more familiar. The walls of the well fell away, but it wasn't until they were very high up that Ellie risked a glance down. Lights twinkled in the distant windows of Sketpoole, and the landscape of Freith was illuminated by a half-moon.

"I think that's Liaflora County," Ellie said, nodding toward it. "That's where I lived with the Alstons for two years. Those were the happiest times of my life."

"That's lovely," grunted Jariel, "but your foot is in my face."

"Oh, sorry." Ellie kept moving.

It was the longest climb of her life. Once Ellie slipped and, true to her word, Jariel kept her from falling. The higher they got, the colder the air grew around them. There was no longer anything to block the wind, and soon Ellie was silently thanking Miss Sylvia for making her wear all these layers.

The steady rhythm of hand-over-hand became monotonous, and an ache crept through Ellie's shoulders and arms. Her muscles trembled with exhaustion. She just wanted to let go of the ladder and go to sleep. *Just keep going. One rung at a time.* She was concentrating so hard that when she bumped her head on something hard, she almost lost her grip in surprise. She clutched at the top rung of the ladder and looked up. Wooden panels. The ship!

"Who's there?" asked a muffled voice from within. Startled, Ellie couldn't remember a word of the greeting Miss Sylvia had taught them. She looked desperately at Jariel.

"For . . . to . . . the Kingdom! The One Kingdom!" Jariel called.

"May it be found."

The panel slid back and a man appeared, silhouetted against a square of yellow light. With a strong hand, he pulled Ellie up, and she tumbled onto a wooden floor. A moment later, Jariel landed on top of her. After climbing so long in the dark, Ellie blinked in the lantern-lit room. It was stacked with barrels and crates of all descriptions, and against the far wall, a few shabby coats hung on a rack beside a flight of stairs.

The man who had helped them pushed the wooden panel back into place and sat back on his heels. He had a square, angular face, sturdy shoulders, and kind blue eyes. Behind him was a small boy who stared at the girls as if they were a new species. The silence stretched out.

"Did . . . did you know we were coming?" Ellie asked hesitantly. "Miss Sylvia sent us to go to the . . . um . . . what's it called . . . "

"The Academy," the man smiled. "Yes, we've been waiting for you all day. Sylvia sent us word this morning."

"Are you the captain?" Jariel asked. "Captain Daevin . . . " She fished for Miss Sylvia's paper. "Captain Daevin Blenrudd?"

"Oh, no!" the man chuckled. "I'm Jude. I'm the ship's doctor."

"Who are you?" the boy behind him asked, squinting at the girls. He looked nine or ten years old, with dark hair and a pinched, inquisitive face.

"I'm Jariel!"

"I'm Ellie."

"Owen," said the boy. "We haven't had any girls here before."

"So you'll have to forgive our bad manners," said Jude, standing up. "I'm sorry; you must be tired. I'll show you your dormitory." He picked up the lantern, making shadows dance on the walls.

The girls stumbled up the stairs after Jude and Owen. They passed through a long room flecked with moonlight. Near the end of the room, Jude led them into a hallway and opened a door on the right.

"This is your room," he said. "If you need anything, Owen and I are across the hall." He lit a candle from his lantern and handed it to Ellie.

"I don't think I'll need anything until the sun comes up," Jariel said sleepily.

Jude laughed. "Good night, then."

Ellie barely had energy to kick off her shoes and blow out the light before falling into a sound sleep.

Chapter 6
Aboard the *Legend*

When Ellie opened her eyes, it was quiet. She couldn't remember the last time she'd woken up in a place where no one was yelling or crying. Light came softly through a round window. Calm lay over the room like a white blanket.

"Good morning!" A head of bright red, upside-down hair burst into Ellie's vision.

Ellie groaned and rolled over. "Morning, Jariel."

"I can't believe I got to sleep in a top bunk! It's like being in a bird's nest! It's the closest thing to sleeping on the roof!" Jariel looked at Ellie. "You didn't want the top, did you?"

Ellie shook her head. "I prefer to have my feet on the ground." She pushed back her covers. "Phew, no wonder I'm so hot. I slept in all my clothes." She sat up and started unbuttoning her coat.

"This is neat," said Jariel, looking around. Her hair was tousled and sticking up like a tumbleweed. "I can't believe we get our very own room. Look, two more empty bunks. There's even a window." She bounded down from her bunk and craned her neck to see out the round window. She gasped.

"Ellie, we're up in the sky! We're flying!"

"Well, that's probably why we climbed the ladder last night," said Ellie, yanking off her spare pair of stockings.

"No, but look! The clouds are right *there,* and there's sky all around!"

Ellie walked over and stood on tiptoe to see out. "Wow. We *are* up high." She stepped back from the window, feeling her head begin to whirl.

Jariel pressed her nose closer to the glass. "Look, birds, Ellie! Big white ones with huge wings, and—is that a *fish*?" Her breath fogged the glass and she scrubbed it with her sleeve. "It *is* a fish—I see its silver scales. Oh look, another one!"

From somewhere nearby, a bell began to clang.

"I think that means we're supposed to be somewhere," said Ellie, hastily pulling her shoes back on. "Hurry!"

Following the sound of voices, the girls entered a long hallway that led into a large dining room. Natural sunlight came through open trap doors in the ceiling, giving the room the feeling of an outdoor picnic lawn. At the table, Ellie recognized Jude and Owen from last night, but at the head was a man with a pointed goatee, and beside him sat a big, stocky boy who wore the sulkiest expression Ellie had ever seen.

"Ah, our new passengers," said the man at the head of the table, standing up. He was tall and had long, white hands.

"Good morning," said Jude, lifting his cup.

"I see you were not informed about the bell for breakfast. In the future, however, it will be obeyed punctually," said the tall man. "I am Captain Daevin Blenrudd. I believe you have met Mr. Jude Sterlen already, and these are Owen Mardel and Connor Wynn."

"Hello!" said Jariel.

"Pleased to meet you," Ellie mumbled, overwhelmed by so many introductions.

Owen waved, but the boy named Connor did not even look at them.

"Now that we are all here, let us sing the blessing," said Captain Daevin. The girls slid into the bench beside Jude and copied the others as they stood and clasped their hands behind their backs. The captain began to sing in a smooth tenor voice. Ellie recognized the first part of the song from Miss Sylvia's, but the second part was new:

To you, our Father King
Our voices do we bring
For this food our thanks we give
Teach us how to truly live.
On this morning filled with light
Our eyes please give true Sight.
And as we sail the seas beneath the sun,
Make your kingdom grow, until it all be one.

After the singing, Jude served porridge from a pot on the table.

"I'm sorry if it's watery," he apologized. "I had kitchen duty this morning. I'm afraid I make a better gardener than cook."

"You have a garden here?" asked Ellie, accepting a bowl of porridge.

Jude nodded. "It's a little greenhouse on the top deck. That's where these raspberries come from. I picked them this morning. Try some?"

Ellie hadn't had raspberries since she had lived with the Alstons in the countryside. The soft, velvety berries dissolved like honey in her mouth. And there wasn't a single screaming baby within earshot. She sighed contentedly.

"So are you heading for the Academy, too?" Jariel asked Owen and Connor.

Owen nodded. Connor looked up and shrugged one shoulder. Ellie tensed. She had the sudden sensation of looking in a mirror. In his broad, square face, under a pair of black eyebrows, were pale blue eyes, almost clear, with faint black rings around the centers. Fascinated and a little frightened, Ellie couldn't look away. They were her eyes.

They narrowed as Connor glared at her. "Whatcha lookin' at?" he growled.

Ellie quickly lowered her gaze. "N-nothing."

Jariel switched her attention to Captain Daevin. "So how long will it take us to get to Rhynlyr?"

The captain stroked his goatee. "It depends on the weather and air currents. But with fair sailing, I'd say . . . perhaps a week."

"A week on a flying ship," Jariel sighed dreamily. "I've never been off of Freith before. May we go explore?"

"After chores," said Captain Daevin. "The *Legend* is functioning with an unusually small crew, and everyone must pull their weight. You'll spend mornings cleaning the ship, keeping the woodwork and sails in good repair, checking the lifeboats, and helping with anything else that needs doing. There are also daily meals to prepare and dishes to wash. Most afternoons, though, will be yours to do with as you like."

"Really?" said Ellie. "There are no lessons? No littler children to look after?"

The captain shook his head.

"This is going to be fun," Jariel grinned. "Can I help check the lifeboats?"

"You don't even know how to check a lifeboat," Connor snapped.

"You may," said the captain. "In fact, Connor will show you how."

After breakfast, Jude went off to work in his greenhouse, and the captain to the navigational instruments in his cabin. Grumbling, Connor trudged up the stairs to the top deck, with Jariel nearly skipping behind him. Ellie volunteered to do dishes, and Owen said he would help.

He showed her to the galley at the rear of the ship, where the dark wooden counters were scored from years of carrot chopping. Huge pots and pans hung overhead, and there was only one narrow window for light.

"So, how did you first come to the ship?" Ellie asked after a few minutes, pouring hot water into the porridge pot.

"Village almsgiver," said Owen, squinting at her.

"Almsgiver? What's that?"

"He was an old man in my village who took care of orphans. Both my parents died in a fire on my farm about a year ago," Owen said matter-of-factly.

"I'm sorry," Ellie said softly. "How did you survive?"

"My father dug a hole in the ground and put me in it," said Owen. "Father Allarants found me there."

"And is he the one who sent you here?"

"Yes," Owen said. "He took care of me, but he was a Vestigian and wanted me to go to school at the Academy. The *Legend* picked me up from the island of Twyrild two weeks ago, and here I am."

There was an awkward pause. Ellie handed Owen a bowl to dry.

"So do you know what you want to study at the Academy?" she asked.

Owen's hazel eyes suddenly caught fire. "Bugs," he said. "I want to be an entomologist someday. I have a collection of bugs, but the bee-skins are my best. The newest is one I found near the island core on Twyrild, and I haven't found it in any of the ship's books. It's got diagonal stripes instead of horizontal. Jude says he thinks it's a new species. You . . . want to see it when we're done?"

"Oh . . . okay," said Ellie cautiously.

"Really? You want to see it? Most people say it's a silly hobby. Connor even tried to ruin my bee-skin collection one time, so now I keep it hidden. Only Jude and I know where they are. I'll show you, though. You seem nice."

Ellie smiled. "Thanks. I promise I won't wreck your collection."

"What do you like to do?" said Owen.

Ellie reached inside the porridge pot to scrub the bottom. "Well, I guess I like to draw."

"You can draw?!" Owen shouted, making Ellie jump and drop the scrub brush. "Then you can draw my collection! I've tried to draw it before, so I can show it to people without revealing its hiding place, but it never looks right. Will you try drawing it? Please?"

"All right," Ellie said uncertainly. "I'll try."

Owen gave a loud whoop and galloped in a circle around the room, waving the dishrag. "Thanks, Ellie!"

They spent the rest of the morning with Jariel and Connor, mopping the long dining room. Owen kept saying how fast the work went with four of them instead of two.

Suddenly Ellie heard a *thud* and spun around. Owen was sprawled on the floor, with Connor's mop stretched out behind him.

"Lying down on the job? That won't get the work done," Connor taunted.

"Did you just trip him?" Jariel said in shock.

Connor smirked. "'Course not. He's just clumsy. Aren't you, Owen?" He began to push his mop again, ramming it into Owen's leg.

Owen didn't say anything. Glaring at Connor, he got to his feet and pushed his mop to the opposite side of the deck.

"Are you okay?" Ellie asked.

He nodded, still glowering. "Fine."

After eating bread and cheese from the pantry for lunch, the children were free to explore. Owen offered to show the girls around, and Ellie was following him and Jariel out of the dining room when she hesitated.

"Do you want to come with us, Connor?"

He barked a laugh. "Ha! And look at silly lineups of bugs? That stuff's for babies."

Owen stiffened. Ellie frowned.

"No, it isn't. That's a mean thing to say."

Connor crossed his arms with a smug look. "Well, maybe I'm mean. And maybe you're ugly."

Jariel's face flushed. She was about to lunge forward when Ellie caught her arm tightly.

"Don't, Jariel."

"But . . . "

"It's not worth it."

Owen turned on his heel. "C'mon. We don't need him, anyway."

The threesome turned their backs and marched away. Halfway down the hall, though, Jariel was still fuming.

"How could you let him talk to you like that, Ellie? To both of you! That boy is so rude!"

Ellie sighed. "I guess I'm used to it. I used to practice with Ewart when he said things like that."

Owen shrugged. "Connor just wants to see if he can get us mad. I ignore him so he doesn't get what he wants."

Jariel let out her breath. "I'd still like to punch him in the nose. I bet that'd teach him to keep his mouth shut."

"Let's not waste any more time thinking about him," said Ellie. "Let's explore."

Owen pushed open the door of the boys' dormitory. "First stop. This is where I keep my pets." None of the four bunk beds inside were made, and it smelled like a nest of furry animals. There was a row of glass boxes hanging from hooks above one of the bunks.

"That one's mine," said Owen. "Come on up."

The girls clambered up the ladder and sat looking up through the bottoms of the glass boxes. They appeared to contain only jumbles of twigs and leaves.

"What are these?"

"My bugs."

As soon as he said it, Ellie spotted them. Inside each box, things were moving—small, crawly things with wings, legs, and many-faceted eyes. She shuddered.

"It's okay; they won't get out," said Owen. He pulled one box off its hook. Inside, an army of red ants was swarming over a dead worm. "These ones escaped the night I arrived here. I kept them in a paper bag then. In the morning, Jude and I were covered with ants and bites. There were more on him than me, though, because he sleeps on the bottom bunk. I've never heard Jude howl like that since," Owen grinned. "But I didn't do it on purpose, I promise. That afternoon, he gave me these boxes to keep my bugs in. See, they have tiny air holes at the top, but the glass is too slippery for them to climb."

"Was Connor here when that happened?" asked Jariel.

Owen shook his head. "He just got here about three days ago."

"Hm. Too bad," said Jariel.

"No, good!" said Ellie. "He probably would have eaten Owen alive if he'd gotten bitten by ants."

"Prob'ly," agreed Owen. He replaced the ant-box on the ceiling and pointed to other boxes. "Those are glowflies and caterpedes I brought from home. The caterpedes are poisonous, but their mouths are too small to bite humans. The glowflies are like night-lights after Jude blows out the candle. That box has a spotted moth in it—you can hardly ever see it, because its spots change color to match its surroundings. Jude caught it for me when we made a stop on Anadyr. And this one" —Owen pulled down a box from above his pillow—"is my very favorite. Her name is Tera."

Ellie peered into the box. Suddenly she jumped as a ball of brown fur crashed into the glass wall. It stuck there with all eight of its thick, hairy, many-jointed legs extended. Ellie jerked away.

"S-s-spider!" she squeaked, barely able to breathe.

"She's a tarantula," said Owen. "Spiders aren't really bugs, but I think that makes her even more special. I caught her right here on the *Legend* when I first came aboard. I have no idea how she got here, but I'm glad she did." He stroked a finger over the glass. Tera followed the movement. Her many-jointed legs did move with a certain mechanical grace.

"How do you know it's a girl?" asked Jariel.

Owen shrugged. "I don't actually know how to tell," he said. "I just guessed. I think she's too pretty to be a boy."

"Do you have any snakes?" said Jariel.

"No," Owen sighed. "I'd give a lot for a snake. But I haven't found one yet. Maybe there'll be some on Rhynlyr."

"Can we . . . go somewhere else?" Ellie asked, staying as far away from the tarantula box as possible.

"What? Don't you like Tera?" Owen batted the box toward Ellie. She shrieked. Owen laughed. "Just kidding. We can leave after I show you one more thing. But we've gotta close the door first."

Jariel did, and Owen pried a loose board away from the wall behind Jude's bed. From inside, he carefully pulled something out. When he turned it to face them, Ellie nearly fainted. It was a board covered with dead bees—papery, hollow heads and bodies.

"These are my bee-skins," Owen said proudly. "Don't worry, it doesn't hurt the bees to take them. The bees just shed them and leave them behind when they're becoming full-grown. Aren't they neat?"

Ellie gulped. Owen laughed again. "Don't be afraid, Ellie; they can't sting you. But you can't tell Connor about my hiding place. Promise?"

Both girls nodded.

"Okay, now we can go. Owen replaced the bee-skins and waved to the boxes above his bed. "Bye, Tera."

They stopped back at the girls' dormitory to get Ellie's sketchbook and colored pencils. Ellie opened to one of the precious remaining blank pages and divided it into four parts. There was a large muddy stain on the corner of the page, but it would have to do. She wanted to capture as many of today's sights as possible.

At the end of the hallway, they climbed a narrow flight of stairs toward a trap door filled with white light. As they stepped out, a cold gust of wind blasted their faces, making Jariel's hair dance straight upward like tongues of flame. They emerged onto the wide wooden deck, where the sun was shining. The wind slammed into Ellie's body and surged through her lungs, sharp and intoxicating. She breathed deeply and grinned, her teeth smarting in the cold air.

Overhead, white sails shaped like half-moons bellied out in the gusty wind. One was directly above them, attached to a mast in the center of the deck, and one was behind them, on a raised quarterdeck over what must be the captain's cabin. Toward the bow of the ship was a tiny house with whitewashed walls and a glass roof that glinted like a jewel in the sun. Outside it stood a few gardening trellises and a shovel. Perhaps that was Jude's greenhouse.

Jariel was already galloping away. "C'mon!" she yelled. "Look what I found this morning!"

Ellie followed her to the bow of the ship, where there was a low platform right behind the figurehead, just big enough for the three of them to stand on. Now that they were closer, Ellie could see that the figurehead had the long, graceful neck and the sharp beak of a *cygnera* bird. They were rare in Freith, but she had once seen one swimming on the lake on the Alstons' farm.

"You can see for miles!" shouted Jariel, leaning forward and hugging the neck of the cygnera. "Look how high up we are!"

"Maybe you shouldn't stand so close to the edge, Jariel," said Ellie, clutching the ship's railing with both hands.

"Aw, it's fine," said Jariel, leaning forward. "Gosh, it's so *beautiful* up here!"

Ellie looked up. It *was* beautiful. She watched a bank of blue-gray storm clouds slide across the sky, gradually shredding apart to reveal strips of clean-washed blue sky. A few gulls soared lazily, their crooked white wings glinting in the light. Cautiously she removed her hands from the railing and took out her colored pencils. As her wrist began to flick back and forth, capturing the shifting cloud-shadows in cobalt blue and charcoal gray, she forgot how high up she was. She added a touch of light green and blended it with the side of her thumb.

When she looked up again, Jariel was sitting on the ship's railing, talking to Owen.

"How do they make ships like this?" she asked. "If I'd known there were ships that could fly, I'd have come here sooner."

Owen shrugged. "I think it's partly the type of wood the ship is made of, and partly the propellers and wing sails." He pointed back toward the center of the ship, where two curved white sails extended from the sides. From here, they did look like wings. Beneath each one was a huge, four-pronged wooden propeller with a brass hub, its blades edged with brass, facing down and spinning like a maelstrom.

"Did you know there are also human-sized wing sails?" Owen added.

Jariel frowned. "So you mean—people can fly, too?"

Owen nodded. "I've done it. It's fun."

Jariel's eyes widened. "Really? Can we try it right now?"

"I haven't finished showing you the ship yet! I'll take you tomorrow. Besides, we'd need to start earlier. Flying with just wing sails is a lot of time and work. The *Legend* has the *lumena* to help it along."

"What's a lumena?" asked Ellie.

"I'll show you! Come on!"

As they headed back to the stairs, they ran into Connor. He made a face and pushed past them, entering the cabin at the rear of the deck.

"That's the captain's cabin," said Owen in a low voice. "Connor's in there a lot. I think he thinks he's first mate."

Ellie kept her sketchbook tucked under her arm, holding on to the ripped cover so it wouldn't fall off. As they explored the ship, she filled her page with sketches: a dusty stack of books in a storage room, the rings on a carrot inside the galley. Last of all, Owen showed them the Oratory.

There was a pair of doors at the end of the dining room decorated with two arching silver trees. Glancing over his shoulder with a grin, Owen pushed them open.

Instantly they were met by the sound of crashing water. From somewhere near the ceiling, a small waterfall plunged down. As it fell, the cascade was dyed a dappled mosaic of colors, from ruby to sapphire to buttercup to salmon to mauve to gold. Looking up, Ellie saw that part of the ceiling was speckled with diamond-shaped panes of colored glass. Light came through them, transforming the whole room to a shifting sea of color. Jariel twirled around, her face purple, her skirt green; Owen turned orange as he squinted upwards. Holding out her own hands, Ellie saw one turn red, the other a light yellow.

Ellie sat down on one of the curving benches against the wall, watching the colors sparkle and shimmer in the water. The light spray of the waterfall cooled her face. She tried to watch a single drop as it fell, but couldn't keep track of it as it mingled with others and was lost in the foamy, stone-ringed pool below. On a sudden urge, she took all of her pencils in one fist, then filled the last corner of her sketchbook page with a loud swirl of every color. Then she wet her fingertips in the pool and rubbed the page with them. The sketch became a smooth rainbow of colors. She smiled.

"That's pretty," said Owen, sitting down beside her. "I like this room, too."

Ellie nodded, listening to the roar of the waterfall, somehow both fierce and musical. "I can see why. It's a good place for thinking."

"It's practical, too," he said. "The waterfall cleans and recycles our water supply, and the light comes from the ship's lumena."

Jariel plopped down beside them, breathless from spinning. "You were going to show us what that was, you know."

"I can't take you right up to it," Owen said. "No one's allowed inside its chamber except the captain. But you can see its light from here." He pointed up to the bright glow behind the many-colored glass chips in the ceiling. "It's alive, but Captain Daevin says it's more like a plant than an animal. It powers the propellers and keeps the *Legend* in the sky. It's kept in a glass chamber right above this room, with sliding panels on the outside. The captain once slid them away to signal another Vestigian ship with the light."

"Hm. Wish I could see it up close," said Jariel, watching the light from beyond the ceiling.

"The captain says it's too dangerous," said Owen, standing up. "There's more to see on the ship, but I have to help with cooking duty tonight. Think you can find your way around from here?"

Both girls nodded.

"Thank you for the tour, Owen," said Ellie as he slipped back through the doors.

"Want to go back out to the deck?" Jariel asked. "I want to climb the rigging and see the view from up there."

"Maybe tomorrow," said Ellie. "I think I've had enough of heights for one day. Besides, I want to see if I can find some string and paste to fix my sketchbook."

"Okay," said Jariel. "See you later!" She let the Oratory door close behind her with a bang.

Chapter 7
Visions

Ellie sat in the colorful room a few minutes longer, running her fingers over the torn cover of her sketchbook and watching the light of the lumena filter through the ceiling. Eventually she slipped out the door, hoping to find some repair materials in the galley.

She was halfway down the hall when she heard raised voices at the top of the stairs. It sounded like Jariel arguing with Connor. The voices stopped, and Ellie heard a heavy step on the stairs. Connor was coming down! She couldn't face him alone. Where could she hide?

Panicking, she turned the handle on the first door she saw and shut it behind her. Her pulse thudded loudly against her temples.

"Why hello, Ellie," said Jude, looking up from the book he was reading. He was wearing a faded brown shirt with sleeves rolled up to the elbow, and he removed a small pair of spectacles. "Are you feeling all right?"

"Yes," said Ellie, trying to catch her breath. "Where am I?"

"This is the infirmary," said Jude, leaning forward in a rocking chair by the low fire. "What brings you here today?"

"Oh," said Ellie. "Well, you see . . . Connor's out in the hallway, and . . . I was by myself and didn't want him to see me. Is it all right if I stay here for a while?"

"Of course." Jude closed his book and set it on a low table beside him. Ellie saw the title *Newdonian Plant Life* on the spine. "Please, sit down." Jude dragged up another wooden chair, this one straight backed, with a frayed blue cushion on the seat. Ellie perched on it, her feet not quite touching the floor, and looked around. Bunches of dried herbs hung from the ceiling, and shelves of glass bottles and jars lined the walls. At the far end of the room were a low sickbed and a desk with a large black instrument on it. The room had a faintly aromatic smell, and the warmth of the small fire was comforting.

"So, what have you been up to this afternoon?" Jude asked, folding his arms.

"Owen gave us a tour of the ship," said Ellie. "We went all over, and I did some drawings of the things we saw."

Jude raised his eyebrows. "I didn't know you were an artist. May I see what you drew today?"

"Uh," said Ellie, pulling her sketchbook to her chest. "They're . . . not very good; they're just . . . quick . . . "

"You don't have to if you don't want to," said Jude, holding his hands up, palms outward. His fingers were short and thick, with close-cut nails and calluses on the palms. Ellie remembered Mr. Matshoff inspecting her hands for mill work, and the thought of losing fingers and never being able to draw again. She glanced down at her book.

"All right," she said, turning to today's page. "You can look at them. But don't laugh if they're ugly."

Jude smiled as he replaced his spectacles and accepted the sketchbook, tilting the page toward the firelight.

"Careful—some of the pages are falling out," Ellie cautioned. "I was actually looking for some string and paste to fix it."

"I have some you can use," said Jude. "It looks like this book has been through a battle."

"Well . . . I guess you could say that," said Ellie.

Jude's forehead wrinkled as his deep blue eyes traveled over the four corners of the page. Ellie flinched. Were the drawings that bad?

"This one's the Oratory, isn't it?" he said at last, tapping the lower right corner with his finger.

Ellie peered over the top. "How could you tell? There aren't even outlines."

"There's nothing else it could be," said Jude. "This is what the Oratory *is*—one big swirl of color. This is exactly right."

Ellie's heart ballooned with pleasure. No grown-up had ever talked about her drawings like this before.

"Oh yes, paste," said Jude, handing the sketchbook gently back to her. "I'm afraid what you really need is a new book, but see what you can do with these." He handed her a dark jar, a ball of twine, and a thick needle.

By the light of the fire, Ellie spread out on the floor and performed surgery on her sketchbook. She brushed dried mud off the pages and pasted the two halves of the cover back together as neatly as she could. Then she sewed up the spine with a new twine binding. The edges didn't exactly line up, and the pages bent when she opened it all the way, but at least she wouldn't lose any more drawings.

When she was finished, she leaned her chin on the book and watched the fire. The flames looked so fluid and energetic, like leaping, red-haired dancers wearing yellow scarves. They reminded her of Jariel, and of red-haired Samanta Alston, whose picture she had lost when her sketchbook was destroyed.

Ellie still remembered the day Miss Nuthers had given her this sketchbook, along with a small box of colored pencils tied with parcel string. She'd been only eight then.

"This is for you, Ellie," said Miss Nuthers, her tiny eyes almost disappearing into her cheeks as she smiled. "It's your very own. You never have to share it or show it to anyone if you don't want to."

"A book! Ellie has a book!" squealed Sam Alston, squeezing Ellie around the waist.

"I've never had drawing things of my own before," said Ellie, dazed.

"Well, we shall see what you do with them," said Miss Nuthers, placing the book in Ellie's hands.

Ellie ran her fingers over the cover, feeling the rough weave of the paper. She didn't remember what happened next, though she hoped she'd thanked Miss Nuthers as she left the one-room schoolhouse. The next thing she knew, she was walking down the road with Sam, clutching the book to her chest.

"Ellie! Ellie! What are you going to put in your book?" Six-year-old Sam danced around her, her short red curls bouncing crazily.

"I don't know," Ellie answered. "There are so many pages. I don't know what to draw first."

"How about me?" said Sam, posing with her fists on her hips, eyes scrunched shut, an enormous grin plastered on her face. Ellie laughed.

"All right. You'll be my first drawing. When we get home, you can sit on the back porch and smile just like that, and I'll draw you."

"Yippee!" Sam twirled out of her pose. "I like your drawings, Ellie."

"I'm lucky Miss Nuthers likes them, too. Otherwise she might not be so patient that I'm slow at reading. You're better at it than me, and you're only six."

"Psh! I'd rather be a good draw-er," said Sam. "And besides, you're getting better at reading."

"Well, I don't know, but I hope so," said Ellie, putting her arm around Sam's shoulders. "But I'll draw pictures for you anytime you like. Now that I have this sketchbook, I could draw anything!"

"Oh no!" Jude cried suddenly, disrupting Ellie's reflections. He seized a wooden spoon and bent over a row of glass cups hanging over the fire. As he stirred them, he muttered, "This one's ready. Oh, Jude, you've let the chamomile tincture go too long." Putting on a big pair of leather gloves, he removed the pole from the fire, setting the cups on the mantelpiece one by one. The ruined chamomile tincture he tossed back into the fire. The room filled with a gentle, soothing aroma that made Ellie feel the slightest bit sleepy.

"Do you spend your days here in the infirmary?" she asked, forcing her eyes to stay open.

"Only parts of them," Jude said, pulling down empty jars from a shelf. "This is where I take care of sick patients and perform the occasional surgery. I also work with wood when carpentry is needed about the ship. And I help with cooking, of course—but only on unfortunate days," he smiled. "The rest of the time I'm in the greenhouse, where I grow my own herbs for medicines. Then I dry them or use them to make healing tinctures or poultices."

"Is that the only thing your greenhouse is for—growing medicines?" said Ellie.

"Oh no," said Jude. "I'd keep a garden even if I didn't need medicines. I love to see things grow. My newest project is growing a dwarf lemon tree aboard ship. I cultivated the hybrid myself. Look! I'll show you its leaf pattern under the microscope."

He hopped to the desk in the back of the room and slid an ordinary-looking, rolled-up green leaf under the black instrument. Putting his eye to the top, he cranked some dials and knobs. "Ah. Look at this, Ellie."

Ellie had to stand on her chair to reach the eyepiece. Through the tiny peephole, rolling green hills came into focus, spiderwebbed with an intricate network of roads. It looked big enough to be part of Miss Sylvia's map.

"That's the leaf? It's so huge!" she said incredulously.

"That's the beauty of the microscope," said Jude. "That dense pattern of veins you saw is what helps the tree to absorb enough sunlight, even though it's small."

Suddenly the dinner bell began to clang.

"We'll have to look at it more another time," said Jude. "Shall we wash up and go in together?"

Ellie put her chair away and scrubbed her hands in his washbasin. She noticed the lemony fragrance of the soap.

They met Owen on his way to the table, staggering under a large platter. Jude lifted it out of his hands and put it on the table, where Connor was already sitting. Captain Daevin stepped out of the galley, and Jariel came galloping down the stairs, her face bright and a bit sunburned.

Captain Daevin took his place at the head of the table and formally intoned the blessing. Supper consisted of white fish, piping hot and flavored with butter and herbs. No matter how fond she was of Jude, Ellie had to admit that it tasted far better than breakfast had.

Owen, sitting next to Ellie, whispered, "We were going to make bread to go with it, but I forgot to put in the yeast. It came out as flat and hard as a board."

Ellie giggled. "Well, the fish is good," she whispered back. "What is it?"

"Cloud trout," said Owen, keeping his voice low. "They swim in the clouds up here and there are plenty for the catching. Captain Daevin said he learned a hundred ways to cook them at the Academy, but they still get old after a while."

"So, Captain Daevin," said Jariel. "The *Legend* is a Vestigian ship, right?"

He nodded, taking a bite of cloud trout.

"But I thought the Vestigia Roi was a rescue fleet. So why is the *Legend* just transporting orphans to the Academy?"

The captain slowly patted his mouth with a napkin. A red flush crept up his neck.

"This ship was not built for long voyages," he said stiffly. "It does not have the weight or capacity to travel long distances."

"Do you ever get bored of shuttling kids around?" Jariel continued. "If I were a captain, I'd want to do something dangerous and exciting."

The captain was seized with a sudden fit of coughing.

"No Vestigian work, however small, is insignificant," said Jude. "Snatching refugees from falling islands is only one type of mission. Some Vestigians spend years on one island, like Miss Sylvia. They feed the coral with caris powder, take care of orphans and the poor, and invite people to become part of the Vestigia Roi. Other sailors simply transport supplies of caris and *lumenai* between the Havens and Vestigian outposts. Yet other members of the fleet spend their entire lives on Rhynlyr, teaching new recruits how to serve in Ishua's fleet. Not all of these jobs are exciting, but all of them help to reestablish the One Kingdom, Adona Roi's kingdom. The *Legend* may not be stationed in the Outer Reaches, discovering drifting islands and rescuing people from death. But if Captain Daevin hadn't taken this assignment, where would you be?"

"Back at the orphanage, I guess," said Jariel, picking at her food. "But I'd still think I'd rather be assigned an adventurous mission."

"Sometimes there is hard work to be done before the adventure comes," said Captain Daevin, clearing his throat. "I would like to sail a bigger ship to the Outer Reaches someday. This was not the assignment I wanted when I completed Officer Training at the Academy. But it is what was given to me, and so I will do my duty until I am reassigned."

"How long have you and Jude been sailing together?"

"It's nearly two years now, eh Daevin?" said Jude.

"Two years, two weeks since the *Legend* brought us together," said the captain, folding his napkin. "And nearly five months since Markos left the crew."

"Markos was our lookout and navigator," Jude explained. "He was a good cook, too."

"He switched to a land position on Rhynlyr when our pay was cut," said the captain. "Too bad. Left us with a lot of work."

"I could learn to be the lookout," said Jariel.

"We'll see," said Captain Daevin. "Now, time for dishes, then singing. Jude, Jariel, you're on kitchen duty."

When the cleanup was completed, the crew filed into the Oratory. Jude moved a carved lectern from the edge of the room to the center, and the captain placed a huge book on top of it. The group formed a circle, facing him.

"What's that?" Ellie whispered to Owen. He blinked.

"You don't know? That's the Song Book."

"The whole book? What song is it?"

Owen raised his eyebrows. "The Song of Ishua, of course!" He raised his hand. "Captain Daevin, Ellie doesn't know what the Song is."

The captain frowned. "I thought Sylvia would have explained it to you. The Song of Ishua is the theme of life, the order that sustains the universe, and the anthem of the One Kingdom. This Book is our copy of it, though more of it is always being discovered. It is the most precious object on board the *Legend,* and it must never fall into the hands of the Enemy. Many Vestigians have devoted their lives to writing it down—and died defending it."

"Oh," said Ellie. It reminded her of her dream. Could this be the same Song Ishua had been singing?

"Tonight we will sing from Canto Twelve, Movement Four." The captain opened the enormous volume to a place near the middle. The pages were yellowed with age and spidered with veins of music.

Captain Daevin began, singing out each line of wordless music and pausing while the rest of them echoed it. The notes were crisp and busy, with a quick pace. Ellie liked the sound of it, but had trouble keeping up with the pattern of notes. It sounded different from the melody in her dream, yet somehow related.

They were only a few lines in when a wave of nausea sloshed in Ellie's stomach. She began to sweat. The music grew distant, the room blurred, and her limbs felt useless, detached from the rest of her body. She took a deep breath, and the sickness passed. But nothing around her looked the same.

She stood in a room whose walls and rafters—even the waterfall itself—were made of light. The crewmembers were bathed in a radiance that pulsed to the rhythm of the Song. But each person also had a unique nimbus of color around them, clinging to them like a hazy cloud. Jariel's was brilliant orange. She was tall and commanding, her playfulness absorbed into a regal bearing. Ellie glimpsed a flicker of gold, like a royal circlet, in her hair. Jude exuded a light green, like summer leaves. But the edges of him—his fingertips and feet—had no color at all. They were as clear and transparent as glass. Connor was small and hunched, as if he'd grown old overnight. His color was charcoal, and there was a great black welt on his back. Captain Daevin was a faded purple, and Owen was as blue as a rain-washed sky. Ellie blinked, but the colors did not go away.

Overwhelmed by this strange vision, Ellie sank down to sit on the floor. The Song abruptly stopped and the vision swept away from her, like the tide going out.

Jariel's arm was around her shoulders. "Ellie! Are you all right?"

Jude knelt down and felt her forehead with the back of his hand. "Do you feel sick?"

Ellie blinked several times. The colors and the lights were gone. She stared dazedly at the waterfall. "That's never happened before."

"What's never happened?" asked Jude, his forehead wrinkled with concern. "Did you get lightheaded or feel like you were going to faint?"

Ellie shook her head. "No . . . it was right when we started singing. I felt sick for a moment, and then everything . . . changed. The room was full of light, and I saw colors around all of you. Jariel, you were orange, and Jude, your feet and hands were see-through. Then the singing stopped and all the colors went away. That's when I got dizzy."

"I think you'd better go lie down in the infirmary for a while," said Jude.

"I'll walk her over," volunteered Jariel.

"Very good. But hurry back. The singing isn't over," said the captain.

"I'll come see how you're feeling afterwards," said Jude.

Jariel helped her down the hall and into the infirmary sickbed. Truthfully, Ellie didn't feel sick or dizzy anymore, but she appreciated the quietness of the room when Jariel was gone. She needed to think. The fire had burned low, and she watched the bed of ruby embers ripple with heat. The lights, the colors, the singing—what did it all mean?

Later on, Jude quietly opened the door and came in, followed by Jariel and Owen.

"How are you feeling?" said Jude, leaning down and feeling her forehead again.

"Better, thanks," Ellie said with a weak smile.

"You look fine to me," Jude said. "After a good night's sleep, you should be good as new. Not too much talking tonight, all right, Jariel?"

Jariel put her hand over her heart and nodded solemnly. As she blew out the candle in their room a few minutes later, all Ellie could think about was the golden circlet shining in that mass of red hair.

Chapter 8
Flying

The next day, Owen kept his promise to teach Jariel to fly. Ellie watched them pull on large, wing-like sleeves made out of dyed, oiled canvas. Owen held them up to the light, checking for holes or cracks.

"How do you use these?" Jariel asked, fingering the stiff boning inside the cloth.

"Like this," said Owen, sliding a green one up to his shoulder. There was a small wooden handle for a grip at the end. "Then two of these for your feet, but save 'em 'til we're on deck." He handed her pair of canvas flippers. "You sure you don't want to come, Ellie?"

Ellie shook her head. "I'm still feeling a little funny after yesterday. I'll watch."

Up on deck, Owen handed Jariel a rope. "Since it's your first time, tie this around your waist. It'll catch you if you start to fall." He climbed up on the railing behind the cygnera figurehead, strapped on his flippers, and unfolded the wings, then carelessly leaped off the ship.

Ellie and Jariel rushed to the railing, wondering if he was already plunging down to the ocean thousands of feet below. But instead he glided into view, green wings spread. He began to pump his arms, gaining height.

"This . . . is the hard part," he puffed, kicking his feet in the air. "Got to . . . get higher."

"All right, I'm going to try," said Jariel, buckling the flippers around her ankles. Ellie watched anxiously.

"Be careful, all right?"

Jariel grinned. "I will. You sure you're not coming?"

Ellie shrugged. "Maybe tomorrow."

Jariel climbed up on the railing. "So I just jump, and then flap my arms and legs?" she yelled to Owen, now a good ten feet overhead.

"Yep!" he called back. "You have tostart right away."

Jariel took a deep breath and looked at Ellie. "Well, here goes. Hullaballoooo!"

She jumped off the railing and didn't pop back up. Ellie leaned over the railing worriedly. Jariel was below the ship, her wings flailing crazily. After a moment, though, she untangled them and began to pump, gradually regaining altitude. By the time she reached Ellie's eye level, she was red with exertion.

Owen glided by in a zigzag pattern, like a floating leaf.

"Hey, good job, Jariel! You're doing it!" he called.

Jariel grunted. "I'm . . . trying."

"When you get about as high as the sails, that's the fun part. Just spread your wings out and let yourself glide," said Owen. "Like this."

A few minutes later, Jariel did. She let out a whoop. "I'm flying!"

"Jariel, watch out for the—"

Owen didn't get a chance to finish. A wisp of cloud swept over Jariel, soaking her. Instinctively she pulled her wings toward her, which caused her to plummet like a stone. She landed in a pile of sailcloth with a thud.

"Jariel! Are you okay?" Ellie ran over.

Jariel sat up, dripping wet and tangled in her wings. "Ugh! That was cold!" She grinned. "Let's do it again!"

Jariel jumped off for another flight, andEllie stood by the railing, watching. Her mind turned over the events of last night again. Her vision had changed as soon as the singing started, and when the singing ended, it had gone back to normal. It reminded her of her dream, when Ishua's singing had made the highways of light appear. Was there a connection? There was no one around, so she began to hum quietly, trying to piece together last night's tune.

She was only half surprised when she began to feel hot and a rush of nausea passed over her. The ship became radiant beneath her feet, the sails blossomed like sunrise clouds, and a wake of golden dust trailed behind it. Jariel and Owen glowed like red and green butterflies in the colorless sky. Far below, the distant islands were speckled with dots of light. One had only a smattering of golden freckles on its surface, while another had them clustered so tightly that they illuminated the nearby ocean. She stopped humming, and the lights faded. The wood of the ship returned to brown and the clouds to white against the blue sky. The dizziness came over her, and she slid down with her back to the railing. So the Song did have something to do with the visions. But what did they mean? She looked at the greenhouse. Maybe Jude would know.

Jude was on his hands and knees with a trowel when she knocked and poked her head in the greenhouse door.

"Jude? Can I talk to you for a minute?"

"Absolutely," he said, wiping his hands on his trousers. "Actually, you're the very person I wanted to see. After what happened last night, I did some research, and I think I may have found something."

"Really? What?" said Ellie, perching on a stool in the corner.

"Well," said Jude, "I was so intrigued by your symptoms and what you said last night that I went looking through the books in that old storage room. I found one by a Vestigian historian who lived nearly a thousand years ago. He said that 'purity of heart may appear as clarity of body for those who have eyes to see.' It made me think of what you said about my feet and hands being clear—though I hardly think I qualify as a good specimen. Then I found a small manual by a mythologist on the significance of colors. She said that colors reflect the conditions of our hearts and motives, and if a person could see the inner self, it would be vividly colored. Red, for example, would display courage or confidence, while blue would reflect calm. Darker shades contain less purity. I'm still not sure what triggered your vision, but I thought this might shed some light on what it means."

"Actually, I think I found out something about that part," said Ellie. "Today—just now, while I was watching Owen and Jariel flying—I tried humming a bit of the music from last night, and the same thing happened to my eyes. I looked down and saw lights on some of the islands, like towns at night. But there were different amounts on different islands. The ship was all lit up, and so was its trail in the sky. But it all vanished the moment I stopped singing. So the Song has something to do with all this."

"Hm," said Jude. "Interesting." He paused. "I don't know enough yet to be sure, but I think you have a gift, Ellie—a special ability to see people and things the way they really *are*. While you're listening to the Song, you can discern past all appearances and illusions to the truth of things—the way Ishua sees."

Nervously, Ellie remembered Ishua's words in the dream: *Do you want to see?*

"I don't yet know the significance of the lights on the islands and the ship," said Jude. "But if my theory is right—" he glanced up through the glass ceiling with a grin—"you could change everything for the Vestigia Roi. You could see through lies to people's true intentions. You could spot the Enemy's soldiers through any disguise. You could identify people who are ready to join the Vestigia Roi."

Ellie dangled her feet off the stool, dumbstruck.

"Oh! That reminds me." Jude reached for a book sitting on a long table against the wall. It was bound in smooth, reddish-brown leather.

"I don't think your talent for drawing is an accident, either," he said. "It means that not only can you see true reality, but you can also share it with other people through your drawings. So here. I made this for you." He handed her the book

"This is for me? You made it?" Ellie ran her fingers over the supple leather of the book. A strap bound it shut.

"It wasn't too difficult," said Jude with a smile. "Just a good thick surgery needle and some twine. You inspired me the other day. Here, open it."

Ellie unwound the strap and opened the cover. Inside was a thick stack of blank white pages. Ellie felt sudden tears start in her eyes.

"A sketchbook," she whispered.

"Do you like it?" Jude asked with concern.

She nodded. "It's just—I've only had one other sketchbook in my whole life. I thought I'd never get another one." She stroked the book's soft cover. "Thank you."

"You're welcome," said Jude. "I hope you'll use it to capture the things you see and share them with others. Many people long for just one glimpse of the kingdom they serve but can't see. You can show it to them. It will give them hope."

"Come on, Ellie!" Jariel called.

It was the next afternoon, and Ellie stood on the deck railing. Chewing her lower lip, she looked down at the islands stretched out beneath them like a tiny strategy board. There was nothing between her and them except for empty air and these flimsy blue wings. She swallowed hard.

"I don't think I can do this, Jariel."

"Yes, you can!" said Jariel, already airborne. She turned a cartwheel, as comfortable as if she'd been flying all her life. "Jump!"

Ellie tightened the rope around her waist.

"Oh, come on, scaredy-cat," said Connor, walking up in a pair of yellow wings. "Stop whining and jump already."

"Leave her alone!" yelled Jariel.

Ellie looked down. "Is that still Newdonia below us?"

"'Course it is, lunkhead," said Connor. "Don't you know your own archipelago?"

Ellie looked over her shoulder. "Yes. I've just never seen it from above before."

Connor rolled his eyes. "It's the same above as it is below. Now will you hurry up and jump so I can go?"

Ellie closed her eyes, trying not to let him rush her. She imagined herself sailing effortlessly among the clouds. She took a deep breath.

Suddenly she felt a shove in her back and lost her balance.

"Connor!" she heard someone yell.

Her stomach scrunched tight in terror as she felt only the air beneath her. She struggled with her wings, but they wouldn't open. Her insides felt jolted around like a shaken jar of jam.

Suddenly the rope snapped taut, knocking the wind out of her. She dangled in space, staring helplessly down at certain death.

"You've gotta pump your wings, Ellie!" came Owen's voice from far above her. "It'll bring you back up!"

The wings felt so heavy. Ellie tried to lift them up, then let them drop.

"Faster!" Owen called. "Use your flippers!"

It felt like hours before Ellie's head came level with the sails. Her arms and shoulders burned. Cautiously she stopped flapping her arms. She dropped a little, then felt the wind steady her and push her into a smooth glide. A smile broke out across her face and she closed her eyes, feeling the breeze sweep through her hair.

When she opened her eyes, she could see everything. Jariel turned cartwheels, and Connor sailed a few yards ahead. Though she was angry with him for pushing her, she couldn't help but admit that he was good at flying. He glided effortlessly on the wind, his feet kicking slow, powerful strokes. A real cygnera bird soared over them, craning its neck at them curiously.

"Look at this, Ellie!" said Owen. He led her over a large gray cloud, so close to it that Ellie could feel its mist on her face. She saw the shadows of fish swimming inside, and underwater plants swaying in the current. A cloud trout with streamers trailing from its fins broke the surface, and Ellie saw its bulging eyes and round silver mouth puckering open and closed. She waved, and the fish dove back into the depths of the cloud. Owen sucked in his cheeks and opened his mouth, imitating it.

Ellie couldn't stop laughing. She checked the rope around her waist. "I'm glad this lets me go so far," she said.

Owen looked back. "Um . . . well, that's why."

Ellie glanced over her shoulder, and her stomach knotted. The other end of her rope trailed loosely in the sky behind her. She was untethered. Nothing prevented her from falling to her death.

"You just needed a little push!" laughed Connor, soaring over her. "Just . . . a little . . . push!" He kicked her in the back, knocking her out of her steady glide pattern. She tried to pump her wings, but she couldn't regain air fast enough. She began to plummet.

"Jariel! Help!" she screamed.

"Grab my ankle!" came Owen's voice from somewhere nearby. Ellie flailed with her hands until they struck skin. Her fall slowed.

"Now grab mine," said Jariel. "Owen, we'll pull her up together. Ellie, you'll have to use your feet. Ready—pump."

Between the three of them, they eventually landed, panting and sweating, on the *Legend's* deck.

"Thanks," said Ellie when she could breathe again. "I guess I just . . . panicked."

"Yeah, I would panic too if it was my first time and someone *pushed* me," said Jariel, fire in her eyes. "That bully Connor could have killed you! You just wait'll I get my hands on him."

"Oh yeah? So you can do what?" Connor landed right behind them, his arms crossed.

Jariel lunged, and the others weren't fast enough to stop her. She barreled headfirst into Connor's stomach, and they tumbled to the deck in a flurry of red and yellow wings. Connor twisted Jariel's left arm behind her back. But Jariel spun around and caught him square in the face with her right fist. Ellie heard the sickening *smack*.

"Stop!" Ellie yelled, but no one listened.

Connor dragged his fingers across Jariel's face, and she kicked him in the shin. Connor was pulling Jariel into a headlock when the ship's bell began to clang sharply. Captain Daevin hurried out of his cabin.

Connor pushed Jariel down and let her go. A purple circle the size of a tomato was forming around his left eye, and four red stripes from Connor's nails stood up on Jariel's cheek. The captain looked at the children, his lips pressed tightly together.

"Children, I want to see you in my cabin immediately. All of you."

Chapter 9
A Mission of Rescue

The four children filed into Captain Daevin's cabin. Jude came in behind them, quietly closing the door. Connor and Jariel glared at each other from across the room.

The captain sat down at his large oak desk. Behind him was a cabinet of pigeonholes stuffed with tubes of rolled paper. There was also an array of gleaming brass instruments, probably for navigation. A smaller desk was pushed against the right wall, and a door in the left wall led off to his private quarters. In the corner was a birdcage on a stand. Ellie recognized the slender white eyret inside.

The captain drummed his fingertips together. "Children," he began. "Something has come to my attention that I must speak to you about."

Ellie looked at the floor. Uncle Horaffe had started many a lecture like this. Out of the corner of her eye, she saw Jariel squirm.

"I have just received a message from Rhynlyr," he said, fingering a roll of parchment no larger than his little finger. "Mundarva, an island from the south of Newdonia, has broken loose from the archipelago. The more time passes, the more quickly the current sweeps it toward the Edge. A speedy rescue is needed. And," he said, his eyes glittering, "we are only three days' sailing from Mundarva, making us the closest ship in the fleet."

Ellie frowned. What did drifting islands and rescue missions have to do with them being in trouble? Was he devising some elaborate punishment for what they'd done?

The captain stood and began to pace, his hands clasped behind his back. "The fleet has asked me to temporarily redirect the *Legend*'s course. Our mission would be to catch up to Mundarva and conduct a rescue mission there, bringing aboard anyone who is willing and transporting them to safety on Rhynlyr."

He turned on them, his eyes sharp and bright as a hawk's. "But I cannot accept this mission without your consent or your help. Sailing toward the Edge and landing on a drifting island is fraught with dangers. Your safety cannot be guaranteed. Furthermore, it would delay your start at the Academy. But"—he stood straight like a military commander—"there is adventure to be had, glory to be won, and should we succeed, our names will have a place in the history of the Vestigia Roi."

"And you will be giving a chance at life to those who do not even realize their own danger," added Jude.

"Of course," said Captain Daevin quickly. "You will also be doing a great service to the One Kingdom. Now, what do you say?"

"So . . . we aren't in trouble?" ventured Jariel cautiously.

"Trouble?" The captain looked at her blankly.

"For . . . fighting?"

"Fighting? Oh—oh yes," said Captain Daevin. "There will be time to deal with that later. But as for now, I must send an immediate response to headquarters. What shall I tell them? Will you be part of this mission?"

"I'm in," said Connor, sticking out his chin. "I don't care if I never start school."

"Me too," said Owen. "I mean, I want to go to Rhynlyr—but we'll go there afterwards, right?"

"Can I be the lookout?" said Jariel.

Ellie looked at the floor. She had come aboard the *Legend* looking for safety and a home on Rhynlyr. After her near escape today, the thought of sailing directly toward danger made her stomach clench into a tight ball. But the crewmembers of the *Legend*—most of them, anyway—already felt like a family. She couldn't lose another one of those.

"I'll go," she said, scraping the toe of her shoe against the floor, "but I don't know if I'll be much good at rescuing people."

Ellie still remembered the day she'd lost the Alston family. From the first day Pa Alston had knelt down to shake her hand at the train depot, she'd known she wanted to keep them. Ma was a thin, faded woman who worked hard and kept good track of scoldings. But Pa, with his bushy beard, large cover-all trousers, and booming laugh, had praised her drawings, taken her and Sam for drives in the buggy, and even let them watch him work at the lumber mill, where the sharp teeth of the saws bit off slice after slice of the long logs. Ellie didn't remember her own father, but she hoped that he'd been a little like Pa.

She and Sam had been coming home from school that afternoon, about six weeks after Ellie had received her sketchbook. They'd had to stay late for dance lessons. The school was holding a special performance at the end of the year, and Miss Nuthers had hired a dancing master to teach them a variety of dances.

As promised, Ellie had completed a drawing of Sam in her book, as well as one of their baby brother Robert and ten or eleven of scenes around the farm and school.

"I want to try drawing the creek again," Ellie sighed, watching the air ripple off the dirt road in the heat.

"Again?" said Sam. "But you already drew it."

"I know, but it looks different at different times of day. Besides, I don't think I got it right last time. I only used blue, and it looked like a blue snake, not a river."

"A blue snake. Sssss," Sam giggled.

"Next time, I'm going to put in green with the blue," Ellie went on, squinting up at the sky. "Maybe some white for light, and a little yellow to show the rocks at the bottom."

"All those colors are in the creek?" said Sam.

"I think so. I don't think I'll really know until I start drawing, though. There are so many ways to look at things, and so many colors to try."

Sam looped her arm through Ellie's. "Well, you'd better start trying them, so I can see if you're right."

They walked the rest of the way home arm in arm, right through the kitchen door.

Ma was sitting at the kitchen table, her head buried in her arms, making awful groaning noises like a hurt animal. Robert sat squalling at her feet, his tiny face beet red and his fists full of his mother's skirts. Behind them stood two men in homespun shirts, their straw hats in their hands. Ellie recognized them from the mill.

"What's wrong, Ma?" cried Sam, running to her mother. Ma raised her head, her eyes red and puffy from crying.

"Oh, Sam," she said, gathering her in her arms.

Ellie's stomach was crawling with fear. One of the men from the mill—she thought his name was Jahn—cleared his throat. His big hands slowly crumpled the brim of his hat as he spoke.

"There was . . . an accident at the mill," he said, his voice thick. "One of the saws, it started runnin' too fast. Splinters were flyin' everywhere." Ellie noticed a trickle of blood on his forehead. "Yer pa, he tried to . . . shut it down." Jahn swallowed. "He didn't . . . he didn't make it."

Ellie's mind went blank. She didn't cry. She knelt down on the floor and pulled the screaming Robert into her lap, patting his back.

"Shhh, Robert," she whispered. "Shhh."

Ellie helped Ma set the table for the funeral supper, helped clean the farmhouse before it was sold, helped Sam and Robert pack as they were shipped off to live with relatives. She knew what was coming for her. But she didn't cry, not even when she said goodbye to Sam, not until she was alone in Bed Fifteen of the Liaflora County Orphanage.

The next day, Ellie helped prepare the *Legend* for the mission to Mundarva. To fortify the ship, they had to nail boards across windows, add bolts to doors, and move the Song Book and other valuable documents to the windowless infirmary for safety. Ellie didn't know exactly what danger they were fortifying against, but she helped with the hammering and tried not to think about it too much.

Luckily, she didn't have to be near Connor at all. He was with Captain Daevin in his cabin, supposedly helping with navigational calculations. Meanwhile, she, Jude, Jariel, and Owen were adjusting the sails to gain as much speed as possible.

"Pull!" shouted Jude. He knotted the end of a rope securely around a cleat on the railing. It was a fresh, blustery afternoon, and the rope snapped taut as the sail puffed out eagerly. The three children were on the sail's other rope, pulling with all their might.

"I *am* pulling!" howled Owen.

"Harder!" yelled Jariel, throwing her weight backward.

Jude came behind them and pulled, and soon the sail was securely fastened. "Good work, mates," he said, winding the excess sail rope around his arm.

"Hey, there's Connor and the captain!" said Owen, leaning over the side. Captain Daevin and Connor were dangling off the side of the ship, strapped into harnesses. The captain was hammering something to the ship, and Connor went behind him with an enormous paintbrush in each hand.

"What are you doing?" yelled Jariel. "Are you *painting*?"

"No, you ninny-head!" Connor yelled back. "We're *caulking*!"

Ellie saw the captain turn sharply to Connor. It looked like they were having a serious talk.

"Caulking keeps the ship airtight and helps it go faster," Jude explained calmly. "Come on; let's let them do their job and we'll do ours."

The *Legend's* pace increased and they clipped along rapidly. The clouds cast spray on the children's faces as they flew by. But what awaited them at the end of their swift journey?

Ellie sat on one of the benches in the Oratory, letting the mosaic of light wash over her. The sound of the waterfall was soothing, muting the din of her thoughts. The water was so colorful that it looked alive.

Rescue. Danger. The Edge. Just thinking about their new mission made Ellie shiver. Why did she have to be so afraid? Why couldn't she be excited for adventures, like Jariel?

She looked up as one of the doors opened. Jude stepped inside.

"May I join you?"

Ellie nodded, scooting over to make room for him on the bench. The two of them watched the waterfall as it changed in the shifting light.

"Thinking about our new mission?" he said at last.

Ellie nodded. "I wish I could be brave like the rest of you. But I'm just—scared."

Jude nodded. "That's understandable. This mission isn't safe."

"Exactly."

"But, if you think about it, there's nowhere in the universe that's really *safe*," he said. "I'm a doctor; I've seen people get injured or killed in carriage accidents or in houses that collapse. I even heard of a man who was attacked and killed by a bird as he walked along the seashore. People drown, get struck by lightning, die in their beds."

"That doesn't really help."

"My point, Ellie, isn't to scare you, but to show you that nowhere is really 'safe.' Nowhere except the King's City, the capital of the One Kingdom, which is beyond the reach of the living. Yes, this mission is dangerous, and it's all right to be afraid. I've been on more than a few rescue missions, and I still get scared sometimes. But members of the Vestigia Roi look for more than safety—we are venturing into danger to bring *others* to safety. We're fighting back against the one who poisoned the islands. We're helping to restore the One Kingdom. Because Ishua will not lead us astray, we can follow him fearlessly." His eyes were kind as he patted her hand. "So take courage, Ellie. Though this life we lead may frighten us sometimes, there is no life more worth living."

Ellie swallowed. She wasn't sure if she could fully believe that, but being around Jude made it a little easier.

Chapter 10
Training

Weapons training began at sunrise the next morning. Owen's hair stuck out at all angles, and Ellie was rubbing sleep out of her eyes as they lined up in the dining room. But Captain Daevin's boots were polished and he was wearing a finely tailored red coat.

"All right, soldiers," he said when they were all assembled. "Salute!"

Ellie hesitated, not sure what a salute looked like. Jariel energetically invented one. Owen hurriedly stuffed a slithery caterpede into his pocket, then began to squirm as it moved.

Captain Daevin sighed. "I suppose we'll have to start from the beginning."

He straightened his shoulders and raised his voice. "You are soldiers now! When I say 'salute,' this is what I want to see!" He snapped his booted heels together, then tapped two fingers of his right hand to his left shoulder and then to his forehead. Ellie recognized the gesture Chinelle had made on the night she and Jariel left.

"Now! Two straight lines! Salute!"

Sleepily, the children shuffled into two lines. Jude gently scooted Ellie to the left. She tried to imitate Captain Daevin's gesture.

"Not good enough!" barked the captain. "You must show discipline!"

They tried the salute nearly two dozen times before the captain accepted it as "good enough." Then he brought out a crate and thunked it down before them.

"Our Enemy will not spare you because you are children. His *urken* and *helkath* and creatures of darkness will do everything they can to keep this mission from succeeding. We must be ready for them. Choose your weapons!"

The crate was half full of armaments, many of them old and rusted. Broken pieces littered the bottom. Connor dove in first. His black eye was beginning to fade. He pulled up four connected rings with sharp points on them. He slipped them on his left hand, where they gleamed like tiger claws.

"I claim these," he said, grinning fiercely.

Jariel was on her knees, rummaging through the box. Suddenly Connor made a second grab, coming up with a slender dagger. Its blade was spotted with rust, but the hilt was inlaid with green stones.

"Hey, I wanted that!" said Jariel.

"I've got it now," Connor shrugged.

She glared. "You always just take what you want, don't you? You're always thinking of yourself first."

Connor pointed the dagger at her. Ellie's heart lurched. Captain Daevin moved like silver mercury and grabbed Connor's wrist, twisting his arm backward until he winced and dropped the dagger.

"Never," the captain hissed, "*ever* let me see you do that again. Even *pretending* to threaten another crewmember is grounds for me to expel you from the Vestigia Roi. Out of mercy," he released Connor's arm, "I will consider this a warning. But I will keep your weapons until training begins."

"*I* wouldn't consider it a warning," grumbled Jariel under her breath.

Captain Daevin turned on her.

"And if I hear another word to *that* effect, you'll be scrubbing out bilge drains until we reach Rhynlyr. A Vestigian crew must be ready to support and defend each other, even to the death. Threats and bickering make us no better than the enemy. Neither of you will be allowed to leave the ship for the duration of the mission. If I can't trust you to respect one another, I certainly can't trust you to rescue others."

Jariel's mouth dropped open. "But—can't I land on the island with the others? Connor started it!"

"Should've kept your mouth shut," said Connor with a smirk.

"Enough!" snapped the captain. "I had intended to spend more time thinking about the mission assignments and announce them later, but I see that only Ellie and Owen are prepared for this dangerous landing. On the ground, my orders must be obeyed without question or squabbling. Apparently neither of you is ready to do that."

"Please, can't I go?" begged Jariel, her eyes welling up with tears. "I'm sorry for what I said, and I won't do it again."

"Not this time. Prove that you are ready, and when the time is right, I will give you another assignment." He looked at Connor. "That goes for you, too."

Jariel sniffed and let out a sigh that was almost a sob.

Ellie chewed on her lower lip. "So . . . Owen and I are going to Mundarva with you?" she ventured.

"Yes! Haven't you been listening?" The captain threw up his hands in exasperation. "Now, hurry and choose something out of the crate. We've wasted too much time already."

Ellie crouched down beside Jariel, who continued to rummage through the weapons. Ellie could see her friend's chin trembling.

"Jariel! How about this?" said Jude, holding up a short bow. He plucked the string and it gave a sharp *twang*. Jariel's face brightened a little.

"Are there arrows to go with it?"

A bit more rummaging produced a leather quiver containing fifteen or twenty arrows. Jariel stood up and proudly buckled it over her shoulder. Owen found a slightly rusty blowpipe and a bundle of darts. Ellie kept searching halfheartedly. She saw nothing she could even imagine herself using. She couldn't even stand up for her friend against a bully. What could she possibly do in a battle?

Owen pulled something up. "What about this, Ellie?"

It was a forked stick, the grip just long enough for one hand, with a stretchy band fastened to both prongs of the fork. *A slingshot.* There was also a soft leather pouch full of pebbles.

"All right." She accepted the weapon uncertainly. She'd never used a slingshot before, but at least it meant she wouldn't have to get close to an enemy.

They spent the next several hours on weapons training. Jude overturned the dining table and padded it with old flour sacks for target practice.

"I wish you did not need to use weapons," he told them. "But the captain is right—our enemies will not show mercy, and so we must be prepared."

As Owen launched his darts with short, sharp puffs of air, Ellie snuck a glance at Connor, who was practicing hand-to-hand combat with the captain. Captain Daevin was using a rapier with a gold basket hilt.

"That dagger's short, so you'll have to make it count," he told Connor. "Keep both arms close to your body. Never raise them above your head. There you go." Metal clashed on metal as they went through the motions of a practice fight.

"Now turn—use the dagger to block your body," said the captain. "Now lunge forward with the claws. Good!"

Connor barreled forward, left fist outstretched. The captain leaped aside just in time, chuckling. "You pick it up quickly."

Meanwhile, target practice was not going so well. All Owen's darts ended up in a clump on the far left edge of the table. Jariel couldn't even seem to hit the table. At the end of her round, arrows were sticking out of the walls, the ceiling, and the infirmary door. Owen, Ellie, and Jude had taken shelter under the staircase. Jariel looked around at her mislaid arrows and put her face in her hands.

"I'm no good at this," she groaned.

Jude helped her with her second round, showing her how to sight down the arrow and aim just a hair above the target. But by the end of the round, she'd still only landed one arrow on the target, and that was dangling loosely from the edge of a flour sack.

"Maybe we haven't found the right weapon for you," said Jude, dragging out the crate again. Looking into it, he pulled out a small rectangular shield and a short, thick knife.

"Try these. You're fast and have strong arms. Ask Captain Daevin to show you a few moves."

Jariel unbuckled the quiver of arrows and slid her left arm through the loops on the back of the shield. It covered her from elbow to knuckles, curving slightly around her arm. She knocked on its hard surface and waved it around. A smile broke out on her face.

"Hey, it's light. I think I like it."

The only one who didn't have any trouble with target practice was Ellie. She sighted the bull's-eye exactly between the prongs of the slingshot, exhaled, then released the stone. Shot after shot clacked off the center of the table.

"Bravo, Ellie!" said Jude when she finished her round. "I had no idea you were such a good shot."

"Neither did I," said Ellie, looking skeptically at her weapon.

"Don't look at the slingshot," Jude laughed. "It's you. Good aim comes from steady hands and clear eyes."

After several hours of weapons training, the fighters were dragging. Jariel rubbed her sore shield arm, and Ellie's eyes were crossing from staring so hard at the target.

"We will take a short rest for lunch, then split up," announced Captain Daevin. "Connor and Jariel, you will go with Jude to learn the defense of the ship. Owen and Ellie, come with me."

"All right," said Jariel sulkily. Connor flashed her a mocking smile.

After lunch, Ellie and Owen followed Captain Daevin to his cabin. He selected a roll of paper from the cabinet behind his desk and began to unroll it.

"Have I already told you how Vestigian rescue missions work?" he asked, not looking up.

"Well . . . I've heard the story about Thelipsa and the islands," Ellie said. Owen nodded in agreement.

"There's a lot more to them than that," said the captain, weighting down the edges of the scroll with smooth stones. "The Vestigia Roi prefer prevention to cure, planting agents on the islands to care for the people and coral over the course of years. But sometimes something interferes with the agent's work, and the coral dies and breaks loose. That's when an emergency rescue is needed. The message I received said that there is a Vestigian agent on Mundarva. But we do not know if that person is still alive, or is free to move. It will be our job to find them, as well as to persuade islanders to come back with us and be rescued from certain death. Ellie, I think this is where your gift of Sight may be useful. Jude told me his theory, and I agree: you may be able to identify those who will be receptive to our message. You can help us choose our conversations wisely and rescue as many people as possible."

"Can the people tell that their island is drifting? Do they know that they're in danger?" asked Ellie.

The captain shook his head. "The motion is so gradual that those on the island cannot feel it. Thus, those you speak to about rescue may think you're out of your minds. To make matters worse, a rescue team usually consists of at least six experienced sailors who have several days to speak to the islanders. We will have only a few hours."

"Captain Daevin? How do you know all this about rescue missions?" Owen traced circles on the desktop thoughtfully. "I mean—you haven't actually been on one, have you?"

Captain Daevin's face flushed. "I may not have been on a rescue mission before, but I spent six years at the Academy, where we became very familiar with mission protocol through simulations under the supervision of high-ranking officers," he said quickly. "So don't think that I don't know what I'm doing. You are still under my authority." His dark eyes flashed.

Owen looked at the floor. "I was just wondering."

"Well, you can stop now." Captain Daevin cleared his throat and pointed to the scroll in front of him. "This is a map of Mundarva," he said. The U-shaped island was drawn in pen and ink, with the V-R symbol in the top left corner. "It is an island of learning. Scholars flock there from all across Newdonia and sometimes even from the other archipelagos. However, sometimes the most learned can be the most blind. It may be very difficult to convince them of their danger."

He tapped opposite ends of the island with two fingers. "The largest village, Saklos, is all the way on the east side of the island. But the Great Library, the hub of Mundarva's learning, is to the southwest. Unfortunately, when we land at the island core, we will have to choose between them."

"Could we—split up?" Ellie suggested. "That way we could go to both."

The captain shook his head. "That would leave one or both of you with no supervision or protection. It's too dangerous."

"Don't worry about us, Captain Daevin. Ellie and I can take care of each other. I think it's a good plan," said Owen.

"It would allow us to cover more ground," said the captain, stroking his goatee. "And it might mean rescuing more people. Do you think you are equal to the task?"

Ellie hesitated. Out of the corner of her eye, she saw Owen nod confidently.

"Very well," said the captain. "I will go through these difficult hills to Saklos, and the two of you will go together to the Library."

"What do we do when we land?" Ellie asked, wiping her damp palms on her skirt.

"Take every chance you have to start conversations. Use your Sight—try to identify people who are willing to listen. Tell them about the danger their island is in, and about the Vestigian ship ready to rescue them if they'll come." He shook his head. "Realize, though, that a fleet of flying ships will sound like a folktale to some people. If one person refuses to listen, move on to another. Be cautious—and above all, don't be late in returning to the island core."

At supper that night, Ellie could hardly eat. She tried to listen as Owen talked about the bugs he hoped to collect on Mundarva, but her thoughts were rushing around like a whirlpool. She wished the mission were over.

Chapter 11
Mundarva

It was mid-morning the next day when Captain Daevin sighted Mundarva through his spyglass.

Fingering the edge of the slingshot in her right pocket, Ellie reported to the ship's hold. Her heart was thudding so hard it made her ribs rattle.

The others were already there. The captain handed Ellie and Owen their coats and a canvas knapsack each. "Each of you has two more coats in these—for anyone we bring back."

Jariel helped Ellie into her coat and hugged her.

"Come back safe and soon," Jariel said with a sniff.

"I'll try," said Ellie.

"Let us sing," said Jude. Arms went around shoulders as the crew gathered into a circle. Ellie's throat was so tight it hurt.

Jude began to sing, his voice low and husky.

Protect them, Father King
As your song they sing
May the islands hear your call;
Keep them from the final fall.

"May Ishua protect you all," he said.

They started down the rope ladder from the trap door. Captain Daevin went first, with Ellie next and Owen last. As they descended,

Ellie noticed the air around them gradually getting warmer. Glancing down, she glimpsed white cliffs and turquoise-blue waters.

They disembarked at Mundarva's island core within sight of the ocean. There had been a stairwell inside the one on Freith, but this core was just a pit dropping down into the earth. It looked like an abandoned well.

"No Vestigian has tended this for quite some time," remarked the captain, poking the edge of the muddy pit with his shoe.

The sun was directly overhead, close and mercilessly hot. Ellie longed to run down to the sandy white beach just a few hundred yards away and plunge into that bright blue water. To the west, south, and east, rows of lush vines spread out in all directions. Climbing up neatly tended trellises, the bright green leaves seemed to glow in the light. They were beautiful, but they also trapped the sticky heat close to the ground and deflected any hint of a breeze. Ellie stripped off her coat, her hair already sticking to the back of her neck. The captain took off his dark blue military coat as well. "We will leave our coats here," he said, stowing his knapsack beneath the vines. Ellie and Owen were only too happy to obey. Cooler, they sat down and ate the sandwiches they had packed earlier.

"What are these plants?" asked Owen, looking around.

"Grapevines," said the captain, lifting a cluster of pea-sized green fruits. "This harvest will never get a chance to ripen, though."

"Too bad," said Owen. "I've never tasted grapes. I'll take some leaves for Tera, though." He picked a few and put them in his pocket.

When they had finished, they stood up and brushed off.

"Do you both remember the plan?" asked the captain.

Ellie nodded, ticking off the items on her fingers. "Find the Library, talk to everyone we can find, be back here . . . "

"Five o'clock exactly," said the captain, pulling a silver disc from his pocket and handing it to Owen.

"Your pocket watch!" Owen exclaimed.

"It's my second-best, so take care of it," said the captain. "Keep careful track of the time. We cannot afford to be late, not even by a few minutes."

"Um—where exactly *is* the Library?" asked Ellie, shading her eyes with one hand and looking around.

"Is that it?" Owen pointed at a distant glint of sunlight. "That might be the sun reflecting off a building."

"Indeed it is, Owen," said the captain, checking his compass. "Exactly southwest. Here, Ellie, you keep charge of the compass. When you return, point the needle northeast—halfway between the N and E—and follow it back here." He handed it to Ellie. "Be careful, both of you. And remember—don't be late."

"Yes, sir!" said Owen, throwing his practiced salute. The captain returned it and marched off in the other direction, toward the village of Saklos.

The going was easy, and Ellie and Owen reached the Library more quickly than they'd expected. They emerged from the grapevines onto a wide, chalky path that circled a wall of white stone. The crenellated wall threw back the sun's light so brightly that it made Ellie's eyes water. A blue-green dome peeped just over the top.

"Uh-oh," said Owen. "We're going to have to get past that wall."

Ellie chewed on her lip. "I don't think we can climb it. We'll have to look for a gate."

They began to circle the fortress, the white path reflecting the sun's heat even more intensely. They soon found a gate, but two men in white livery were slouching in the shade of the gate's arch. The guards stepped forward when they saw Ellie and Owen approaching.

"What is your business?" asked the first guard. Under his peaked white hat, he had swarthy skin and a clean-shaven face. He looked younger than Captain Daevin.

Ellie looked at Owen, but his face was blank. She licked her lips, her mind whirring. "Please—sir," she said, surprised at how pitiful her voice sounded. "We've come a long way . . . " she trailed off, pointing back the way they had come. *It's not a lie,* she told herself.

"Villagers," grumbled the young guard. "Varian, you know what the Masters say about unauthorized villagers entering."

"Tsk, Cobal!" The second guard, an older man with a dark beard, leaned down. "Are you children here to visit someone?"

Ellie nodded, trying to play along.

Cobal narrowed his eyes. "*Who* are you visiting?"

Ellie's mouth opened and closed. "Our . . . mother," she said, her heart sinking. *Now it's a lie.*

"What did I say?" said Varian. "They're only children wanting to find their mother. Use your head! You're leaving them fainting in the heat out here."

"Oh, very well," said Cobal, pushing on one of the doors behind them. It opened with a deep groan.

"Good luck finding your mother," said Varian. "It's busy inside—market day."

"Thank you, sir," said Ellie, bobbing a curtsy.

Varian chuckled. "See, Cobal? Polite as can be."

Ellie and Owen hurried inside, and the gate shut behind them. Owen looked at Ellie with a grin.

"That was amazing! They believed everything you said!"

Ellie winced. "I'm just sorry I told that fib about our mother. Let's not waste any more time. Where should we start?"

The main building in the enclosure had to be the Library. It was a circular building with smooth white walls encircled by a ring of white columns. Narrow windowpanes glittered like gems in the sun, and at the very top was a metal dome, weathered to a light blue-green patina. Around it were many low, whitewashed buildings. Compared to the Library, they looked squat and plain. But people were bustling all around them, wearing white robes and carrying baskets.

"Market day," muttered Ellie. "Owen, I think we're going to have to split up."

"Split up? But I told Captain Daevin I'd stay with you!"

"Well—" Ellie looked helplessly at the people milling around the courtyard. "Look at all these people. We can't talk to both them and the people inside the Library."

Owen looked up at the imposing structure of the Library. "I think I'll stay out here." He grinned. "This is where the bugs'll be."

"All right. Let's meet back here at four o'clock. That should give us enough time to get back."

"How will you keep track of time?" said Owen. "I've got the pocket watch."

"There has to be a clock inside. I'll see you then," said Ellie. "Now go!"

Casting a backward glance at her, Owen hurried off toward the outbuildings.

Ellie faced the formidable Library dome and took a deep breath. To bolster her courage, she began to hum a simple tune from last night's singing.

The nausea was over almost before she noticed it, but the change in her vision was drastic. The blinding whiteness all around her dimmed to an old, weather-beaten gray. The white-robed people looked small and drab. In fact, the only light came from the double doors to the Library. One of them was half-open, and light burst from it like a shout. Golden tendrils branched out on the path before her feet, curling in the dust like letters of fire.

Ellie let go of the Song and the vision disappeared. She stepped inside the half-open door.

The entryway was dim, with only one high, small window for light. Inside, a young woman in a black robe sat behind a desk, reading. There was a pucker between her eyebrows, and she did not seem to notice that anyone else was there. Her glossy brown hair was pulled back in a knot, but one rogue strand slipped down, and she puffed it absently out of her eyes. Ellie studied the woman's dark eyes, high cheekbones, and pointed chin, and thought what a good charcoal portrait she'd make.

At last Ellie stepped forward. "H-hello," she said nervously.

With a gasp of surprise, the woman snapped the book shut and hid it under the wide sleeves of her robe.

"Can I help you?"

"Um," Ellie swallowed, her tongue like sandpaper. She had to think of something that would get her inside. "I'd like to see the Library—please."

The woman relaxed and pulled a tall black book from a drawer. "A prospective novice, then. Wonderful. And what is your name?"

"I'm Ellie."

She entered the information with a quill pen that squeaked. "And what are you interested in studying here, Ellie?"

"Uh—art. You know . . . drawing."

"Drawing?" The young woman looked up, her brown eyes flickering with interest. "Are you an artist, then?"

"Oh, no. I mean, I hope I will be someday. I do like to draw, though," said Ellie.

"I suspect you'll be interested in our collection of paintings, then," said the woman, closing the book and replacing it in the drawer. "I am Scholar Edrei, and I will give you a tour of the Library." She lowered her voice to a whisper. "You'll be my excuse to get out from behind this desk. And you can call me Vivian." She winked, the light of her smile making her eyes twinkle.

Vivian slipped the book she had been reading into an inner pocket of her robe. Ellie caught a glimpse of red leather and letters she didn't recognize.

Vivian led Ellie into a cool, dim hallway, walled on one side with a series of leaping arches. The pillars were covered with colored mosaics that glittered with hints of gold. Ellie cleared her throat. Maybe this would be a good place to bring up the *Legend*.

"Miss Vivian—"

"Just Vivian, please. Oh, Wark! I need you to take over the desk for the afternoon," she called to a leathery old man tipped back in a chair. He opened one eye.

"None of my business."

"But I am giving a tour for a prospective novice," Vivian entreated. "Please?"

Grumbling, the little man got up from his chair and headed toward the entry hall, his short black robe swishing.

"Thank you, Wark," called Vivian with a grin. "All right, follow me, Ellie."

They approached an arched door in the hallway. Vivian stopped.

"Close your eyes."

"My eyes?" Ellie hesitated. "Why?"

"Just trust me."

Ellie obeyed, and Vivian's smooth hands drew her forward into a space filled with light.

"Ready . . . open!"

They were standing directly under the dome of the Library. From overhead, a round skylight bathed the entire rotunda in tranquil white light. The rest of the dome was painted with alternating panels of starry skies and mythical scenes—wars, weddings, judgments. The room was like a grand cathedral to knowledge. A spiraling ramp circled the entire rotunda, descending past floors and floors of workspaces lined with books. In some, she could see black-robed people writing with long quill pens or poring over open books. Even the floor was intricate, a grand mosaic formed of thousands of colored tiles. There were long strands of triangles, squares within lozenges, spirals of swirling gold, green, and turquoise, but Ellie couldn't see what shape they formed from this level.

Vivian began to climb the spiraling ramp, and Ellie followed. It was made of the same bluish metal as the dome, and a continuous inscription scrolled around the railing in strange, foreign letters. Ellie looked down at the floor mosaic as it shrank beneath them. Now she could tell that it was a giant sun on a background of ocean. The light from the dome made the rich colors gleam and sparkle.

About two floors up, a fat man with a gray beard approached them. He was dressed exactly like Vivian, except that his robe had a red stripe running from collar to hem.

"Blessed be the Search," he said, holding up his palm.

"And fruitful be the mind that seeks, Master Elgin," answered Vivian, pressing her palms together and bowing. Ellie did her best to imitate the motion.

"Who is this, Scholar Edrei?" asked the fat man, gesturing to Ellie.

"Her name is Ellie, Master Elgin," said Vivian, putting a hand on Ellie's shoulder. "She is a prospective novice, interested in the study of Art. I am giving her a tour of the Library."

Master Elgin frowned. "You know the lower age limit is ten, Scholar Edrei," he said, tucking his hands into the wide sleeves of his robe. "How old are you, little girl?"

"Twelve," answered Ellie, lifting her chin. "I'm small for my age."

"Certainly not too young to learn from the Library's wealth of knowledge," Vivian added. "I will take personal responsibility for her for the duration of the tour."

"Then I suggest you remain watchful," said Master Elgin, his eyes narrowing, "if you value your scholarly career." He swept past them, bumping Ellie's arm on the way. Vivian steered Ellie up the stairs. They stopped off at a doorway marked *Fifth Level.*

"Well," said Vivian in a low voice, "Master Elgin may be a Scholar Seventh Level and the Library's Master of Manuscripts, but I am sorry for his rudeness. I have all confidence that you will conduct yourself appropriately in the Library."

Ellie nodded. "I will. I just hope you don't get in trouble because of me."

They entered a marble-floored gallery, lit by a series of windows and mirrors. The walls were lined with paintings, and Ellie exhaled with pleasure. The only paintings Ellie had ever seen up close were the ones in the home of the Beswicks, the wealthy couple who had been her first adoptive parents. She'd been only four at the time and had known nothing about technique, but she still remembered a painting of a full moon shining on a lake. Now, in the Library's gallery, she paid close attention to the blending of the colors, the weight and thickness of the brushstrokes, the detail in the facial features. Portraits of old men in black robes made up most of the collection, but there were some landscape paintings as well. A small one of an ocean wave shattering into a plume of spray sent a thrill through her. She examined it.

"Blue, green, white, yellow—is that brown? I can see *through* this water. And the spray—it looks just like air." Ellie sighed. "I wish I knew how to do that."

"Maybe you just need the right tools," said Vivian. "We have a treasure trove of books on painting here. If you can identify five different colors in a picture of water, it seems you have an eye for it." She smiled.

Ellie looked up into that smiling face, longing to pour out all she knew about the Vestigia Roi. But suddenly she found that that her mouth was dry.

When they reached the end of the gallery, they continued up to the sixth floor, one short of the top.

"I am a Scholar Sixth Level, so my workspace is on this floor," said Vivian. "I'll show it to you. I also have limited access to the classified research materials on the seventh floor." She grinned. "There are some *wonderful* books up there. Someday, when I am a Master, that is where my workspace will be. Then I'll be able to read those books as much as I like." They stopped in front of a door, and Vivian turned the knob.

"For now, though, welcome to my castle."

The room was full of the warm, sweet, dusty smell of old books. Vivian lit a match, dispelling the half-gloom of the waning afternoon, and touched it to a strange contraption, a candlestick surrounded by mirrors.

"I brought this from my home," Vivian explained. "I much prefer the smell of candles to oil lamps. They give better light, too."

As the flickering light grew stronger, illuminating the desk, ceiling, and walls, Ellie surveyed the room. It was *crammed* with books. There were books everywhere: shelved in double layers against the walls, stacked in wobbly towers on the floor, covering the seat of the only chair, lying open on the desk. There were books on the steps of a wheeled ladder attached to the bookshelf, and books on the ledge of the window into the rotunda. There was even a wooden machine in the corner that had rotating shelves attached to a wheel, allowing multiple books to remain open at once.

"Are all the workspaces like this?" Ellie asked, overwhelmed by the presence of so many books. She liked the way they looked and smelled, but the thought of so much reading made her head swim.

"Well," said Vivian, scooping the books off the chair, "to some extent, though the others may look less like storm wreckage. Please, sit down."

"What do you do in here?" asked Ellie, studying the machine with the crank.

"I do research, copy manuscripts, translate." Vivian perched on the edge of the desk, sending two or three papers drifting down to the floor. She looked affectionately over the room. "Languages and Linguistics is my area of expertise. I'm fascinated by the words and languages people have invented to communicate with each other. I especially love dead languages, those with fewer than two speakers left alive. Those are like the voices of long-gone civilizations. When I learn those languages, I can hear the past speaking."

"Wow," Ellie breathed. "How many languages do you speak?"

Vivian shrugged. "Not as many as some Scholars in my field. I can read in about eighteen, but I only speak five or six well enough to converse." She laughed. "In the others, I would just end up insulting people."

Ellie's mind reeled. *Eighteen languages?* "Do you have a favorite?"

"A favorite?" Vivian laughed. "That would be like asking a mother to choose her favorite child. I like them all, except perhaps Guduk—speaking it feels like choking. I do like Knerusse—it's been dead for over two thousand years, but I wish I could speak it all day. It's mostly vowels."

"Can you say something in it?"

Vivian thought for a moment. "*Ssiali lythassu elyrium hala,*" she said, pronouncing each word lovingly. Ellie listened, enthralled.

"What does that mean?"

"It means 'Under our trees, you are a friend.' It's a greeting."

Ellie sighed. "It sounds like blue streamers in the wind. Or water running through reeds."

"What a lovely way to picture it!" Vivian exclaimed. "You really must be an artist to see pictures like that."

See. Ellie looked at Vivian, already feeling a bond of friendship growing between them. She wished Vivian would come back with her, join the *Legend*'s crew, and be safe. Her heart hammering in her throat, Ellie took a deep breath.

"Vivian? Can I . . . tell you about something?"

Vivian leaned forward. "Of course."

Ellie swallowed, blurting out the words before she lost her courage.

"I—I'm not really here to see the Library or study art. I mean, I do love art and want to learn about it, but that's not—I mean, there's a Song, and ships that fly—and Ishua, and—and your island is drifting, and you have to—you have to escape, and—" *I sound like a lunatic,* Ellie thought. She saw Vivian's eyebrows tilt upward, pity written on her kind face. In desperation, Ellie began humming the Song. It was the first part, the one Ishua had begun in her dream.

Her voice started out cracked and whispery, but the familiar melody gave her confidence. Her vision changed, and the Library went dark, as black as the closet Ewart had once locked her inside. The only light in the whole building came from Vivian, outlining her in golden penstrokes. The vision lasted only a moment, though, because then Vivian's hand clamped over Ellie's mouth, stifling the Song.

"Shhh!" Vivian hissed. "What are you doing? Don't you know the Masters could have you flogged, or me expelled, for that? That is dangerous music!"

Ellie blinked as Vivian removed her hand. "You—you know the Song?"

Vivian looked hard at Ellie. "Close the door." Ellie did so, and Vivian locked it with a key from her desk. Then, from the inner pocket of her robe, she pulled the red book she had been reading earlier.

"I found this book on the seventh floor, bound for the incinerator heap. I thought it was there by accident, and since it was a valuable specimen of Antoth, whose last speaker died two hundred years ago, I rescued it. Then I started reading. It's about the Prince of the Islands, a man named Ishua, who founded a rescue fleet of flying ships after Thelipsa's Rebellion. It's a history book, but it reads like a fairy tale—bravery, friendship, sacrifice. I couldn't stop reading. And then I found this."

She thumbed carefully to the last page. There, in flaking black ink, were a few hand-written bars of music.

"When I was a novice here, the Masters taught me that there were many kingdoms—the arts, the letters, the sciences—and that the human intellect ruled over them all. But this book claims that there is only One Kingdom, and Ishua and Adona Roi rule it. And—well—I know it sounds silly, but when I learned the Song, I knew the story was true." Her eyes flicked upward, wide and frightened. "Please don't tell anyone about this. The Masters would call this book treasonous. If they found it in my desk, I would be expelled from the Library forever."

"I think you have bigger things to worry about," said Ellie. "Mundarva's coral foundation has broken loose, and this very second, the island is drifting toward the Edge. It only has a few hours left. Please come back with me—I came from a flying ship that can take you to safety. I know it sounds strange, but it's the truth. Please come?"

Vivian stared absently into the rotunda.

"You *do* believe the story, don't you?" asked Ellie.

Vivian bowed her head. "Yes."

"Then you have to come. It's all true." Ellie was surprised to feel tears sting her eyes. "Please say yes. This is the only way you can be saved."

Vivian looked at the wall, where a clock with wrought-iron hands ticked steadily. "Then I guess I'd better start packing."

At that moment, there was a loud banging on the door. Vivian turned pale. "Quick, hide this," she said, shoving the red book into Ellie's hands. The pounding came again. Vivian walked slowly toward the door while Ellie stuffed the book in the bottom drawer of the desk and covered it with loose papers. She barely had time to close the drawer before Vivian opened the door.

Master Elgin stood in the doorway, his face livid with rage.

"Master Elgin! Whatever is the matter?" asked Vivian with a hurried bow.

His cheeks puffed out, turning his whole face red. "The matter! As if you didn't know! Master Antal's portrait in the gallery, defaced with quill ink! Two hundred years of history, destroyed in a moment! It is an outrage, and *someone* is responsible." He turned his glare from

Vivian to Ellie. "Did I not warn you about keeping that child under supervision?"

"Master Elgin, please! Ellie could not have defaced Master Antal's portrait, even if she had wanted to. She has been with me since the moment she entered the Library."

Master Elgin's face went from red to purple. Vivian looked like a willow reed before the tempest of his wrath.

"Then you were party to the crime! You are hereby stripped of your rank and expelled from the Library, effective immediately!"

Vivian drew herself up to her full height, her eyes flashing. "Now, just a minute. There are hundreds of novices in this Library who could be responsible, yet without evidence, you single out the one in my care. If you carry a personal grudge against me, then bring it out and don't mask it with this hollow accusation! The Library is my home, and I would never be party to its harm. If you cannot see that, you must be even more blind than I thought."

"If defacing Library property wasn't enough, this alone would expel you!" Master Elgin roared. "Lying, defiance, and insulting a superior! And don't think I don't know about your meddling with seventh-floor materials." His eyes narrowed. "Pack your things and get out immediately. You can never return here."

Vivian held her chin up, her face a mask of calm. "Very well. You need not expel me—I resign. If I had known this institution of enlightenment was so blind to the truth, I would have left sooner. You need not fear. I will never return."

Quivering with fury, Master Elgin stormed out of the room, slamming the door so hard that the bookshelves trembled. As his heavy footsteps died away, Vivian sank to the floor.

"Wow! I'll bet no one's ever talked to him like *that* before," said Ellie, crouching down beside her. "You were so brave!"

Vivian put her face in her hands. "I shouldn't have said any of those things. Now I'll never become a Master or finish my research." She gave a quiet groan. "Everything I've dreamed of and worked for, gone in one day."

Ellie put an arm around her shoulders. "But Vivian—you were going to leave anyway, weren't you? Remember the ship, the Edge?"

Vivian sniffed. "Yes. But I'd rather not have left in disgrace."

"Nobody will care about that where we're going. And at least Master Elgin didn't find your book." She trotted over to the desk and pulled it out from under the papers.

"That's true," Vivian said, wiping her eyes with the sleeve of her robe. "He probably would have burned it and put us both in prison as traitors."

"Then let's get out of here," said Ellie. "I'll help you pack."

At four o'clock sharp, Ellie and Vivian stood outside the closed doors of the Library. The westering sun warmed the walls with a golden glow. Vivian, carrying a bulging knapsack, gave the stones a last wistful caress.

Just then, Owen came up, limping. His shirt was unbuttoned and wrapped around a bundle on one side.

"Owen! Are you all right?" Ellie cried.

He winced. "I don't think I did a very good job of talking to people. All I got was a beating in the marketplace. But you'll never guess what I found." He looked at Vivian, noticing her for the first time. "Who're you?"

"This is my friend Vivian," said Ellie. "She's coming with us. Vivian, this is Owen." Ellie lowered her voice. "Vivian, do you think—could you pretend to be our mother? Just while we get through the gate? We told the guards we were looking for her so they would let us in."

"Are you two brother and sister?" Vivian asked.

Ellie shook her head sheepishly. "That was part of the act, too."

"Well, I have no experience, but I'll try," said Vivian, extending a hand to each of them. Her grasp was calm and confident. It wasn't hard to pretend.

As it turned out, the gate guards had changed, but they took one look at the three figures hand in hand and let them pass through. Ellie glanced over her shoulder for one last look at the white-walled city of knowledge. She remembered her vision of the darkness inside the Library, with only Vivian outlined in light. They had done all they could here.

Ellie and Owen held on to Vivian's hands until they were deep in the grapevines. Then they dropped hands and stretched. Ellie felt a twinge of disappointment that this family was only make-believe.

"I don't think I'll be needing this anymore." Vivian cast off her black Scholar's robe, letting it lie where it fell, half-draped over a vine trellis. Underneath, she was dressed in the baggy white shirt and brown trousers of a field laborer. She shook out her tight bun, letting her glossy, waist-length hair fly free, and hitched up the straps of her heavy knapsack.

"Why are you wearing boys' clothes?" Owen asked.

"Well, if you were going on a journey, wouldn't you prefer trousers, too? My stars, but dresses are a nuisance."

Owen turned to Ellie. "Want to see what I found?" He took off his shirt, keeping it carefully wrapped around the bundle he had knotted in one side.

Ellie gasped. "Owen, your back!" Angry red welts stood up from Owen's pale skin, and between them were some nasty cuts. "What *happened* to you?"

He shrugged. "I tried to talk to a big man about Ishua and the Edge, and he chased me away. When I came back, he started beating me with a stick. Then his wife came out with a leather belt that stung like blazes. Luckily, I'd collected a few spiders that I dropped on the man's hand. They were harmless, but he didn't know that. He started to jump around and scream, and I made a break for it. I lost the spiders, but I found something better."

"I'm just glad you weren't hurt worse," said Ellie. "I'm sure Jude'll fix you up when we get back."

"Prob'ly. Now look what I found." Owen untied the bundle in his shirt. He slowly lifted out a wriggling white coil striped with blue rings.

Ellie stifled a scream. Vivian bent closer.

"That's quite a find. What kind of a snake is it?" Vivian asked.

"It's a bluestripe ribbon snake," said Owen proudly. "I've seen it in books. Don't worry, Ellie, it's not poisonous. I found it by the well outside the Library. I've wanted a snake for *so* long."

"Is it . . . safe there in that pocket?" said Ellie, steadying herself.

"Yep," he grinned. "I'm calling him Mobius, Moby for short. I can't wait to introduce him to Tera."

When they reached the island core, Captain Daevin was already there, along with another man. The stranger was shorter, with a swarthy complexion and the coarse shirt and trousers of a field laborer.

"Are we late?" puffed Owen as they reached them.

"Ten minutes," growled the captain. He looked up and noticed Vivian for the first time. "And who might this be?"

"Vivian Edrei," she said, hitching up the heavy pack on her shoulders.

"An honor to have you with us, madam," said the captain with a bow. "May I take your knapsack for you?"

"Oh, don't trouble yourself. It's quite heavy." She shrugged it up on her shoulders.

"All the more reason. Please."

Ellie raised her eyebrows. The captain was already carrying a knapsack of his own.

"Well—if you insist," said Vivian, letting the pack slip to the ground. "Please be careful, though. Its contents are very precious."

The captain tried to lift it with one hand, then dropped it. He reddened, then lifted it with both hands.

"What *do* you have in here?"

"Books," Vivian grinned.

"Vivian's a Scholar from the Library," Ellie explained.

"Ah. I am Captain Daevin Blenrudd, and this is Manul, the Vestigian agent on Mundarva."

Manul made the Vestigian salute to Ellie and Owen and the Scholar's bow to Vivian. They each returned in kind.

"You all are a gift from Ishua," he said. There were dark shadows under his eyes. "I have been on Mundarva for three years. I did my best to speak to the people, first in the Library compound and then in the village, but the people only seemed to grow more hostile to my message. I was under house arrest when the captain found me. I would have fallen with the island if you had not come."

"Let us speak of such things when we are safely aboard our ship," said the captain grimly. "Coats on."

Ellie handed Vivian a coat from her knapsack and began buttoning up her own. A sudden movement, seen from the corner of her eye, made her look up.

At the ocean shoreline, only a few hundred yards away, black shapes were beginning to rise out of the water. Ellie blinked, wondering if the heat was playing tricks on her eyes, but the shapes grew larger and larger. There were nearly a score of them.

"Um, captain?" She pointed at the shapes. "What are those?"

The captain squinted in the direction of her hand and hissed something under his breath. He dropped the knapsack of coats.

"What's wrong?" said Owen.

The captain was still for a moment, staring at the shoreline, his jaw clenched so hard that a muscle twitched in his cheek.

"Urken," he muttered. He ran a hand through his hair, not taking his eyes off the shore. "The Enemy has followed us here. We cannot climb this ladder with them behind us—they could follow us or cut us down. We'll have to fight here."

"F-fight?" Ellie stammered, thinking of the flimsy slingshot in her pocket.

"Ooh, a real battle!" said Owen, taking off his shirt containing Moby and stowing it safely among the coats. "I can't wait to try out my blowpipe."

The captain pulled two long knives out of his boots. Manul turned to the nearest grapevine and broke off a thick, sturdy branch. Seeing it, the captain seemed to relax.

"Have you engaged the Enemy in combat before, Manul?" he asked.

Manul shook his head. "I have never seen the Enemy's creatures for myself. But I think I know what to do with them." He gripped the branch in his broad, solid fists.

Sweat stood out on the captain's forehead. "Then you and I will take the offense. The rest of you—cover us with missile fire. Owen, you find a spot on our right flank; Ellie and Vivian, take the left. These creatures fight by no code of laws or rules. We must destroy them or be destroyed ourselves."

Ellie stood frozen, watching in terrified fascination as the black shapes barreled across the beach toward them.

"I wasn't expecting this when we left the Library," Vivian said to her. "What are we supposed to use for missiles?"

"Um . . . I have these," said Ellie, pulling a handful of slingstones out of her pocket.

"Those will do," said Vivian, grimly weighing a stack of them in her hand.

It was less than a minute before the band of urken were upon them. Shaped like short, stocky humans with hunched backs and gangly arms, they carried nasty hooked weapons and angular shields. The shields had a reflective coating that shrank and distorted their enemies' images. Ellie caught a glimpse of herself, and she looked tiny and terrified.

Captain Daevin's knives moved like twin bolts of lightning, felling the first attacker instantly. The urken's thick body crumpled, and the captain stepped over it and moved forward. Manul shoved another one and it fell, shrieking, into the pit of the island core. The two men seemed to be everywhere, harrying the enemies with sharp blades and heavy blows. The urken band hesitated, unprepared for such fierce resistance.

Owen had wriggled under a trellis of grapevines, and was using his concealed position to pick off enemies with his blowdarts. His aim was still skewed to the left, and most of his shots only managed to annoy as they glanced off hands or shoulders. But one stuck fast in an urken's neck, and the creature made a horrible gurgling sound as it went down. When all his darts were spent, Owen gave a yell and jumped into the fight. He picked up the sword of a fallen urken, nearly as long as he was, and began swinging it in a large circle, slashing at anything that dared to get too close

Vivian pelted the enemies energetically with stones. She flung a rock at the nearest urken, missing its eyes but delivering a stunning knock to its forehead. Ellie held the slingshot, but it hung limply in her hand. Her arms felt pinned to her sides, too heavy to lift. All she could see were the enemies' slitted yellow eyes and the wiry hairs sticking out of their flat skulls. Her breathing was loud and ragged in her ears.

The urken pressed forward, pushing against Captain Daevin and Manul. An urken followed a quick block with a punch, shoving the captain backward. He reeled and fell, close to the trellis where Ellie and Vivian stood.

"There are so many of them," he muttered.

Vivian sent a stone whistling through the air. It found an urken with a sickening *crack*. "We'll win if we keep fighting!" she told the captain. "Don't give up!"

Captain Daevin stared at Vivian for a moment as if considering her in a whole new light. Then he got up with a grunt and trooped back to the fray.

"Come on, Ellie, use that slingshot!" Vivian shouted. "We need you!"

Ellie looked at her slingshot. Her pulse was thundering in her ears and her hand was trembling, but she loaded a stone and let it fly. It only glanced off an urken's shield, but it gave her courage. Her second shot knocked the sword out of an enemy's hand.

A cry drew Ellie's attention. Owen lay on the ground just yards away, an urken's many-stranded whip biting into his back. He screamed as lines of blood crisscrossed his skin. Ellie started to duck under the grapevine trellis, trying to help him, but Manul was already on his way. The big man shoved aside the urken he was fighting and crashed through the battle toward Owen. Manul struck the attacker with his club and the urken reeled back. Owen crawled to safety under some sheltering vines.

Suddenly Manul winced and pressed a hand to the back of his neck. A black, fist-sized shape plopped to the ground.

"Helkath," he muttered, kicking the fallen shape into the pit. "Blast."

Ellie stared in horror as a puffy purple welt began to form on his neck. He lowered his club and stared out at the ocean with strange, listless eyes.

"It's no use. We cannot win this fight."

"Manul!" yelled Captain Daevin, struggling to reach him. Urken kept crowding in front of him, blocking his progress.

"Might as well die sooner than later," Manul muttered. He dropped his club. The earth shuddered faintly, and the weapon rolled into the island core and was lost.

An urken charged toward Manul. The big man watched passively as the attacker came on, lifting its hooked sword. Captain Daevin shouted, trying to warn him, but it was no use. When the weapon came crashing down on his head, he offered no defense.

Ellie screamed and covered her eyes with her hands. She had just watched a brutal murder. Why, oh why, couldn't she wake up from this bad dream?

"Ellie! Climb the ladder!" yelled the captain. Forcing her eyes open, Ellie saw a pile of black bodies—and Manul's limp arm extending from beneath a grapevine. The others pushed her forward, and Ellie almost fell into the pit of the island core, but the captain caught her and forced her up the ladder. She began to climb doggedly, feeling the weight of the others behind her. She didn't risk a backward glance until she was high up. The turquoise sea lapped at Mundarva's white shores, oblivious of the death and violence that had just occurred there. And far out in the water, a single boat bobbed like a dry leaf. In it, a standing figure stood watch, its black cloak billowing like wings in the sea wind. A knot of cold dread tightened in Ellie's stomach.

Chapter 12
Discoveries

Ellie's arms were stiff and heavy by the time she reached the wooden bottom of the *Legend.*

"To the One Kingdom!" she yelled hoarsely.

"May it be found!"

Jude appeared in the opening. One by one he helped the rescuers up, and they lay sprawled on the floor, panting for breath. Ellie's muscles trembled, and she felt sick to her stomach. Jariel's face appeared in front of hers.

"Ellie! You're alive! Are you all right?"

"Mmm," Ellie groaned.

The rescue party was in sorry shape. Jude sat them around the dining room table and took care of them as they told the stories of their mission. He cleaned and bandaged the whip cuts on Owen's back, and frowned as he gave the captain a foul-smelling poultice for a gash in his arm. Ellie wasn't hurt, and he just gave her a cup of chamomile tea to calm her nerves. Jariel sat next to her, patting her back.

"What—what happened to Manul, Captain?" Ellie ventured at last. It felt awkward even to say his name. "He changed so suddenly during the battle—just dropped his club and stopped fighting."

The captain rubbed his forehead. "He was bitten by a helkath, a creature of the Enemy. They're like big spiders. Their poison doesn't kill, but it does cause their victims to lose hope, to forget what they believe in. To make matters worse, helkath bites are almost impossible to prevent, since the creatures are invisible until after they release their poison and die."

Ellie shuddered, reliving scenes from the battle all over again.

"The effects aren't permanent," offered Jude. "Black borrage root, used as a poultice and a tea, draws out the poison in about two weeks."

"Well, Manul didn't have two weeks," observed Owen.

"No," agreed the captain. "Which is one more reason why helkath bites are so dangerous."

Jude came to Vivian last.

"I'm fine," she insisted, pushing loose strands of hair out of her face. "Tend to the others; nothing happened to me."

"I'm just making sure," said Jude. "I'm a doctor; it's my job." He checked her face, then her hands, which had a few small cuts. In spite of Vivian's protests, he gently applied a mild antiseptic and several bandages.

"There. That wasn't so bad, was it?" Jude looked up into her face.

"I suppose not. You are very gentle."

A pink flush climbed up Jude's neck and into his face. "Hm-mm," he cleared his throat. "All—very—thank you."

Breakfast the next morning was unusually delicious. There were sweet rolls brushed with cinnamon and sugar, fragrant mugs of herbal tea, and fresh blueberries from Jude's garden. Vivian sat between Ellie and the captain, taking everything in.

"Who made these?" Ellie asked as a bite of bread dissolved in her mouth. It was like biting into a cloud.

"Connor did," said the captain. His neck was still bandaged, and he looked a shade pale, but his beard was freshly trimmed and he wore his dress coat.

"Dey aw dewicious," mumbled Owen through stuffed cheeks. Moby was draped around his neck.

"Would you like another?" the captain offered Vivian, lifting the plate.

"Watch out!" shouted Connor. From underneath the plate crawled a huge, hairy spider. Ellie screamed. Everyone jumped up at the same time, knocking over the benches.

"A tarantula!" cried Vivian.

"Stand back!" shouted the captain, lifting the plate.

"No!" screamed Owen.

But it was too late. The captain brought the plate smashing down. There was a huge crash.

Broken china lay everywhere. A large piece covered the center of the table, where the spider had been. Owen's eyes were fixed on it. A fragment of broken plate crunched under his shoe as he stepped forward.

"Tera?" he said hoarsely.

He lifted the big piece of crockery. Underneath, in a mound of shattered china and mangled rolls, lay the flattened shape that had been Tera. She was crushed into the tabletop, and two of her legs were missing. Owen's face lost its shape. Tears began to dribble down his face. He let out a moan.

Ellie put her arms around him, feeling as if she were going to cry herself. She'd never liked spiders, but Owen had loved this one. It felt like a funeral. Jariel joined in, wrapping her arms around them both.

"Well, it seems that *someone* has some explaining to do," said the captain crossly, surveying the table full of broken china and ruined sweet rolls. "What is the meaning of this?"

From across the table, Connor shrugged. "I don't know, sir. Owen's the one who keeps bugs for pets."

Captain Daevin looked at Owen. "Is this your doing, young man?"

Owen couldn't stop crying. He buried his face in his hands.

"It isn't Owen's fault!" said Ellie. "Tera was Owen's favorite pet. He would never hurt her."

"Well, whoever it was has a lot of sweeping to do," said the captain, narrowing his eyes.

Suddenly Jariel stepped forward. "*You*," she said, pointing at Connor. "You planted the spider!"

Connor pointed to himself. "Me? I hate bugs."

"But you stole Tera and put her on the table." Jariel's face was red. "You did it to get Owen in trouble. You killed his favorite bug, just for spite. You're the meanest, most selfish person I ever met. I wish we'd left *you* on Mundarva to fall off the Edge!"

"That's enough!" bellowed the captain. "I don't care who did this. You will all spend the morning cleaning up this mess. He turned to Vivian. "I am terribly sorry that this was your first impression of the *Legend*. While this gets settled, may I offer you some breakfast in my cabin and then a tour of the ship?" He offered her his arm.

"Are you sure? I can help— "

"Perfect," said Captain Daevin, sweeping her toward the stairs.

Ellie stood on a stool, glumly scrubbing one of the surviving plates. It was cloudy, and the morning light coming through the scullery window was weak and gray.

"Well, this is the last I could save," said Jariel, sliding a plate and mug into the washbasin. "Owen's cleaning up the rest of the trash. Poor kid. He looks pretty bad."

"I know," said Ellie. "I'm glad you found out Connor's plan, though."

Jariel gritted her teeth. "Oooh, that Connor makes me so mad. Of all the mean things to do. If Jude hadn't posted him on deck and me downstairs while you were gone, we prob'ly would've killed each other."

"Sometimes he reminds me of Ewart," said Ellie. "But then . . . other times he doesn't. Even though he sometimes does horrible, mean things like he did today, there's also another side to him I can't figure out. It's hard to explain."

"Well, let me know if you find it," said Jariel dryly. "I think he's just a big bully who toadies to get on the captain's good side."

"Speaking of the captain, did you see him and Vivian this morning?"

Jariel laughed. "Did I? 'Another roll, madam? A tour of the ship, milady?'" Jariel made a loud kissing noise, making Ellie double over with laughter. "He's a goner."

Ellie groaned. "Now I'm never going to get Vivian to myself. You should hear her stories, Jariel. She knows all sorts of things about languages and books, and she actually makes them sound interesting. And now Captain Daevin's going to steal her away."

"Maybe." Jariel shrugged. "Maybe not."

When the dishes were clean, Ellie went to look for Vivian and Captain Daevin. She found them as they were leaving the Oratory.

"Oh, Ellie, have you seen that beautiful room?" said Vivian breathlessly. "The waterfall, and—and the ceiling!"

Ellie smiled. "It's my favorite room on the *Legend*."

Captain Daevin frowned at her. "Don't interrupt, Ellie. I've several things left to show Vivian, and I don't need your help."

"She can come," said Vivian. "She's not harming anyone, and I like her perspective."

The captain grunted, and they continued down the hallway. Captain Daevin gestured to two or three closed doors without stopping.

"These rooms were used as extra dormitories when the *Legend*'s crew was larger," he explained. "Now they are used for storage. Of course, we could convert one into a private room for you, if you'd like."

"There's no need for that," said Vivian. "I like sharing the dormitory with the girls—that is, if you and Jariel don't mind, Ellie."

Ellie shook her head energetically.

"May I have a look inside these rooms?" Vivian ran her fingers down the third door.

"What for?" said the captain. "They're nothing more than disorganized closets."

"I love closets!" said Vivian. "Closets are adventures. You never know what you'll discover inside."

"All right, then," said the captain, turning the knob on the door. "But don't say I didn't warn you."

The storage room was dim and surprisingly large. Several bookshelves stood empty, while equipment, books, and furniture lay in jumbled heaps on the floor. Cobwebs clung to the corners.

Vivian knelt down by one pile, gently pulling out a book with a crusty leather cover. She blew a puff of dust off it. Captain Daevin sneezed.

"This ought to go in your ship's library," Vivian said.

"We don't have one."

Vivian spun around to face the captain, horror on her face.

"Er—" he coughed. "Not yet, anyway."

But Vivian didn't seem to be listening. She stood up and paced the length of the room, navigating around some crumpled-up sailcloth and a chair with a missing leg. She measured a bookshelf with her arms. Then she turned to face the captain, her face glowing.

"I think I could turn this room into a library. A combined library and scriptorium." Her eyes swept the dingy ceiling and walls. "I'll clean it all up and make a proper home for these books. It'll be my project. May I? Please?" She clasped her hands entreatingly.

A small smile curled Captain Daevin's lips. "This room is yours. Do whatever you wish with it."

A grin broke out over Vivian's face. Impulsively, she flung her arms around him. "Oh, thank you! Can we save the rest of the ship tour for tomorrow? I can't wait to start on this."

"Very well," agreed the captain with a chuckle.

"Can I help?" Ellie offered.

"Of course!" A few strands of hair had escaped from Vivian's braid, and her eyes were sparkling. "Are you ready to start?"

Chapter 13
In the Library

Ellie and Vivian began by moving all the clutter out of the new scriptorium and library. They worked until their backs were sore and their sweaty skin was coated with dust. Captain Daevin helped for a while, but the dust made him sneeze and soon he retired to his cabin. The others, drawn by the noise, dropped in one by one to watch or help. Jariel used her long arms to pull down the moth-eaten curtains, flooding the room with light. Connor paused to loiter a moment in the doorway, casually asking if there were any books on astronomy. Owen was still wandering in the fog of his grief, but his eyes lost their listless glaze for a moment when he trapped a small spider in one of the cobwebs. Vivian told him she'd seen a pictorial encyclopedia of insect life that he could borrow.

Mid-afternoon, Jude dropped in to bring the laborers some tea.

"So this is to be the new library?" he said, looking around. The floor was mostly cleared, and Ellie had opened the round windows to let in some air. Dust motes drifted in the shafts of light.

"And scriptorium," said Vivian, standing up and stretching. "Then we'll not only be able to organize existing books, but copy and illustrate more. There are plenty of shelves, and those windows will let in lots of light—once they're clean, that is. I'll see if I can find some reading chairs and a desk or two. It's too bad I couldn't bring my book wheel with me—that was such a useful research tool." She wiped her forehead with her hand, leaving a dirty streak behind. "Phew, it's hot in here. I'm going to go up on deck for a breath of fresh air."

When she was gone, Jude crouched down next to Ellie. "What's a book wheel?"

"It's a machine that Vivian had in the Library. It was about this big," Ellie held up her hands at her eye level, "and it had shelves that moved when you turned a crank."

Jude glanced at the door through which Vivian had left. "Do—do you think you could make a drawing of it?"

"Yes." Ellie nodded slowly. "I got a pretty good look at it in the Library."

"Well," said Jude, "I have an idea. If you can draw it and give me some rough measurements, I think I can build another one. We could do it secretly and surprise her."

"She'd love that! Of course I'll help."

"Help with what?" Vivian came in, twisting her hair back into its braid.

"With . . . his garden!" Ellie said quickly. "I help Jude with his planting and weeding." She winked at Jude.

"I have yet to see your garden," Vivian said, smiling. "Would you show it to me? Perhaps tomorrow, to complete my tour of the ship?"

"I—you're—of co—yes." Jude wiped his forehead. "I'd—better go. I should—get back to work." He turned and hurried out.

"Is he all right?" Vivian looked after him with concern.

It was all Ellie could do to contain a fit of laughter. She knew exactly what was wrong with Jude.

The crew was just finishing supper when there was a distant *boom*. Captain Daevin rushed up the stairs, followed by the others, who clustered around his spyglass.

"What's happening?" asked Connor.

"Mundarva—it's falling," said the captain.

Ellie froze. The terrible event she'd heard about only in stories—it was happening right in front of their eyes. The captain offered the children turns at the spyglass, but Ellie didn't want one. Seeing the vague, dark fleck on the horizon was enough for her. She didn't want to watch the beautiful island fall to its doom.

"It's tilting up in the air!" cried Jariel, who had the spyglass.

Everyone watched the horizon breathlessly. Then Jariel lowered the glass.

"It's—it's gone."

Vivian had tears on her cheeks, her nose red in the numbing wind.

"Fruitful be the mind that seeks," she whispered. Captain Daevin put his arm around her.

Then Jude began the Song, a new part that was slow and sad. Ellie closed her eyes, listening to the music. When she opened them, her vision had switched. The amber sunset had absorbed into the people around her. The crewmembers glowed, and the *Legend* itself left a glittering wake. But the rest of the sky was dark. The Edge seemed much closer, and there was a dark, empty pit where Mundarva had been. It wasn't dark like a room with all the lights out—it was a *living* darkness, a darkness that ate light. The total blackness made Ellie shiver. Then, inside of it, ghastly flowers that glowed with an unhealthy green-white light began to appear. They began to wriggle and move, away from the black hole and toward the *Legend.*

Ellie collapsed to the deck and covered her head with her hands. Abruptly the music stopped.

"Ellie! Ellie, what's wrong? What do you see?"

She felt herself being gathered into strong arms and carried, but it was a long time before she dared to open her eyes. When she did, she was in the infirmary, her face against Jude's rough shirt. The others were all there, watching her anxiously.

"What did you see, Ellie?" asked the captain, his forehead lined with worry.

Ellie buried her face against Jude's shoulder. "I don't want to talk about it."

"How about a cup of tea first?" said Jude.

The chamomile tea was calming, and when she had finished it, Ellie asked for her sketchbook and colored pencils. She chose the black one and took a deep breath.

"After the island fell," she began, coloring in a black circle, "I saw this black hole—darker than anything I've ever seen." She switched her pencil for a stick of charcoal and rubbed it hard over the black circle. "This still isn't dark enough. It was like . . . the darkness was swallowing up the light around it." She squeezed her eyes shut. "Then lights began to appear in the hole. I don't even have a color for them. *Dead* is the best word I can think of—like ghosts. But then they started to move—toward us." Tears sprang unexpectedly to her eyes. "I was so scared."

Jariel wrapped her arms around her. "Shhh," she whispered. "It's over now."

Captain Daevin and Jude exchanged a grim nod, and the two of them got up.

"We have some business to take care of," said the captain. "Don't wait up for us." They left the room together.

"What are they doing?" asked Owen.

Vivian looked at the closed door. "I don't know. But I think we'd better get some sleep. It's been a long day for all of us."

Ellie shivered. "I don't think I can sleep after all that."

Vivian stroked Ellie's hair. "What do you say we leave a candle burning tonight? I wouldn't mind a little light myself."

As Ellie lay in her bunk, trying to sleep, the ship pitched and rocked in a sudden storm. The candle's orange flame leaped crazily up and down, and gigantic shadows billowed and shrank on the walls. Finally Ellie got up and blew out the light. Those jumping, looming shadows were worse than the dark. Listening to Jariel's peaceful snores, Ellie eventually drifted off to sleep.

She was scrambling up a steep slope studded with rocks. Out of the corner of her eye, she glimpsed a ghostly green flower floating toward her. She tried to climb faster, but the dirt shifted under her feet and she slid backward. A second flower joined the first. Her heart pounded and she gasped for breath. Would she ever reach the top?

She looked up and saw a ledge, just a few feet above her, where a man was sitting on a bench. He stood up, leaning on a pair of crutches.

"Ishua! Help me!"

He reached out his hand and helped her over the ledge. The pale flowers fell back and vaporized as she held his hand. She leaned against him, and they sat down on the bench.

"Ishua, why do I have to see these things? The golden lights and the flowers and the darkness—what do they mean? And why me?"

Ishua put his arm around her. His soft, checkered shirt smelled of fresh grass clippings.

"You already know what your Sight means, Ellie. You see the truth of things."
"I know, I know, things as they really are. But what *are* they? I don't understand."

"Many people live their whole lives without even trying," Ishua said wryly.

"But I want to know!" cried Ellie. "What about the darkness I saw today, and those flowers that grew out of the hole?"

Ishua sighed. "There is only One Kingdom, ruled by Adona Roi, and nothing can change that. But there are some who try. Our Enemy, Draaken, imagines a world he calls Khum Lagor: a world in which all the landwalkers on the islands obey and serve him. But if they will not bow, then he wishes to see them destroyed, snatched forever from the One Kingdom. When an island falls over the Edge, it is a site of great triumph for him—he loves to watch the agony of people who realize their blindness too late." Ishua bowed his head, his forehead lined with pain.

"And the flowers?"

"In the space left by a fallen island, Draaken's power is strong. He cannot create slaves for himself—only Adona Roi has the power to make new things. But he can call back the souls of the rebels who have fallen and bend them to his will. In his underwater dwellings, they are given unnatural new bodies and made into soldiers for Draaken's army."

Ellie shuddered convulsively. "So they're . . . not really dead, but not really alive? And they're after us?"

"I'm afraid so," said Ishua grimly. "Draaken hates you. The Vestigia Roi steals his victory, rescuing souls who would otherwise belong to Khum Lagor. He will do whatever he can to stop you."

Ellie scooted closer to him. "What about the golden lights, then? I see them around the ship, and sometimes around the crew. I even saw them around Vivian on Mundarva."

"There is evil in the world, Ellie—much evil. But there is also good. Those lights are a sign to show you where the One Kingdom is growing. Vestigians who have sailed a long time with the fleet begin to develop a sense for it—but you have been given the gift of seeing the Kingdom with your eyes."

"Why me?" Ellie moaned. "It would be so much easier if I didn't see any of these things."

"The burden of Sight is heavy," Ishua said, his brown eyes full of compassion. "I know, because I carry it, too. But the gift was not given for your benefit alone. Do you remember the orphanages where you've lived? You were frightened there, because you didn't know if there was anybody who cared about you or was watching over you. That same thing scares everybody sometimes, even if they don't show it. Your Sight isn't going to take away your fear, but it can give you hope that the Kingdom is growing and that you have a part in it. And through your drawings, you can share that hope with other people. You are their eyes." He smoothed her hair. "You are not alone to face the world, Ellie. You are watched over. Although the Enemy is strong and real, I am never far away."

Ellie looked up at him. "But I can't always see you."

He smiled, stroking her cheek with his calloused thumb. "If you ever wonder where I am, all you have to do is sing."

In the morning, the tired crew gathered for breakfast. No one had slept very well except for Jariel, who could sleep through a war and a double earthquake. Connor looked slightly green.

"Are you—okay?" Ellie asked.

"Mind your own business," he grumbled.

"If the rocking last night made you sick, maybe some tea would—"

"I said, mind your own business!"

Ellie sat down quietly. She watched Connor staring at the thin, sloshing layer of porridge in his bowl. He looked so miserable that she almost felt sorry for him.

The captain had dark circles under his eyes.

"I apologize for the turbulence last night," he said. "I do not wish to frighten you, but Ellie's vision last night revealed to us that we are not alone in these waters. We are—being followed." He paused. "Last night, Jude and I let out the sails, threw our extra equipment overboard, and charted a zigzag course in hope of throwing the Enemy off our trail."

"Did it work?" asked Jariel anxiously.

The captain sighed. "We will find out, probably later today. In the meanwhile, no one is to go up on deck without my permission. Connor, I need your help with navigational calculations. The rest of you—go about your regular work, but keep your weapons at hand."

As dishes were cleared away and chores were done, a thick, heavy silence settled over the ship. Ellie tucked her slingshot into her pocket, but she didn't feel much safer.

When she was done with chores, she wandered into the new library. Vivian was on her hands and knees, her face shiny with sweat as she scrubbed the floor with a stiff brush. She looked up when Ellie entered.

"Hello, Ellie. Come back to help again today?"

Ellie nodded.

"I'm trying to get everything clean today so we can start moving books in. Would you like to wipe down the shelves?" Vivian tossed her a wet rag. "I've never seen so much dust in my life."

"All right," said Ellie. It felt good to have something to do.

After a while, Owen drifted in, looking for the entomological encyclopedia. All the books were still in stacks, but Vivian remembered where she'd seen it.

"How—how are you?" Ellie asked him. "I mean—about Tera."

Owen stroked Moby's tail, which draped down from his shoulder. "I miss her. I don't think I'll ever find such a beautiful tarantula again. But Moby's a good pet, and I still have my other bugs."

"Would you ever want a pet that wasn't a bug or a snake?" Ellie asked, keeping her distance as Moby poked his head into Owen's shirt pocket.

Owen shrugged. "Maybe. I really like bugs. But I'd kind of like to try a dog someday." He smiled. "I'd just have to keep my pet fleas in a separate box."

Ellie smiled back. It was good to see his eyes lose that distant, empty look, even for a moment.

Owen curled up to read his encyclopedia in the hallway, pulling the fat book close to his nose. Ellie went back to scrubbing shelves, and Vivian began moving furniture into the room.

A few minutes later, Jude almost collided with a huge oak desk as Vivian tried to drag it through the doorway. Jude picked up the other end of it, and the desk floated lightly into the room.

"Thank you," Vivian panted when the desk was settled beneath one of the windows. "I wasn't sure how I was going to get that all the way over here."

"You're welcome." Jude quickly turned to Owen.

"Oh, there you are, Owen. I've been looking for you."

Owen looked up from the encyclopedia.

"This is a great book, Jude. It's got scientific classifications and pictures of every bug in Newdonia. You'd like it."

Jude smiled. "I'm sure." He produced a small, narrow package from his shirt pocket. "I have something for you."

"It's not my birthday," said Owen, but his fingers were already undoing the cloth wrapping. A pair of small, round spectacles fell into his hand.

"Glasses! Are these for me?"

Jude nodded. "I think they may help with your aim in target practice. And you won't have to hold your books so close to your nose." He pulled the encyclopedia an arm's length away. "Give them a try."

Doubtfully, Owen slipped the glasses on, pushing the bridge up on his nose. He squinted at the faraway encyclopedia, then slowly relaxed and sat back.

"Wow, it's so . . . clear!" he said, his eyes roaming around the room. "I can read the titles of those books over there, and . . . and Ellie's eyes have black rings around the blue."

Ellie laughed. "Those are good glasses!"

Jude rumpled Owen's hair. "I had a spare pair in the infirmary. I guessed you might be nearsighted, so I fixed them up for you. I hope they work."

Owen was still looking hungrily around the room, as if he were eating it with his eyes. Jude laughed and headed back to the infirmary. Ellie noticed Vivian watching him go.

Later that afternoon, Captain Daevin appeared in the library doorway.

"Vivian," he nodded. "You look lovely, as always."

Vivian was washing the windows. Up to her elbows in soapy water, she looked at him as if he'd gone crazy.

"I must ask to borrow your apprentice. Ellie, I need to see you in my cabin."

Ellie climbed down from the last bookshelf and wiped her sleeve across her forehead. "I'll be back soon, Vivian."

The captain's navigational instruments were set up before the window in his cabin, and papers were strewn over his desk. Against one wall, Connor sat at a small slanted table, a sheet of figures before him and a pencil in his left hand. When he saw Ellie, he made a cross-eyed face, but Ellie ignored him.

"It is time to look," said the captain, holding out his spyglass to Ellie. She licked her lips. What if she saw those flowers again?

The captain began to sing, his voice soft and controlled. Her heart pounding, Ellie took a deep breath and put the glass to her eye.

The bright blue sky instantly paled to gray. The *Legend*'s golden wake trailed behind them. The rim of the spyglass glowed gold, making it hard to see.

But the horizon was empty.

Ellie pivoted the spyglass from side to side, but there was not a living thing in sight—just the empty gray sky and the golden froth behind them. She lowered the glass.

The captain searched her face. "Well?"

She shrugged. "There's nothing out there—just us and the sky."

Connor let out an undignified whoop of joy.

"We're safe!" cried the captain. "Let's tell the others."

On their way out of the cabin, Captain Daevin clapped a hand to Connor's shoulder and whispered something in his ear. Ellie couldn't hear what the captain said, but Connor's face broke into a smile that melted away the hardness of his appearance. She paused, noticing the dimple that appeared in his left cheek. It recalled something, a whisper from the deeps of her memory, but it was just beyond her reach.

Connor caught her staring and the smile disappeared. "What are you looking at?" he snapped.

She shook her head and turned to go.

Chapter 14
A Holiday

There were exclamations of relief and gladness as they told the crew the good news. They were going to make it safely to Rhynlyr! The captain declared the next day a holiday, free from all chores, which caused even more whoops of delight. Ellie let herself daydream about what she would do with a whole day off.

The flush of excitement faded, however, when the captain shooed her out of the library and shut himself inside with Vivian. Ellie stood in front of the closed door, annoyed. She hoped Vivian would stir up lots of dust and send the captain into another sneezing fit so he would leave.

When she got tired of waiting, Ellie wandered off in search of Jude. When she found the infirmary empty, she tried the greenhouse, where she found Jude on his knees beside a bed of flowers. He looked up.

"Oh, hello, Ellie. How are you?"

She frowned. "The captain shut me out of the library so he could talk with Vivian."

A shadow darkened Jude's face. "Oh."

"Can I help you in here?"

He offered her a trowel. "Of course."

For a while they worked together in silence as Ellie helped transplant red, blue, and purple flowers from tiny pots into a larger wooden box. The soil was warm and dark, and the flowers nestled comfortably into their new home. Ellie liked the feel of tangled roots and living leaves.

"Jude?" she asked after a while.

Jude didn't answer. His hands moved, but he was staring vacantly at the wall.

"Jude!"

"Hm?" Jude looked down. He was starting to plant a flower sprout upside down. "Oh dear." He turned the sprout right side up. "My mind must have wandered."

"Are you all right?"

Jude sighed. "I think so. What were you asking?"

"I just wanted to know what these flowers are called. Oh! And I almost forgot." She handed him a folded square of paper.

His face lit up when he saw the drawing inside. "The book wheel! This is a very good drawing, Ellie. Just what I need." He folded the paper and put it in his shirt pocket. "And these flowers are called *yrania*. They're pretty, aren't they?" Jude tilted one toward the light. "They're very hardy, asking nothing but a little water and enough earth to grow in. They're perfect for growing aboard a ship." He scooped a hole in the dirt and placed the roots of the flower inside. "Someday maybe I'll have a real garden—settle down on one of the islands and build a little house. But the yrania will have to do for now."

"They smell good," said Ellie, sniffing the sprout in her hands. It had a light, clean fragrance, like a breath of fresh air. "What are those over there?" She pointed to a tall plant with tiny blue hanging flowers.

"That whole section is medicinal," he said. "The blue flowers are called *rilia,* or more commonly, 'falling stars.' They have tiny berries inside them that can be ground and taken for stomach pain. Beside it is an *aton* plant, which is a wonderful fever reducer. Which reminds me, I need to dry some more of that. Would you collect about fifteen leaves for me?"

Ellie combed over the plant for the longest and darkest of the slender green leaves. When she accidentally bruised one, it gave off a sweet, aromatic scent that made her shoulders relax.

"You can fix everything, Jude," she said, breathing in the sweet fragrance. "Your plants are like magic."

Jude chuckled softly.

Plants are a gift, but I'm afraid neither they nor I can fix everything. I've seen patients so sick or injured that there's simply nothing I can do." He grew quiet, and his face looked sad.

"So if a person is too close to dying, you can't bring them back?" Ellie asked.

Jude started to shake his head, then stopped. "Well, popular mythology has it that there is one way. It's more legend than science, and there are no reliable reports of it actually working. But there are some sages who swear that every healer has an ultimate sacrifice that they can make for one person. They call it the Kiss of Life."

"What does it do?"

"From what I've read, it's a trade. The healer breathes into the dying patient's mouth and in return, absorbs their wounds or disease into himself. Then the healer dies, which is why the Kiss of Life can only be given once." He shrugged. "I don't know why I'm telling you this, though. It's not something you need to worry about." He rumpled her hair, dirt still clinging to his fingers. "What you do need to know is that these over here," he led her to a bush starred with plump purple berries, "are ripe and delicious."

To celebrate their holiday, the children brought out the wings and flippers and went flying again. Ellie found that she'd grown stronger and was able to keep up better with Jariel in the air. As they drifted high above the ship, they looked down on Captain Daevin and Vivian, who were having a picnic on deck. Vivian was wearing a white dress and a big straw hat. Jude was nowhere to be seen.

"Ugh, just look at them," said Jariel. The girls watched as the captain handed Vivian a bouquet of yrania flowers. "The captain's making a fool of himself."

"Vivian doesn't seem to like it much," observed Ellie as Vivian put the flowers to the side and turned her face away.

"I don't like it either," said Jariel. "The captain's turning into a buffoon. He acts like a clown around Vivian and is sour with the rest of us. I like Vivian a lot, but she's definitely made things more complicated around here."

"I can think of one person who's glad she came," said Ellie, pumping her wings to gain altitude.

"Who?"

"Jude."

"How do you know?"

"It's obvious! He almost planted some flowers upside-down yesterday because he was so distracted. And he can hardly get words out whenever she talks to him."

Jariel laughed. "You're right. It's funny to watch." She paused. "Do you think Vivian likes him too—in that way, I mean?"

Ellie glided thoughtfully. "I don't know. I think she might."

"Well then, it's all settled. Since Jude acts a lot nicer than the captain and Vivian likes him back, they need to be together. And we need to help them. Otherwise we'll never get any peace around here."

"How do we do that?" asked Ellie.

"Oh, spy on them, think up ways to get them together and keep the captain away. We should get Owen to help us."

"What about Connor?"

Jariel scowled. "Are you kidding? The first thing he'd do would be tattle on us. We don't need him."

When they were done flying, the girls went to look for Jude. But first they found Owen and told him about their plan. He didn't care much about what Vivian did, but he did agree that the captain was acting nasty, especially after the Tera incident. He agreed to help.

Jude was in the infirmary, making pencil marks on a long piece of wood.

"What's this project, Jude?" asked Ellie.

"This," he held up a folded, varnish-spotted piece of paper.

"The book wheel!" said Ellie. "You're really going to build it?"

"Your drawing was very helpful. The design has a lot of pieces, but I think it's going to work," said Jude.

Ellie grinned. "Vivian's going to love this."

"Really? You think so?" Jude asked earnestly.

"Of course!" said Jariel.

"It'll help her out in the library a lot. I bet it'll remind her of her home, too," said Ellie.

"Mmm," Jude grunted, setting a saw to one of the pencil marks and beginning to push it back and forth.

Just then, there was a light tap on the door. Everyone froze.

"Ah, so this is where you're all hiding," laughed Vivian, entering the infirmary like a spring breeze. Jude scrambled to his feet, wiping sawdust off his hands.

"This is the infirmary," grumbled Captain Daevin. "Not much to see. Would you like to—"

"Oh, but there *is* lots to see!" Her eyes swept the shelves lined with bottles and jars, the dried herbs hanging from the ceiling, the microscope, the half-sawed plank. "This doesn't just look like an infirmary," she said. "It looks like a workshop. What are all those?" She pointed to the shelves.

"Mm—ah—those are—my medicines and—well, I keep the garden upstairs, so the herbs—they go—"

Ellie glanced at Jariel, who was struggling to contain her laughter.

"You make your own medicines? How fascinating! Where did you learn to do that?" Vivian asked.

"Anadyr—I grew up there," Jude said. "I was apprenticed to a healer—a foreign master—and trained not only in surgery but in the power of herbs." His words began to calm, as if talking about his trade gave him confidence. "Master Zu was a member of the Vestigia Roi—it was because of his stories that I joined the fleet instead of becoming a city physician, as my family wished."

"And now you're a renowned Vestigian healer," said Vivian, smiling. "And what is this?" She pointed to the plank.

Jariel stepped in front of it. "Oh, it's nothing. Just a . . . project."

"Jude is teaching us about carpentry," Ellie added.

"Can I help, too?" Vivian asked eagerly.

"You?" Captain Daevin laughed. "It's awfully dusty work, and you'd get your dress dirty."

She turned.

"I beg your pardon? What do you think I am, a painting on the wall, existing only to be admired? Thank you, but I have no fear of a little dust, dress or no dress. Here, hold this."

She thrust her straw hat into his hands and turned her back on him.

"Now, what can I do to help?"

Jude silently handed her a measuring stick. Captain Daevin, blinking in surprise, backed out of the room, still holding Vivian's hat.

Chapter 15
Illuminations

The next afternoon, Ellie visited the library. She was amazed at what Vivian had already accomplished. Light from the sparkling-clean windows glanced off the polished bookshelves and the desks on either side of the window seat. A few comfortable chairs sat in the corners.

"It's beautiful!" said Ellie with a smile.

"Isn't it?" said Vivian proudly. "It looks just as I imagined. Of course, it's not the Mundarva Library—nothing can ever replace that. But once I get all these books shelved, it'll be a cozy place to read and write and imagine. And draw, too. You left your sketchbook open in the dormitory this morning, and I couldn't help seeing your sketch of the golden ship. It was beautiful."

Ellie blushed and looked at the floor. "It was just a sketch. I was trying to draw one of the visions."

"Ellie, you have a gift, and it's all right to admit that," said Vivian, smiling. "I want to show you something." She lifted a book, bound in white leather, from one of the desks.

"This is one of the books I saved from the Library," she said. "You won't be able to read it—it's in Tehber, a dead language—but open it."

The thick, yellow pages crackled as Ellie opened the book. It smelled like warm vanilla cookies, and it tickled her nose. Unrecognizable black marks marched down the page in rows, but the border was what caught Ellie's attention. It was full of light.

Lush green vines swept up the sides of the pages, sprouting ripe fruit and large colorful flowers. Wide-eyed animals peeked out from among the foliage. Red, yellow, white, and blue; four-footed and two-footed and no-footed, they examined the script curiously, even clambering onto some of the outermost letters. A funny creature that looked like a dog with purple feet looked straight at Ellie. And the page's first letter posed regally at the top, displaying all the majesty of a king presiding over his subjects. Shaped like a sideways V, it was penned in graceful crimson strokes against a background of gold. The metallic ink shimmered in the light. The page reminded Ellie a little of her doodles in the margins of her schoolbook, but much more magnificent.

"This is . . . beautiful," breathed Ellie. "The pictures . . . " She traced a dark green leaf on a vine. "They bring the book to life."

"It's an ancient art called illumination," said Vivian. "It's art done on the inside of a book to magnify the meaning of the words, to fill them with light."

"To help people understand them?" said Ellie.

"Exactly—and to reveal their beauty." A smile spread across Vivian's face. "And I think you have the makings of an illuminator."

"Me?" Ellie blinked.

"Yes. Here, have a seat." Vivian pulled out a chair at the desk and Ellie sat down.

"I want to make this room a scriptorium as well as a library," Vivian said, pulling down a few jars from a shelf. "If a library is a house where finished books live, a scriptorium is a nursery where they're born."

The jars were filled with brightly colored powders. Vivian sprinkled some of each into shallow cups and mixed them with a few drops of water. Pools of brilliant red, green, blue, white, and yellow formed. Ellie's eyes fed hungrily on the liquid colors.

"I thought books were printed by machine," she said.

"Most are, these days. But illumination is for special books—books so rare that they have to be handmade, each one one of a kind. Before there were printing presses, that was how all books were made. I've even heard that in remote parts of the Orkent Isles, that's still how they make books."

Vivian placed a half sheet of what looked like thick, brown paper in front of Ellie. There was a small block of curly black writing at the top.

"This is vellum," Vivian explained. "It's paper made from leather. We use it for illuminating because it's sturdy, but it's very precious because it's made from animal hides. This piece is a scrap. I started copying a page from a ship's log, but I made a mistake. I'd like you to read the words—these ones aren't in Tehber!—and use these paints to breathe life into them, to fill them with light. Do you think you can try that?"

The black letters were beautiful, with long slanting tails, but they all curled together until they looked like a big knot on the page. Ellie looked longingly at the cups of color, her heart sinking.

"Vivian, I . . . I really want to illuminate. But I can't."

Vivian looked disappointed. "You can't? Why not?"

Ellie sighed. "Because . . . I can't read. Not very well, anyway. The letters just start to mix themselves up, and then I can't make sense of anything." She looked at the floor. "I really want to learn to illuminate, but I can't. I'm sorry."

To Ellie's surprise, Vivian laughed. Ellie felt hurt. "I don't think it's funny."

"Oh, darling, I wasn't laughing at you," said Vivian. "But is that the only reason you think you can't illuminate?"

Ellie nodded.

"What if I were to read the words to you?"

"Read *to* me?"

"Hasn't anyone ever read to you before?" Vivian asked incredulously.

"Miss Sylvia did sometimes, for all the children at the orphanage. She never had time to explain the parts I didn't understand, though."

"Well, difficulty reading shouldn't keep you from doing what you are gifted to do," said Vivian. "Why don't I read you this passage, just so you can try illuminating? Then, if you like it, we'll do it again tomorrow. We can even practice reading together. I'll bet that with some good reading material and some help, you'll find that the letters behave a little better for you."

"Really?"

"Well, we can try, can't we? Now, let's read." Vivian picked up the scrap of vellum and pulled up a chair across from Ellie.

"Tenth day of sailing. Yesterday we encountered the cruelest tempest I've seen in all my years as a sea captain. The waves were as high as hills, sweeping over the deck and washing sailors overboard. But just when we thought all was lost, a crack appeared in the clouds overhead and a bird swooped down, a white gull with wings that flashed in the light . . . ”

Vivian’s clear voice was like a silver brush, painting the words into pictures in Ellie’s mind. When she stopped reading, Ellie stirred.

“Then what happened?” she asked.

Vivian shrugged. “That’s all I copied. The rest is up to your imagination—and your pen.” Vivian handed her a long, gray quill pen with a sharpened tip. “Ready?”

Ellie took the pen and let it hover above the page. *Fill the words with light.* Where on earth to start? She closed her eyes, remembering the story. Instead of curly black letters, she saw sailors fleeing from giant waves, a salty hurricane of spray overtaking them. But then the clouds broke and the white gull came wheeling down in a shaft of golden light. The fearsome waves were turned to translucent turquoise mountains, capped with snowy foam and gilded with light like the *Legend* in her visions. She dabbed her pen in the dish of blue ink and began to draw.

Her first attempt was a failure. The ink was runny and dripped off the quill pen in an uncontrolled blob, ruining a whole corner of the page. Ellie gasped and tried to wipe it out with her finger, but it only spread the stain. Carefully turning the blob away from her, she started on a new corner. This time she dipped the quill less deeply into the inkpot and wiped it off before starting to draw. The lines still came out fat and wobbly, but at least she could control them better.

It was the moment of the clouds breaking. Ellie mixed blue and green here, and yellow and white there. She found that by tilting the quill tip forward to its sharpest point, she could get very fine lines, while if she held the pen at a more relaxed angle, the lines were thick and bold. The grippy surface of the vellum held the colors in place. When she heard footsteps behind her, she looked up, as surprised as if she had been sleeping. Late afternoon light filled the scriptorium. How long had she been drawing?

She turned around and found everyone standing behind her: Jariel and Owen, Jude and Connor, Captain Daevin with his hand on Vivian's elbow. Ellie looked from one to another.

"What are you all doing here?"

"I saw your drawing, Ellie," said Vivian softly, "and I brought them to look."

Ellie looked back at the page, and everyone crowded around her. Blue-green waves crashed at the bottom of the page, peaked with gilded foam. The tip of one even looked a little transparent, like the painting she'd seen in the Library. A bird's wing, a slice of white no thicker than a nail paring, flitted through a shaft of golden light, a sign of hope that the tempest rocking the ship would not overwhelm it.

"May I?" Jude picked up the page and examined it more closely. "Ellie, this is—brilliant," he said.

"It's so real, it makes me feel seasick," said Jariel.

Ellie wasn't fully pleased with the illumination. The edges of the light weren't blended enough, and most of the water was too blue, too flat. But it was a start. Vivian would read her more manuscripts, and she would dip her quill into the array of vivid inks and paint the pictures that appeared in her head. She was going to be an illuminator, vested with the power to breathe life into stories. A thrill went through her like a firework.

"When you've had a little more practice, Ellie, you ought to illuminate the Song Book," said Vivian. "I was looking at it today, and it would make a perfect illumination project. The words are so beautiful, but they're lying fallow on those huge pages."

Captain Daevin turned. "Words? There are no words in the Song Book."

"Yes, there are," said Vivian. "Almost every line has them."

"Where could there be words?" said the captain. "I've seen the Song Book, sung from it a thousand times."

Vivian lifted the Song Book down from its shelf of honor and opened it to the first page. Ellie saw nothing but the familiar notes. But Vivian pointed to a set of squiggles between the bars of music.

"These are Knerusse graphemes. The syntax is unusual, but the symbols are unmistakable."

"Those just look like decorations," said Ellie.

"What do they mean?" asked Jariel.

"Each symbol represents a sound. So this line reads, *Syath elphara elssoo.* And the next one: *Syatha! Nirial elphara evansua lythassu.*"

"Well, we don't all speak Ne-what's-it-called," said Connor.

"You could learn if you listened," said Vivian. She closed her eyes, wrinkling her forehead. "It's poetry. *Listen, O heavens, and hear the Song. The Good King's song*—no, *the Good King's making-words. Listen! They fall like the rain.*" She frowned. "It sounds much more musical in Knerusse. If I worked on it, I'm sure I could come up with a closer translation."

Ellie felt dizzy. She felt swept up like a leaf in a whirlwind. Images battered her senses: glowing bars of music swirling in a cyclone, golden words pouring down in a thunderstorm. The vision was trapped inside her, its sharp elbows poking at her, its wings flapping in circles behind her eyes. The walls of her mind stretched and an ache built inside of her. Suddenly she ran from the room. She needed more paper.

Chapter 16
The Ball

The discovery of the words in the Song Book was a momentous occasion—not only for the crew of the *Legend,* but also for the Vestigia Roi. How famous Vivian would be when they reached Rhynlyr! To celebrate the discovery, the captain declared a celebration for the next evening. They would sing the Song with the new words, and then there would be feasting and dancing. The *Legend's* food supplies were starting to run low, but as they were only a few days' sailing from Rhynlyr, it seemed fitting that they should celebrate.

The next morning, regular chores were forgotten as everyone scurried about, transforming the dining room into a ballroom. Owen and Jude worked together, scrubbing the floor until it shone. Captain Daevin headed up the cooking, with Connor as his assistant. The girls put themselves in charge of decorations, collected all the bedsheets and candles they could find, and held a secret meeting in their dormitory.

As evening fell, Ellie, Jariel, and Vivian were getting ready together in their dormitory. Vivian, wearing her white undershift, was picking a comb through Jariel's tumbleweed of hair. Ellie and Vivian had their hair wrapped in rags to make it curl.

"You have such beautiful hair, Jariel," said Vivian. "The question is, what shall we do with it?"

Jariel sat on a chair in her nightgown, dangling her feet. "Chop it off? I know where the scissors are."

"I have a better idea." Vivian plucked her yrania bouquet from its vase on the windowsill and started to braid Jariel's hair from the side.

"What are you going to wear tonight, Vivian?" asked Ellie, pulling on her clean stockings. "You're singing in front of everyone."

Vivian squeezed her eyes shut. "Don't remind me."

"Why not? You're the one who discovered the words. You deserve it."

"I know I'll be bad at it. I'm not a good singer."

"You'll do fine. Don't think about the singing. Do it for us—we need to hear the words."

Vivian took a deep breath. "I'll try."

Ellie opened the doors of the narrow wardrobe. "You could wear your white dress tonight. Or…oh!"

Standing on her tiptoes, she lifted out a shimmering, midnight-blue length of fabric. It fell like water over her hands and made a slippery rustling sound.

"What's this?" said Ellie.

Vivian shook her head. "Oh, that's much too fancy for tonight. I had that before I became a Scholar."

Ellie held the gown up as high as she could. The skirt pooled on the floor, and the bodice glittered in the light. "What did you use it for?"

"Well," Vivian said slowly, her hands lacing the flowers into Jariel's hair. "My father was a senator on the island of Vahye in Arjun Mador. My mother died when I was very young, and my father's politics were his life. I realized that if I ever wanted to talk to him, I'd have to learn his language, and that was government. I picked it up rather quickly, and for a while I thought I wanted to be a senator myself. My father began to take me with him to political meetings and fancy state dinners. He gave me that dress to wear to an outdoor banquet at the First Minister's summer palace," she said, a distant look in her eyes.

"But eventually I realized that my father didn't want me to be a senator—he wanted me to marry a wealthy businessman or lord so he could gain power. He made me dance with the son of the First Minister, who had eyes like a fish and breath like a goat. I was just a pawn in his game. Then I knew that I was finished with politics—I wanted a life of learning. And where better to pursue that than the Mundarva Library?" She sighed. "It's a long story, but eventually I told my father I would starve myself until he let me go to the Library to become a Scholar. When I started to become ill, he finally gave in."

"Where is he now?" asked Ellie.

Vivian tied off Jariel's braid thoughtfully. "He died suddenly, just before I was promoted to the rank of Scholar. I went home, put his affairs in order, and then moved to Mundarva permanently. We were never very close, but I wish—I wish things had been different." She shook her head as if rousing herself.

"But why am I standing around blathering? I have a surprise for you both." The twinkle returned to Vivian's eyes, and she pulled a silver box from under her pillow. She opened it, revealing glittering coils of rings, necklaces, and bracelets inside.

"You can each pick something to wear tonight," she said with a smile.

Ellie's eyes nearly jumped out of her head. Aunt Loretha had had a jewelry box, but Ellie had never been allowed to go near it, let alone wear anything out of it. Her hand was halfway toward a sapphire necklace when she stopped, an idea forming in her brain.

"I'll only borrow something if you wear the blue dress."

"Oh, don't be silly. Tonight isn't about me! I want you girls to have a good time."

Jariel sat on her hands. "Well, I'm not going to have a good time unless you wear your beautiful dress. I'll just sit in a corner and sulk all night." She winked at Ellie.

Vivian cocked her head, looking puzzled. "Well . . . all right, since you insist. But I don't understand why you're so keen on it."

Ellie grinned. "Just because we want to see how pretty you'll look. I'd like to borrow the blue necklace, please."

Ellie and Jariel's clothes were worn, but with Vivian's jewelry they felt like princesses. Ellie's sapphire droplet glittered at the end of a silver chain, and Jariel chose a clinking pair of gold bracelets studded with rubies. Jariel's flower-studded braid circled her head like a crown, and Ellie twirled around, her halo of curls thick and shiny.

Vivian was stuck inside her gown.

"I'm lost in here," came her muffled voice. "Can someone help me?"

Ellie helped guide her to the head-hole and Jariel fastened the eighteen satin-covered buttons. When Vivian turned around, the girls clapped their hands. She looked like a piece of the night sky, her pearl earrings sparkling like stars. Her hair fell down her back in long, glossy curls that smelled like jasmine flowers.

"I don't know about this," said Vivian nervously, tugging at her bodice.

"You look beautiful," said Jariel, taking one of her hands.

"You'll do fine," said Ellie, taking the other.

The girls exchanged a knowing smile.

Ellie and Jariel helped Vivian enter the dining room, lifting the train of her skirt so it didn't drag. They had transformed the room this afternoon. Now it looked like a page from an illuminated manuscript. Potted plants from the greenhouse lined the walls, turning the room into a lush garden. Candles glittered on stands in the corners, and even the little-used chandelier had been lit. Surrounded by gauzy swathes of bedsheets, the lamp looked like a galaxy of stars reflected in the polished wooden floor.

Across the room, Owen tugged on Jude's sleeve. The doctor looked up, and when he saw Vivian, his face kindled to an expression of amazement and wonder. He stood up straight, tucked in his shirt, and started across the room. But before he could reach Vivian, Captain Daevin entered the room, carrying a tall stack of plates. He was wearing his best red waistcoat, and his slicked-back hair shone faintly in the candlelight. He looked at Vivian, then at Jude.

"Here," he said, loading the plates into Jude's arms. The doctor's face fell. Captain Daevin swept Vivian a flourishing bow.

"Milady, you are the embodiment of loveliness. Would you do me the honor of sitting beside me after the singing tonight?"

"Well, I—"Vivian's eyes wandered across the room.

"Good." Not waiting for an answer, the captain tucked her arm under his elbow and pulled her toward the Oratory.

The singing was wonderful. Vivian had translated Canto One, Movement Three. At first her voice was weak, drowned by the rush of the waterfall, but as she sang, she gained confidence. As the crew echoed back each line, the Song began to take flight. Not wanting to see any visions tonight, Ellie closed her eyes and simply let the cascade of music sweep over her.

We will proclaim the name of the King!
Oh, let us shout of his greatness!
For the justice of Adona Roi,
His mercy and uprightness,
Are the bedrock of the Kingdom,
Of the ocean and its islands.

How shall we serve him?
With faithless rebellion?
Is that how we shall repay,
Shall return his boundless goodness?
He shelters the Kingdom under mighty wings;
His wisdom and kindness shield us.

Let us show him our love by sailing,
By taking his name to the islands.
Foolishness may reign for a time;
Darkness may last the night.
But his name proclaims hope to the farthest seas,
And the One King shall reign forever.

The words and music made Ellie's insides feel squeezed, pressed down beneath the weight of something crushing and glorious. The beauty of the Song ached inside of her, sharply sweet, but she never wanted it to end. She wanted to catch this moment and hold on to it like a butterfly in a jar.

When the singing did end, Ellie opened her eyes. The faces of the crewmembers were full of light, their backs straight, their eyes bright. The Song brought them hope.

Their hearts full to bursting, everyone trooped into the dining room. The rest of the night was for feasting and dancing, celebrating the great discovery Vivian had made. But though Ellie laughed and talked with the others, carrying silverware and baskets of bread, the peace of the Song continued inside of her. It filled her with quietness like water within a clear jar.

Captain Daevin steered Vivian toward the table, but Jariel hurried ahead of them and took the seat to the captain's right. He frowned.

"You are sitting in Vivian's seat, young lady," he said sternly.

"But I want to sit next to you," said Jariel innocently.

"Oh, let her stay," said Vivian. "I'll sit on her other side."

"Not tonight," said Captain Daevin gruffly.

With a sigh, Jariel scooted down one seat. She shrugged across the table at Ellie.

The banquet was scrumptious. Connor and the captain had outdone themselves. There were bowls of vegetable soup and plates of garden salad, fresh fish in a sauce of crushed walnuts and caramelized honey, mashed potatoes with rosemary and garlic, and long loaves of fresh bread. Ellie ate so much that she thought she'd never be able to eat again. Not since she'd lived with the Beswicks had she tasted such a feast.

When all that was left on the platters were streaks of sauce, when the bread basket contained only crumbs, when Owen was feeding the last shred of lettuce to Moby, Connor disappeared into the galley. He reappeared carrying a masterpiece on a cake plate. It was so tall he could barely see over the top. He grunted as he set it down on the table.

"Double-chocolate layer cake with a raspberry filling. The frosting is melted butterscotch."

"Wow," said Jariel, licking her lips. "Who made this?"

"I did," said Connor without emotion. He sliced into the center of the cake, and raspberry jam and warm butterscotch dribbled down together.

Ellie swallowed, trying not to drool. "You know how to bake?"

"I made the bread, too."

"Really? I think baking is hard."

"It's not. Not if you can measure and count," said Connor. When he looked up to hand her the plate, his cold blue eyes had a different look in them—softer, maybe.

One bite of the cake, and Ellie heard singing all over again. It was warm and gooey, and she thought all the desserts she'd ever tasted were just preparation for this one. All the faces around the table were rapturous. Compliments to Connor abounded, and though he just shrugged, Ellie saw the dimple beginning to appear in his left cheek.

Then the dancing began. Owen surprised them all by producing and playing a small set of panpipes, and Jude overturned a bucket and kept rhythm on it like a drum. Captain Daevin, Vivian, Ellie, and Jariel danced together in a circle, following the lively rhythm. Ellie beckoned Connor onto the dance floor, but he stubbornly crossed his arms and sat down on a bench.

"Never mind him," Jariel said. "Watch this!" She jumped into the middle of the circle and began hopping on one foot and waggling her head, her bracelets jangling crazily. Ellie laughed until she couldn't breathe. Owen abandoned his panpipes and joined them for one dance, and the three children took hands and twirled until they were tangled up in a knot. But out of the corner of her eye, Ellie saw Captain Daevin dancing with Vivian. She sent Owen a meaningful look, and he trotted back to his instrument.

"We don't need a drum for this one, Jude," he said. "It's a waltz." Owen struck up a slow, plaintive tune. Captain Daevin again claimed Vivian as his partner. Jude's hands hovered awkwardly at the sides of the drum. Ellie went up to him.

"Come dance with me, Jude."

Jude shook his head. "I don't dance."

"Why not?"

He cleared his throat, redness creeping into his face. "I just don't like it. I'm not very graceful on my feet. Besides—I don't—I don't know how."

Ellie grinned and put her hands on her hips. "Well, that can be fixed." She held out her hand.

She'd only had a month of real dancing lessons, back when she'd lived with the Alstons. But though all the fancy work was long forgotten, she remembered the basic steps.

"Here," she said, facing Jude. "Hold my right hand and put your other hand on my back. Like this." His arms were as stiff as wooden beams, but he complied.

"Now move your feet like this: one—two—three." They walked in the shape of a box. "Ouch!" Ellie jumped back as Jude stepped on her toes.

"I'm sorry!" Jude dropped her hands. "Are you all right? I knew I shouldn't have tried this."

"I'm fine," said Ellie, shaking out her foot. "Try again. One—two—three."

Owen kept up the music, and soon Jude was mastering the steps. He still looked rigid, but he wasn't stepping on Ellie's toes anymore.

Ellie glanced across the room, where Captain Daevin swept Vivian around in graceful circles. He was a good dancer, but her smile looked forced. It was time. As Ellie and Jude spun around, she threw a giant wink in Jariel's direction.

Jariel trotted out onto the dance floor. "Dance with me, Captain Daevin! I haven't had a chance yet."

The captain frowned, pausing mid-waltz. "Go ask Connor. I'm busy."

"Connor won't dance. And besides, he hates me." Jariel stuck out her bottom lip so far that she looked like a clown. Ellie giggled.

"Oh, look at her, Captain," said Vivian, chuckling. "Give the poor girl a chance."

"But—"

"Please?"

"Well . . . " Captain Daevin looked from Jariel back to Vivian. "If you insist."

"I do insist." Vivian walked away and sat down on one of the benches by the table. Still frowning, Captain Daevin took Jariel's hands and reluctantly started to waltz.

Seizing the chance, Ellie steered Jude straight toward the table. When they were next to Vivian, Ellie made an enormous false yawn.

"I'm *so* tired! I think I need to rest a while." She plopped down next to Vivian.

"Are you all right?" Vivian looked at her with concern.

"Oh—oh yes. I just need to sit down. Why don't you two dance together?"

Vivian smiled up at Jude, her dark brown eyes sparkling in the candlelight. Jude's face turned beet red.

"Ah—hm—er—would you—hm—would you like to—dance?" Jude asked, plunging his hands into his pockets.

"I'd like nothing better," said Vivian with a grin.

They took the floor, and Ellie watched them with satisfaction. Jude took Vivian's hand and held it as gingerly as a fragile seedling. At first he couldn't seem to remember the steps he'd just learned, but Vivian gracefully helped him along. Their heads leaned close together, and Jude's shoulders relaxed as Vivian laughed.

At the sound, Captain Daevin looked up. Forgetting Jariel, he marched up to Jude and Vivian.

"*May* I cut in?" he said, sliding between them with knifelike smoothness. He swept off with Vivian, glaring at Jude over his shoulder.

Jude stood alone on the dance floor, sliding his hands back into his pockets. Ellie went up to him.

"Come on, Jude, keep dancing. One-two-three." She took his hands and lowered her voice to a whisper. "You have to get her back."

Jude glanced over his shoulder. "How?"

"Just do what the captain did," Ellie said. "Cut in next time he spins her."

Vivian twirled, and Jude caught her hand.

"May I?" he said, pulling her away. She laughed and followed him.

Now Captain Daevin was the one standing alone. He didn't look sad, though—he looked angry. His mouth pressed in a tight line, he marched across the dance floor, straight toward them.

Just then, Owen ended the music. Jude spun Vivian around and made an awkward bow. Vivian curtsied, laughing, but straightened up when she saw Captain Daevin, pale and trembling with fury.

"Captain . . . are you all right?"

His face went red as his mouth soundlessly opened and closed. Then he turned on his heel and stalked up the stairs to his cabin. Ellie heard the distant slam of a door.

Chapter 17
Crossroads

When the captain came downstairs the next morning, dark circles ringed his eyes and his jaw was rough with stubble.

"Did you sleep well last night, Captain?" Owen asked cheerfully.

The captain didn't answer. He slopped a ladleful of porridge into his bowl and took a huge bite.

"Aren't we going to sing first?" Jariel asked.

The captain's eyes flicked to Vivian. "Ask her," he said, his voice rough as gravel.

Vivian looked startled. "Yes . . . yes of course, we're going to sing. Who will lead us? Ellie?"

Ellie didn't even have time to think of an excuse before Connor said, "I will."

Everyone looked at him. He lifted his chin. "What? Don't you think I can?"

Without waiting for an answer, he launched into the mealtime song. Ellie had never noticed his voice before; it was pleasant and smooth, and he kept the rhythm perfectly. She was so surprised she almost forgot to join in.

The rest of breakfast was virtually silent. The drooping bedsheets from last night still hung from the ceiling like storm clouds.

The captain did not break his sulky gloom. Jude's porridge seemed even thinner than usual.

Ellie and Jariel were just getting up to clear the dishes when the door to the upper deck banged open. A cold draft of air blasted down on them. A strange figure began to descend the stairs, half cloaked in shadows.

"Who's there?" called Jude.

The figure jumped down the rest of the stairway, opening a pair of great feathery wings to slow his fall. Ellie's mouth dropped open. It was a man—or something like one. His skin was as dark as polished walnut wood, and his only clothing was a pair of black leather breeches. Powerfully built, his chest and arms were covered with swirling blue tattoos that shimmered faintly when he moved. Another tattoo curled just above his eyebrow. The hilt of a slender, dagger-like *sai* extended over each of his shoulders.

He tapped two fingers of his right hand to his left shoulder, then to his forehead in the Vestigian salute.

"To the One Kingdom." His voice sounded like a rumble of distant thunder.

The entire crew stood up and returned the salute in unison. "May it be found."

The stranger folded his wings. They were muscular yet graceful, their tips reaching just below his knees. The feathers at his shoulders were the shade of a deep twilight, but they lightened to a pale robin's-egg blue at the tips. Light passed through their edges. Ellie itched for a drawing pencil. He was majestic: as beautiful as a statue, yet as wild as a hunting lion coiled to spring.

"I am Kiaran," he said. "I carry an urgent message from Lord Ishua, Commander of the Winged Armies."

"You've seen Ishua?" Ellie burst out.

Kiaran's eyes pierced through her. They were as clear as two panes of washed glass. "He gave me this message personally."

Ellie felt a thrill pass through her. She had a sudden urge to hug the winged man.

"Would you . . . like to join us for breakfast?" asked Vivian.

Kiaran shook his head. "My message cannot wait. I must speak with Daevin, captain of the *Legend*."

"I am honored to receive it from one of the *Alirya*," said Captain Daevin. "I am the captain. What is your message?"

"An island called Suor has just broken loose from the southern tip of Arjun Mador. It is now three days from the Edge, at best. Eight hundred souls drift upon it. Therefore, Ishua commissions you, along with the other Vestigian ships in closest proximity, to go after it. If your ship is the first to reach it, you will conduct a rescue mission and return to Rhynlyr with any survivors who are willing to depart."

Captain Daevin frowned. "We have just outrun a large detachment of enemy soldiers. If we double back, they could pick up our trail again and catch us."

"Not to mention the risk of the Edge," said Connor.

"And our food supplies are almost out," added Owen.

Kiaran crossed his arms gravely. "If you accept this mission, you do it at great risk."

No one spoke. The captain bowed his head, rubbing a hand over his stubbly chin.

"How much time do we have to decide?" he asked at last.

"Every minute is precious," said Kiaran. "The island is already drifting."

The captain looked up. "Everyone to the Oratory. We must sing."

Minutes later, they all stood in a circle around the waterfall, Kiaran included. Ellie shifted from foot to foot, her heart pounding as if it would fly out of her chest. She'd been through so many dangers to get to Rhynlyr and have a home. Couldn't Ishua commission somebody else to be the rescuer this time?

The captain began the familiar, wordless call-and-response of the Song. Vivian had not had time to translate this section. Ellie closed her eyes, waiting for the change to take place in her vision.

When she opened her eyes again, the walls of the ship were gone. The seven other people in the room were suspended in space, their bodies so swallowed in light that she couldn't even make out their faces. But the Song Book on its stand commanded her attention: its Knerusse words danced off the huge, gleaming-white pages, and to her surprise, she could read them.

Proclaim the name of the Deliverer!

His wings cover the islands; his great wings shield them all.

Faithful and kind, he catches the falling.

The Good King saves; his name is Deliverer.

Ellie looked out through the invisible walls of the ship. Far away, she saw an island that flickered like a distant star. It faded, burst forth again, shone brightly, then dimmed as if going behind a cloud. Then a dissonant sound started to conflict with the music. It made Ellie wince. It grew louder and louder, drowning out the singing. It was the sound of screaming, thousands of voices crying out in fear. Ellie covered her ears, trying to shut out the awful sound, but it was inside her head, filling her brain.

"Stop!" she cried.

The singing died away. Everyone looked at her.

"What is it, Ellie?" Jude asked with concern.

Ellie squeezed her eyes shut. "We have to go."

"Why?" Captain Daevin's voice was sharp.

"The people on Suor—I heard them screaming. They're afraid. If we don't answer, how can we call ourselves part of the Vestigia Roi?" She closed her eyes and swallowed hard. "I don't want to go. I just want to make it to Rhynlyr and be safe. But—" she took a deep breath. "But the Song says Ishua's name is Deliverer. And if we call ourselves part of his fleet, we have to go rescue his people, danger or no danger."

"It is a terrible choice," said Jude, rubbing at a wrinkle in his forehead.

To Ellie's surprise, it was Connor who responded. "But how can we call ourselves rescuers if we run away from a rescue mission just because it's dangerous? Are we Vestigians, or aren't we?"

Ellie stared at him. His blue eyes were fierce, and his jaw was set. Whether he was fighting for a bad cause or a good one, Connor certainly commanded authority.

"You're right," said the captain, his face grim. "If we sail in Ishua's fleet, there is only one choice for us. But I will not give the order without unanimous consent. What do the rest of you say?"

A chorus of *ayes* agreed, however solemnly. Though Ellie had argued for this course of action, her stomach twisted into a knot. She had the sinking feeling that she was about to lose another family.

There had been a painting on the wall in Ellie's first home, outside the city of Harwell. She had been little then, with fine straight hair and dimples in her elbows. She remembered standing in front of the painting in a ruffled pink dress Nevin and Darling Beswick had given her. The dress itched, but she liked the way it twirled when she spun around. The painting was of a still nighttime lake with white flecks of moonlight floating on it. Ellie edged closer to the gold-framed picture, wondering if the painted moonlight would move with her as the sunlight coming through the window did.

Nevin jogged down the staircase in his black woolen overcoat, briefcase in hand. Ellie ran to hug him around the knees. His long overcoat smelled like sweet pipe smoke.

"Goodbye, Ellie," he said, patting her head like a dog's.

"And where do you think you're going?" Darling spun around on the stool in front of her gold-rimmed vanity mirror. Half of her lower lip was painted red, and she held the paintbrush in one hand.

"Darling, I have to go to work," said Nevin, holding up his hands. "I have a meeting with the Board this morning, remember?"

"So who's going to stay with *her*? I'm going to the dressmaker's with Elmyra and Laralyn, *remember*?"

"Can't she go with you?" Nevin swallowed. "Just this once?"

"Nevin, whose idea was it to adopt a child in the first place? Who wouldn't stop bothering me until it was done?" Darling's eyes narrowed into slits. "You promised me it would be no trouble. I'd hardly even notice it was here. Certainly I wouldn't be stuck in the house or dragging the little brat along every time I went out. And now you're leaving it on my hands while you go to the office without a thought. I should have known your promises would come up empty."

Nevin glanced nervously down at Ellie. Ellie saw the worried lines in his forehead. He didn't want her.

"Oh, I suppose it'll be all right," he said quickly. "I'll bring her with me, this once. You'll be a good girl and not bother me at work, won't you, Ellie?"

Ellie nodded so hard it made her neck hurt.

"Well, let's go then. We've got to hurry." Nevin took her hand and Ellie grabbed on without a word. She curled her bare toes into the rug.

"Goodbye, Darling," called Nevin.

"G'bye, Mama," said Ellie.

Darling did not answer. She had turned back to her mirror again.

It wasn't until they'd hurried down three flights of stairs and stepped out into the snowy street that Nevin stopped short.

"Ellie, you're barefoot! And with no coat!"

Ellie looked up at him, trying to keep her teeth from chattering. If she was very, very good and quiet, maybe he wouldn't be sorry he'd brought her. Maybe he'd bring her every day.

Nevin sighed, glancing at his pocket watch. "Well, no time to go back. The train won't wait."

Nevin picked Ellie up and hurried to the corner, where he purchased two tickets for the little train that stopped there. Ellie paid little attention. She rubbed her cheek against the rough collar of Nevin's overcoat. She was glad not to have shoes today.

When the train arrived, Nevin sat Ellie down by the window and tucked a lap robe around both of them. Gradually, Ellie's teeth stopped wanting to chatter. As the train lurched out of the station, she looked out the window at the bustle of people. They looked cold, trudging around frowning in the hard winter sunlight.

"Busy place," said Nevin, following her gaze. "Not like what you were used to at that country orphanage, eh, Ellie?"

She shook her head, keeping her lips tightly pressed together.

Nevin smiled wanly. "You don't have to be quiet until we get to my office, Ellie."

She relaxed her mouth and snuggled closer to him. His hand absently smoothed her hair.

"Can I call you Papa?" she blurted out. He took his hand away, and Ellie looked at him, confused. Had she said something wrong?

Nevin shifted uncomfortably in his seat. "I . . . well . . . " he rubbed the back of his neck. "I don't see why not. I suppose it's all right, at least for now."

Ellie leaned back against him. "All right, Papa." Saying that felt so comfortable. The only thing she didn't like were his words, *for now.*

Nevin's hand resumed stroking her hair, and she was almost asleep by the time they pulled into the next station. Nevin picked her up again and carried her into a nearby clothing shop. He bought the first girls' coat and pair of shoes he saw, and a handful of toffees as well. The white coat was furry, and the shoes had satin bows on the toes. Ellie's feet slipped around in the too-big shoes, but she felt like a princess. A lady in Nevin's office exclaimed, "What a beautiful little girl you have!" Ellie beamed and said, "This is my papa. Isn't he beautiful, too?"

But the big men on The Board were not so kind. Their frowning foreheads said *no children allowed,* and when Nevin left the office, his shoulders sagged. That night, Ellie overheard Nevin and Darling yelling in their bedroom. When she looked at the painting of the lake the next morning, she was sure she saw waves that hadn't been there yesterday.

And so, three months later, Ellie stood in her white coat and shoes in the yard of the Harwell Home for Orphans, waving as Nevin and Darling's black hansom cab drove away. She was crying so hard she could hardly see. She wasn't good enough for her new family to keep her. Darling never looked back, but Nevin leaned out of the cab and waved once before the vehicle turned a bend. Ellie soon outgrew the coat as her arms lengthened and her elbows lost their baby dimples, but she wore the shoes until their dirt-gray bows fell off and the soles wore to shreds.

Kiaran left them as soon as he had their answer. For the rest of that morning, the crew worked to chart their new southwest course and bring the *Legend* up to top speed. Captain Daevin gave orders that food would be rationed down to two meals a day to stretch their dwindling food supplies. Ellie felt as if she had a gnawing animal in her stomach.

At lunchtime, she wandered into the library, feeling hungry, lonely, and unsure of what to do with herself. Vivian was working at one of the desks.

"Hello Vivian," said Ellie.

"Ah, hello, Ellie. You're just the person I was looking for. I have a project for you. Do you remember when I talked about you illuminating the Song Book?"

Ellie nodded.

"Well, I'd like you to begin. I know you haven't had much time to practice, but . . . I think you should start now. Where would you like to start? Beginning, middle, end?"

Ellie shrugged, glancing out the window.

"Ellie?"

Ellie met Vivian's concerned eyes. She chewed on her bottom lip. "Vivian—do you think this really matters now? I mean, I know it's good to keep busy and everything, but we're sailing into a battle we might not win. No one has time to look at pictures now. And if we . . . well, if we don't . . . make it home, no one will ever see them at all. Drawing just doesn't seem like a very important thing to do."

"Oh, Ellie, it's more important now than ever." Vivian sank to her knees, taking Ellie's hands in both of hers. "You have a gift—a gift of seeing truth and sharing beauty. Those are the things that give people hope. And it's in dark times like these—times of battle and suffering and fear—that people need hope most of all." She released Ellie's hands. "Even if no one on Rhynlyr ever sees your illuminations, the crew of this ship needs them now more than ever. There's never been a more urgent moment to draw."

Ellie looked at her fingers as if they could shoot lightning.

"You really think so?"

"I know so. You were brought to this ship for a reason."

Ellie took a deep breath. "Then . . . I think I'd like to start at the beginning of the Song Book. Will you read it to me?"

Together they mixed the colored ink powders with water. Ellie retrieved her sketchbook and opened it to the sketches she'd done the first time Vivian had read from the Song Book—whirlwinds of music and rainstorms of words. She paused.

"Vivian, how do you make gold ink? Like that letter in the Tehber book?"

"It's costly," Vivian said. "You have to grind real gold flakes into powder and blend them with glue, one drop at a time, until it forms a thick paint. The ink is so precious that it's only used for the most special pages. It's magnificent, though. It makes the words shine as if they're full of light."

Light. "I think I need some for this page," Ellie said cautiously. "I know it's expensive, but . . . "

" . . . it is the first page of the Song Book," Vivian finished for her. "Let's go look in my jewelry box."

Using a large mortar and pestle from the galley, they ground a gold necklace clasp into chunks, then flakes, then powder. When Vivian had carefully mixed the gold with glue, Ellie selected a quill and closed her eyes. Vivian began to read the words of the Song and Ellie listened, letting them form pictures in her mind.

The Good King's making-words, listen! They fall like the rain.

The *Legend* might be racing hopelessly toward the edge of the world. All the forces of the Enemy might be after them. But Ellie dipped her quill into liquid gold and began to illuminate.

Supper had never felt more welcome, even if it was only watery soup and thin slices of bread. The animal in Ellie's stomach growled less ferociously as the warm soup went down her throat.

"This soup sure is delicious," said Jariel, who was sitting next to her. "I was out in the rigging all afternoon, keeping watch with the spyglass, and the wind out there whips up a real appetite." She licked her fingers and looked at her empty bowl. "Wish there was more of it, though."

Ellie nodded. "Vivian promised she'd tell us some Tehber fairy tales before bed, though. At least that should keep us from *thinking* about being hungry."

"I'm going to be starving by the time we get up for the night watch, though." Jariel wrinkled her nose and lowered her voice to a whisper. "It wasn't fair for the captain to cut our rations *and* assign us night watches at the same time."

Ellie shrugged. "I don't think he had a choice. None of us expected all this to happen. At least you and I get to do our watch together. And we're the last watch, so by the time we're done, it will be almost breakfast time."

Jariel sighed. "That's something."

No one felt much like staying up late with rumbling stomachs. Everyone was saying good night after supper and heading off to their dormitories when Captain Daevin put a hand on Vivian's arm.

"Vivian, I must speak with you." He cleared his throat. "Alone."

"I'm sorry, Captain; I promised I'd tell the girls some stories before bed," said Vivian, pulling her arm away.

The captain took her hand. "This is more important."

"But—" Vivian looked desperately at the girls.

"Please. You'll have time for stories later." He led her toward the stairs. She followed reluctantly.

Ellie and Jariel looked at each other.

"Do you think we should follow them?" said Jariel. "Vivian looks kind of scared."

Ellie shook her head slowly. "I think that would just make the captain angry. Whatever he's got to say to her, he wants to say it alone."

Jariel grumbled something under her breath and headed to the dormitory. Ellie started to follow her, but glanced once over her shoulder. She was just in time to see Jude padding silently up the stairs.

Unfortunately, whatever the captain wanted to say took a look time. Ellie and Jariel changed into their nightgowns, cleaned their teeth, blew out the candle, and got into bed, their stomachs already gnawing again. The longer Vivian was gone, the more Ellie wondered if she was all right. She was just resolving to go look for her when the door burst open and Vivian stormed into the room.

"Vivian! We were worried about you!" said Ellie in the dark.

Vivian slammed the door. Her footsteps rapidly crossed the room.

"What happened?" Ellie asked.

Vivian exhaled violently. "The captain just asked me to marry him!"

The bunk bed creaked as Jariel sat up. "What?"

"He did?" said Ellie.

Vivian's voice was trembling with fury. "Oh yes, he did. He said that he wanted to 'confer upon me the honor' of being a captain's wife. Ugh!"

"What did you say?" said Jariel.

"No, of course! I could never marry that man. I know he's the captain, but he's an insufferable, pompous dandy who cares more about his waistcoats than other people's feelings." She kept pacing. "When he asked me to speak with him, I was actually frightened, after the way he acted last night. But tonight he just gave me a fat letter and told me to read it."

"What was in it?" said Ellie.

"Oh—pages and pages of his flowery sentiments, along with some rather awful poetry. It finished with the question of marriage, if we survive this mission." Vivian's feet beat the floor like hammers. "When I finished reading, he crossed his arms and asked me what I thought. That was it." She sighed. "I tried to be gentle, but I made it very clear that I do not love him and never can." The other bunk bed squeaked as Vivian sat down.

"What happened then?" asked Jariel.

"He didn't say anything. He looked sad, and for a moment I thought he might cry. But then he just got up, said 'all right,' and opened the door to let me out. Then I almost tripped over Jude outside." There was a moment of silence, and when Vivian spoke again, her voice was softer. "He was hidden behind the door, and the captain didn't see him. I think he was waiting there to make sure I was all right."

More silence. Two thumps as Vivian pulled off her shoes.

"Would you mind if I told you girls those fairy tales tomorrow? I'm very tired."

"That's all right," said Jariel.

"Night," said Ellie. She rolled over on her bunk, glad that the darkness hid her secret smile.

When Owen shook her awake two hours before sunrise, Ellie could barely open her eyes. She woke Jariel, and the two of them bundled into their coats and dragged themselves out to the deck. A freezing wind numbed their ears and fingers, but the stars blazed brilliantly overhead. At first they walked together, scanning the horizon and talking quietly about the captain's proposal to Vivian. Then Jariel stretched and rubbed her arms.

"We should probably split up for a while. I don't think we're actually getting much watching done."

Jariel patrolled the front half of the ship, and Ellie circled the captain's cabin quietly. Now that she was alone, she felt jumpy. She hunted through the dark with her eyes, half-expecting a shadowy form to spring up before her at any moment. As she rounded the corner of the captain's cabin, she froze. A hunchbacked shape with a long, deformed nose was silhouetted against the sky. Her heart pounded wildly and her mouth went dry. Should she scream and try to draw attention? Or just sneak off quietly and try to get help before the creature saw her? She decided on the second option and was just retreating when she tripped over a coil of rope, falling to the deck with a thump. The dark figure turned to face her. It came toward her, looming large. Ellie couldn't make a sound, let alone scream. She squeezed her eyes shut.

"What are you doing out here?"

Ellie opened her eyes. She recognized that voice.

"Connor?"

"Who did you think?"

Ellie let out a deep, shaky sigh. "I thought . . . I thought you were an enemy. Jariel and I are on night watch. I was about to go for help."

Connor chuckled.

"What are *you* doing out here?" Ellie asked, standing up and brushing herself off.

"None of your business."

Ellie started to back down, then stopped. "Actually, it is my business. It's the middle of the night, and I'm on watch."

"Too bad."

"I'll scream," Ellie warned.

"Fine! I'll show you. Just—don't tell anyone about this, all right?"

"That depends if it's something they should know about," said Ellie suspiciously.

"It's not like that, okay? Can't you believe that I do anything besides get in trouble?"

Ellie crossed her arms. "Well, you *do* get in trouble a lot."

Connor sighed and stepped back to the railing. A dark tube was slanted up at the sky.

"It's a telescope," Connor said. "The captain let me borrow it. It's much more powerful than an ordinary spyglass, and I've been using it to chart the skies between Newdonia and Rhynlyr over the last few weeks. I'm filling in the early morning star positions."

"I didn't know you liked astronomy," said Ellie, looking curiously at the telescope.

Connor looked up at the sky, clasping his hands behind his back. "It's nice out here when there's nobody else around. It's quiet. It was never quiet at the orphanage where I lived." He looked at her. "Do you want to look through the telescope?"

"I—don't know how," she faltered.

He pointed to the eyehole on the side of the scope. "Just put your eye here and don't bump the scope. You'll see the Calix Cluster. With just your eyes, it looks like one big, bright star, but through the telescope, you'll see that it's a whole cluster."

Ellie followed his instructions. Through the eyehole, sparkling tendrils like cresting waves came into her view, curling into a spiral pattern like a whirlpool. Each tendril was made up of dozens of stars, glittering like blue diamonds.

"Beautiful!" Ellie breathed, filling her eyes with the glorious sight. "Maybe you have an artist in you after all, Connor."

"Me? Ha!" said Connor. Ellie looked at him. "No, the sky is like a huge machine, full of moving pieces. You can use the stars to chart the ship's movements because the stars are always in their places, always following the same patterns. Once you understand those patterns, you can depend on 'em. They'll take you anywhere you want to go."

As they watched, a shooting star streaked across the sky. Ellie looked at Connor with a grin. "But sometimes things happen that we don't expect."

He shrugged. "Maybe." There was a long pause. "Guess I didn't expect Captain Daevin to come for me when I ran away from the orphanage."

"You ran away?"

"Yup."

"Why?"

Connor sighed heavily. "I guess . . . I couldn't stand the bullies anymore. You were either with 'em or against 'em, and they wanted me with 'em because I was big and tough. But . . . where'd that leave all the other kids, you know? The biggest bully of all, Tison—he kept making me beat up kids, take their food and stuff. I was good at it, too. All the other kids were scared of me. But sometimes . . . I didn't want to stop. I got too angry, and I hurt 'em bad. I was . . . scared of what I could do. So I ran away."

Ellie was silent, looking up into the sky. Suddenly Connor's past behavior was making so much more sense. "Where did Captain Daevin find you?"

"Under a hedge. I'd been out there for days. I was wet and starving. He offered me a coat and told me about this ship." Connor patted the *Legend*'s railing almost tenderly. "If it wasn't for him, I'd prob'ly be dead."

"Does he know about your astronomy?"

Connor nodded. "His idea. He said I should think about studying it on Rhynlyr."

"So why don't you want the others to know? I think it's neat."

"They'd think it's silly. I've had enough of teasing."

Ellie sighed. "I don't think they're like that. Still, if you don't want people to find out for themselves, you'd better head inside." She pointed to the eastern horizon, where the black velvet of night was already paling to a charcoal gray. "It'll be dawn soon."

"Then . . . you won't tell anyone?" Connor asked hesitantly.

Ellie shook her head.

His eyes studied her intently. "Thanks."

Chapter 18
On the Brink

The rising of the sun had never come as more of a relief. Storm clouds on the horizon turned pearly white, then blushed rosily, then flamed into brilliant gold. A gust of damp wind swept through the girls' hair.

"I think we're in for some rain," said Jariel.

The rain started during their meager breakfast, at which Vivian and Captain Daevin sat as far away from each other as possible. It looked like the beginning of a long, hungry, gloomy day.

After a short nap, Ellie headed to the scriptorium, hoping to paint out her growling stomach and jittery nerves with gold ink. Vivian read to her from the Song Book when she needed it, and the other crewmembers drifted in and out as the rainy afternoon wore on. Owen found a book called *Medicinal Potions: Help and Harm.*

"I think I've figured out how to extract poison from my caterpedes without hurting them," he said. "I want to use it to coat my blowdarts. I wish I could to figure out how to extract stinging juice from my red ants, but I don't think they'd survive the operation."

Jariel stopped in and loitered around Ellie's desk for a few minutes, but after she upset a pot of purple ink, Vivian asked her to go see what Jude was doing. Even Connor dropped by for a minute, looking for a book on advanced rudder maneuvers for the captain. Captain Daevin himself did not appear.

It wasn't until late afternoon that they had another visitor. Ellie was completing the last of a series of intricate, intertwining blue-and-gold swirls when Jariel popped her head into the library again. A grin kept wiggling its way onto her face. She winked at Ellie.

"Can we come in, Vivian? We have a surprise for you."

Ellie watched as Jariel, Owen, and Jude worked together to bring a bulky, oddly-shaped object, hidden under a sheet, into the room. Jariel and Owen were working hard to keep straight faces. They set it down against the wall by Ellie's desk. Vivian frowned.

"What is this? I don't think any more furniture will fit in here."

Jude looked at the children. "Shall we show her?"

Their grins escaping, Jariel and Owen yanked off the sheet.

"Oh!" Vivian cried.

It was the finished book wheel. Ellie stared at it in amazement. It was just like the one in the Mundarva Library. Jude had brought her drawing to life in shades of rich amber and honey. Nearly as tall as Ellie, the polished wheel gleamed in the light.

Everyone looked at Vivian, who approached it slowly. She dropped to her knees beside the wheel, her fingers skimming over the butter-smooth wood. She tested the crank and watched the shelves rotate. She looked up at Jude and the children, her eyes brimming with tears.

"Please—please don't cry," said Jude, wringing his hands nervously.

"Don't you like it?" asked Owen.

"It's the most beautiful thing I've ever seen," said Vivian, dabbing at her eyes with her sleeve. "It's even better than the one I had on Mundarva. Did all of you make this together?"

The children nodded proudly.

"This was our carpentry project," grinned Jariel mischievously.

"You weren't supposed to see us working on it, but at least you didn't see the whole thing," said Owen.

"Jude did most of the work," said Ellie.

Vivian turned to him. "How did you figure out the design? It's just like the one I had at the Great Library!"

"It was Ellie," said Jude, a smile tugging at the corners of his mouth. "She had seen your wheel and did a very good drawing of it, along with some approximate measurements. After that, my job was easy."

"You drew the wheel after seeing it just once?" Vivian asked Ellie. Ellie shrugged shyly.

"Well, it's wonderful," said Vivian, running her fingers over the new book wheel once more. "This is the loveliest gift I've ever received. Thank you all." She hugged Jariel and Ellie, though Owen wriggled away before she could get him. The girls followed Owen out of the room, but Ellie glanced over her shoulder and paused. Jariel tiptoed back to join her. Vivian turned and hesitated awkwardly in front of Jude.

"Thank you . . . thank you so much," she said, her cheeks turning pink.

"It was . . . no trouble. Glad to," said Jude, looking at his shoes. There was an awkward pause.

"Vivian, I . . . " Jude began suddenly, looking up and meeting Vivian's eyes. In that look, Ellie saw all the kindness and care he poured into his gardening, his doctoring, his listening. But there was something else to it, too—a longing that looked almost like pain, but with a light in it, too, like the sun rising from behind the mountains.

Vivian studied his eyes.

"Yes . . . ?" she said slowly.

Jude looked at her a long time. He opened his mouth several times, but no sound came out. At last he sighed in frustration, and the light in his eyes went behind a cloud.

"I hope you like the book wheel," he said. "I hope it makes you feel . . . at home." Then he turned quickly and went out.

Vivian stood looking after him for a long while, looking disappointed. Eventually she turned, letting her fingers linger a moment on the book wheel, and went back to work.

It was nearly suppertime, but Ellie went to find Jude. He was in his greenhouse, hacking at a box of plants with a garden fork.

"What are you doing?" Ellie cried. "You're ripping up your garden!"

Jude shook his head. "The aton's gone to seed," he grunted. "Have to turn it under."

Ellie sat down on a stool and watched him. The muscles in his jaw were tense as he struck the plants again and again. Then he picked up a trowel and started forcefully shoveling the green fragments into the soil.

Finally he dropped the trowel and leaned on his curled fists. "I'm such a coward sometimes."

"What? You're one of the bravest people I know!" said Ellie.

Jude's voice was tight. "No, Ellie. I'm not brave. When it comes down to it, I just don't have the courage to do the right thing."

Ellie thought about her slingshot, tucked under a corner of her mattress. She didn't even want to think about using it again. "I know how you feel," she said. "I'm afraid that when we meet the Enemy, I'll be too scared to fight—that I'll just hide under the covers or something."

Jude smiled grimly. "That's exactly it. I always choose to hide under the covers."

Ellie crossed her arms. "Not always. What about when Owen's back was covered with whip cuts and you bandaged him up? Or when I was so scared after my first visions? You were the first one there, telling me it was going to be all right."

Jude sighed. "I don't think healing takes much bravery."

Ellie shrugged. "Sure it does. I think everything takes some kind of bravery. Healing people, drawing, even . . . talking to someone." As soon as those words were out of her mouth, Ellie regretted them.

Jude sighed deeply and painfully. His breath stirred the top layer of dirt in the box. "Hand me that bag of seeds on the wall?"

Ellie hopped up from the stool, glad to have something to do. "Maybe you just need one more chance. You'll find that you're brave after all; you just needed a chance."

Jude smiled stiffly and took the bag of seeds. "Thank you, Ellie. Now I'd like a little time to be alone. I'm just going to finish planting these." He scooped out a tiny handful of light brown kernels and sifted them in his hand.

Ellie quietly let herself out the greenhouse door, feeling hurt and confused. What would it take for Jude to find out that he was brave?

And with the evil armies so close behind them, would the seeds he was planting ever have a chance to grow?

Between her rumbling stomach and the events of the day, it took Ellie a long time to fall asleep that night. When she finally drifted off, she dreamed.

She was walking through a great hall with a vaulted ceiling that faded into dimness, even though many candles were lit. The walls were lined with mirrors that flickered in the candlelight. Ellie glanced at her reflections as she walked past. One of the mirrors made her look short and fat, flattened as if by a great weight. In another mirror, she was tall, but horribly stretched and gaunt as if she'd been pulled end from end. Still another mirror was spiderwebbed with cracks, fracturing her reflection until twenty pairs of her own eyes stared back at her. The reflections were everywhere, surrounding her. She couldn't remember what she actually looked like. From above one mirror, a tiny blue bird chirped *Sing!* But she couldn't stop to sing here. She began to run.

At the end of the hall was a great archway. Ellie plunged through it and suddenly found herself outdoors. She was standing in a field of white lilies, waist-high, that swayed like a pale ocean under the moon. The flowers were silky under her fingertips as she passed through them, the stalks as graceful and slender as dancers.

Suddenly the field ended and she was standing on the edge of a stream. The water was low, just a trickle, and she crossed it easily. Her feet slithered on the underwater stones.

On the far shore, a man was lying with his back to a rock, a pair of crutches beside him.

"Ishua!" Ellie cried, running toward him. He looked all wrong, sick and small there on the ground. As she dropped to her knees beside him, he opened his eyes. They glowed yellow, with tiny black pupils where she saw her own reflection. Cold fear clutched her chest.

"Ishua?" she said hesitantly. From what sounded like a great distance away, she heard a bird chirping.

Ishua sat up, his yellow eyes glowing. Unfolding one hand, he held out a white lily to her.

"For you, Ellie," he said, his voice unusually deep and rich. It was a warm and pleasant sound, and she reached for the flower.

Her hand passed right through it. It was empty air. Instead, her hand touched Ishua's. His fingers were as slimy and cold as death. Ellie pulled her hand away in horror. Ishua started to laugh, a shapeless, rattling sound. His feet fused together into a tail, and his skin melted away into a coat of black-and-yellow scales. The red tongue of a great serpent flicked toward Ellie. The lily he had held fell to the ground. Its stem turned black, then the color seeped up into the flower until it was all dark with a red edge.

"How dreadfully easssy," the serpent gloated, its eyes narrowing into yellow slits. "Deceiving one who cannot be deceived. What good is a gift if you don't ussse it?" The snake slithered around her, encircling her with its coils. Now all the Sight in the world will do you no good."

Paralyzed by fear, Ellie stood frozen as the snake's cold, whispery scales brushed against her legs, wrapping them too tightly to move. Glancing over her shoulder, she saw blackness surging up the stems of the lilies behind her, the serpent's toxin eclipsing the whole field of moon-white flowers. The serpent's coils began to squeeze, and she gasped for air.

"Should have looked before leaping, eh?" The serpent's rattling laugh began again, its tremors echoing inside Ellie's constricted rib cage. "Now it is too late."

Ellie's eyes snapped open and she sucked in a breath of air. She was lying on the cold floor, wound tightly in her blankets. She let out a deep, shaky sigh and sat up, pushing off the tangled fabric. It was still dark outside, and Jariel was snoring. She settled her blankets back on her bed and crawled under them, but she didn't dare to close her eyes. The distorted mirrors, the poisoned lilies, Ishua turning into a snake . . . what had it all meant?

Sing! The chirping blue bird had warned her.

Ellie rolled over, burying her face in the pillow.

How dreadfully easy, the serpent had said. *What good is a gift if you don't use it?*

Illusions. That was what the dream had been about. And she'd been deceived by every one of them. She, who had the ability to see things as they really were.

"Ishua," she groaned softly. "How can you want a coward like me in your fleet? I don't even think to use your gift when I'm in danger. Why didn't you give it to someone braver?"

She was quiet, half-listening for an answer, but the only sound was Jariel's snoring.

She was still awake when Owen poked his head in the door.

"Time for watch," he whispered.

Ellie shook Jariel, and both of them bundled up, but it was even harder to stay awake than it had been last night. Ellie felt as if there were giant weights on her eyelids. Jariel paced the deck, slapping her arms against her legs to keep warm, but Ellie sat on a crate outside the captain's cabin, too tired even to walk around. Still thinking about her dream, she began to hum a few bars of the Song. She wanted to stay in practice. Maybe it would help her stay awake, too.

As she hummed, she saw something fluttering by the prow of the ship, where Jariel was walking. It looked like a dim white . . . bird, or something. Ellie stopped singing and squinted into the darkness. There was nothing there. Was she falling asleep after all?

Ellie picked up the Song where she'd left off, feeling a little more awake. Instantly the white shape snapped into view again, but now it was closer. It wasn't a bird after all, but a large butterfly that looked as if it were made of lace. It was pretty, making graceful, lazy swoops through the air. But something about it wasn't right. Ellie drew back, but the butterfly was not coming toward her. It was headed straight for Jariel.

"Jariel, look out!" Ellie cried, cracking the still night air.

Jariel turned. "What?"

"Get down; it's coming!"

Jariel looked confused, but she obediently lay down on the deck. Ellie walked toward her, humming nervously and looking from side to side. There! The butterfly was perched on the railing, not three feet from Jariel, its wings bobbing up and down. Ellie swallowed hard. Catching sight of a stack of empty clay pots outside Jude's greenhouse, she grabbed one. Noting the butterfly's exact spot, she stopped singing and crept up quietly. Then she brought the pot down with all her might. It broke on the railing with a loud *crash.*

"What on earth are you doing?" asked Jariel, her arms covering her head.

Ellie slowly poked at the shards of pottery. Underneath was a white shape that was rapidly shriveling.

"What *is* that?" breathed Jariel.

The door to the captain's cabin burst open, and there was a sound of commotion from below decks. Captain Daevin reached them first.

"What happened? I heard a crash."

The girls watched in riveted horror as the butterfly's lacy wings shriveled to ash. Its swollen body was turning black as its eight legs curled inwards. It was a spider, nearly the size of Ellie's palm. Three red dots marked its upturned abdomen.

Just then, the others came running up the stairs.

"That is a big spider," said Owen, his eyes sleepy and his hair sticking straight up.

"It's a helkath," said the captain. Whipping out a small knife from his belt, he speared the bug's body and flung both the helkath and the knife overboard.

"Why'd you do that?" said Owen. "I could have kept it for my collection."

"Get me a wet rag," said the captain.

Owen brought the rag, and the captain immediately scrubbed down the railing where the bug had been. Ellie noticed a faint scorch mark on the wood. When he was finished, the captain tossed the rag overboard. "Dead helkath emit a scent that attracts other enemy creatures. With luck, we've now erased all traces of this one." By the look in the captain's eyes, though, he did not think that was likely.

"Are you two all right?" Jude asked the girls.

"We're all right," said Ellie shakily. "That—*thing*—was coming toward Jariel. I only saw it because I was singing."

"And you smashed it!" said Jariel. She flung her arms around Ellie and squeezed. "You saved my life!"

"That was brave of you," said Vivian, slipping an arm around Ellie's shoulders.

Ellie tried to smile. She didn't feel brave. She felt like going back to bed.

Jude and the captain relieved the girls for the rest of their watch, so Ellie got her wish. However, she slept only fitfully, with glimpses of white wings darting uneasily through her dreams.

At breakfast, everyone looked pale and ghostly. It was the third day of their mission. The Suor rescue would most likely be complete by nightfall—unless the Enemy found them first.

"Today will require our utmost," the captain said, his voice rough and low. "Our rescue mission must be ready to depart the instant Suor comes into view. I will lead the mission. Ellie and Vivian will accompany me, to help with Sight and translation. I would not ask either of you to come if your skills were not absolutely necessary."

"Can I go, too?" begged Owen. "I don't have any bugs from Arjun Mador yet."

"No," said the captain. "Not this time." He looked at Jude. "If we do not return within two hours, you are the new captain. Turn the ship around and sail for Rhynlyr with all speed. Connor can help you with the navigational instruments and charts."

Ellie's mouthful of porridge stuck in her throat. Turn around? And leave them stranded on Suor, to fall over the Edge with the islanders? Would they never make it to Rhynlyr? She looked at Jariel, whose eyes were already red and puffy.

Captain Daevin scraped back his chair and stood.

"I do not think it will be long before we sight the island. Carry your weapons with you and be constantly alert."

"I don't have a weapon," said Vivian.

"What?" the captain turned on her impatiently.

"I was never given one," she said, crossing her arms.

"Very well. Girls, show Vivian the weapons chest and see that she gets something."

The old crate that held the weapons looked pitifully empty.

"Here's my bow!" exclaimed Jariel, pulling it out. "I mean, I wanted to use a bow at first, but I didn't, because my aim was too awful. You try, Vivian."

"Hm," said Vivian, testing the string. "I did have a few lessons in archery when I was younger. It was a fashionable sport for young ladies at the time. I wonder . . . " She fitted an arrow to the string and pulled it back, squinting at a mostly empty sack of flour across the room. The string twanged, and the arrow smacked into the lower left corner of the sack. Vivian rubbed the inside of her left arm.

"I forgot how the string burns. Well, my aim isn't going to win any prizes, but it'll do." She retrieved her arrow and buckled the quiver around her waist.

Shouts from upstairs startled them.

"Hurry!" Connor appeared at the top of the stairs, his eyes wide and frightened. "Everyone up on deck, quick!"

Chapter 19
Under Attack

When the girls scrambled up to the top deck, they didn't need the spyglass to tell them what had happened. The stricken faces of the other crewmembers and a glance at the horizon revealed it instantly.

Far below on the sea horizon, yet close enough to see with the naked eye, a black hump was growing. A wave of nausea swept over Ellie. It was a falling island.

The crew watched helplessly as Suor teetered on the edge of the world, silhouetted against the sky. Then, without a sound, it slipped from sight. Ellie covered her eyes. She had hoped she would never have to witness that awful scene again. And thinking of the enemy spawn that were already springing up there made her skin crawl.

There was a long moment of silence.

"We're too late," Vivian whispered. "Suor is gone."

The captain stood with his head bowed. "But still we must pay." He raised his head, his face grim.

"Set a new course! We must flee from here immediately. Speed is our only chance."

Feeling sick, Ellie stumbled to help the others haul in the sails. The captain was already at the helm, turning the ship's wheel.

Suddenly Owen, looking over the railing, pointed at a spot below them.

"Uh . . . Captain? I think you should see this."

From far below came a sound that Ellie didn't recognize. At first it was only a low, ominous bubbling, but it built into a dull roar. Hardly daring to look but unable to resist, the crew leaned over the *Legend*'s railing.

The glassy turquoise surface of the ocean below was being churned into a white froth. Out of the raging whirlpool rose what looked like a gigantic tentacle—a scaly, iridescent arm as big around as an oak tree. As it came closer, they saw a platform affixed to its tip like the top of a siege tower.

"That thing can't . . . reach us, can it? We're too high up, right?" asked Ellie, nervously watching the tentacle continue to extend.

"Look, it's stopped," said Connor. The platform hovered in space about sixty yards below them.

"What are those on the platform?" said Jariel, pointing.

"Urken," said Ellie with a shudder. They were packed in a dark mass on the wooden platform—she couldn't tell how many. "They've caught up to us."

"Good thing they can't—" Owen began. A whistle in the air cut him off, and Ellie jerked him away from the railing. A thick, black, three-pronged hook with sharp barbs hit the *Legend*'s railing and dug into the wood where he had been standing. A rope trailed behind it.

"Grappling hooks!" shouted the captain. "Cut the ropes!"

He whipped out his sword, but Connor was faster. He hacked at the rope with his dagger, but the rope was strong and thick and took many strokes to cut. When it finally fell away, the blade of his dagger was notched.

"I think we're going to need more knives," he said.

"I'll get some from the galley," said Vivian.

A dozen more grappling hooks appeared in the air, thudding with sickening solidity into the wood of the *Legend.* Far below, many dark, broad-shouldered bodies began to climb, their reflective shields strapped to their backs.

"Prepare for battle!" shouted the captain. He grabbed a rope and began lashing the helm in place. "We must face the enemy this time. Boil pots of hot water, oil, anything you can find. And keep your weapons at hand!"

The crew scrambled to obey. Ellie ran downstairs to help Vivian boil huge pots of water in the galley. When they returned to the deck, lugging a scalding pot between them, Connor pointed at the horizon. "Captain! Look!"

Ellie looked up. There was a speck on the horizon, so far away she couldn't tell what it was. But it was moving.

The captain whipped out his spyglass. Without a word, he bolted for his cabin. Moments later, he reappeared with a paper-wrapped parcel.

"What is it, Captain?" asked Owen.

"A ship," said the captain, ripping open the brown paper. Inside was a small black tube with a red cap. He set it on its end and fumbled in his pocket. "Too far away to tell if it's Vestigian, but we'll have to take our chances."

Producing a book of matches from his pocket, the captain struck one and lit a string coming from the bottom of the tube.

"Get back!" he yelled.

There was a loud explosion, a plume of fire, and a cloud of blue smoke.

"If that's a Vestigian ship, it'll know a distress flare when it sees one," muttered the captain, shading his eyes with his hand.

Ellie worked to carry the rest of the hot water to the deck, then took her place beside Vivian. Owen had disappeared. She had a pouch full of stones for her slingshot, but she hadn't even touched it yet. All she could think about was the battle on Mundarva, and Manul's arm lying limp under the grapevines.

"Keep them off the deck as long as you can," said the captain, pacing up and down the deck. "The longer we have the high ground, the better our advantage."

Ellie swallowed. Her tongue felt like sandpaper. She glanced at Jariel, who was tightening the buckles on her shield. Jariel looked up and smiled grimly.

"See you when this is over," she said. "Good luck."

"Ready—pour!" shouted the captain.

Bending her knees, Ellie lifted a pot of water from the floor, her muscles straining. She had barely raised it to the railing when her hold slipped. The climbing urken screamed as scalding water poured down on them. Then the pot followed with a great *clunk* and two or three urken lost their grip, their screams fading as they fell.

"Missiles!" yelled the captain.

Her hands shaking, Ellie's first few shots went wide. But firing stones at the heads of climbing urken was much less frightening than fighting hand-to-hand. When she didn't have to stare into their glazed yellow eyes, it was almost like a game of skill. She began to concentrate, and nearly every stone she shot found its mark. Beside her, Vivian sighted down arrow after arrow.

"Watch this," said Owen. He was tugging on a pair of wings.

"Owen, wait! Don't—" Ellie cried. But he had already jumped over the railing. Ellie looked down. Owen swooped down from behind the attackers like a bird of prey, firing his poisoned blowdarts. Urken fell, screaming, from the ropes, some taking others down with them.

When Ellie was out of stones, she fired garden pots, silverware, anything she could find. When Connor rushed up with a pile of heavy books, though, Vivian gasped.

"We can't throw those!"

The captain looked at her dryly. "If we don't fight this battle with everything we have, neither the books nor we will survive."

"Well," said Vivian wistfully, "at least leave them for last. Don't throw them until there's nothing else left."

Rolling his eyes, Connor ran to find more debris they could throw.

More grappling hooks flew, and soon there were simply too many climbers to hold off. Owen reappeared and tumbled to the deck, one wing slashed through the middle.

"Are you alright?" said Ellie in alarm. One of the lenses of his glasses was cracked.

He winced, moving his left arm gingerly. "Yeah, I think so. But I don't think I can fly anymore. Can't see so well, either. But I never really wanted to see those ugly beasts again anyway."

"Me neither," Ellie agreed.

She turned back to her post and suddenly came face to face with a pair of leering yellow eyes, inches from her own. She screamed.

"We're under attack!" yelled the captain. "Archers to the quarterdeck! Cover us!"

The first urken clambered over the *Legend*'s railing. Ellie, Vivian, and Owen retreated to the platform over the captain's cabin, and Connor and Jariel dashed forward with a yell. Connor's tiger claws glinted, and Jariel's hair streamed in the wind like a banner of flame. Jude lashed out with his quarterstaff, and the captain's rapier was like a bolt of silver lightning. From her new post, Ellie had a hard time firing without hitting her friends.

Wave after wave of urken broke over the railing in a black tide. Forcing their reflective shields together, they pushed their way forward. The distorted mirrors made the crew of the *Legend* look like isolated stars fighting the blackness of the night sky. Jude's quarterstaff and the captain's sword worked back and forth. Connor punched and lunged, a weapon in each hand, while Jariel whirled like a tornado. But little by little, the enemy pushed the crew of the *Legend* back. An urken maneuvered around Connor and ran for the deck where the archers were standing. Vivian aimed an arrow and fired, but the urken ducked and kept coming. Ellie's heart pounded in her throat. Suddenly she couldn't remember what to do with her slingstones.

Just then, it howled and stumbled on the stairs. Jariel stood behind it. The urken swung at her with its hooked sword, but she ducked nimbly. Her knife moved and she gashed its leg a second time. The urken fell prone on the stairs, writhing in pain. Jariel hesitated for a moment, grimly eyeing her knife. Then she stabbed it in the neck. The creature twitched and went still.

"You did it!" Ellie cried above the din of battle.

Jariel hastily wiped her knife on the urken's tunic. "Welcome."

A shrill whistle pierced the air, and as if in answer, a cloud began to form around the *Legend.* At first it looked like brown vapor, but soon Ellie could make out individual flying bodies about the size of dragonflies. More enemy creatures?

With a low, ominous hum, the dragonfly creatures closed in on the ship. Ellie saw one with thick pincers and a curling tail like a scorpion's. It flew straight toward an urken, landed on its arm, and stung it with its tail. The urken howled, dropped its sword, and clutched the arm, which now hung limp as though paralyzed.

It appeared that the scorpionflies did not discern sides, however. Just feet in front of Ellie, Jariel groaned, her knife clattering to the deck. A scorpionfly whizzed away, and the fingers of Jariel's right hand curled inward, freezing in a claw-like position.

"Jariel! Are you all right?"

"It won't move," Jariel said, trying to force her fingers outward. "I can't feel it."

A shadow loomed over them. An urken leered down, its long, gangly arms almost brushing the deck. Jariel tried to reach for her knife, but her right hand was still frozen into a claw. She glanced up at the urken in fear. It took one ambling step toward them.

"Jariel, run," Ellie whispered. Feeling out of her mind, she ran a few steps away from Jariel. "Over here! Hey, you!" She picked up one of the abandoned books and threw it, hitting the urken in the shoulder.

The ugly creature's slitted eyes slid off Jariel and focused on Ellie. She took a step backward, heading around the captain's cabin. "Right. This way. Follow me." Not taking her eyes off the beast, she picked up another book and kept backing up, not sure exactly what she was planning to do. Out of the corner of her eye, she saw Jariel grasp her knife with her left hand. She would be all right now.

Suddenly Ellie backed into something hard. It was a small barrel wedged into the corner of the railing. Her heart skipped a beat. The urken closed in. There was nowhere to go. Ellie cringed, covering her head. But then there was a flash of light from the ship in the distance. Ellie had just time to see the puff of smoke before she dove into a corner, covering her head. There was a loud *boom* and she was slammed against something hard.

She must have lost consciousness, because the next thing she remembered, she was in the dark. She tried to move her arms and legs, but there was something heavy on top of them. Her heart began to pound. Out—out—she couldn't get out.

Ellie let out a soft whimper. Her face pressed to the deck, she felt the stuffy air closing in around her. Would anyone come to find her? No—they were all too busy fighting. She was trapped. She would die all alone in here.

Or—Ellie listened, and the sounds of battle came faintly through the walls of her prison. Or she could fight.

She wiggled her shoulders. She felt something shift around her right arm. Wriggling harder, she gave a sharp yank and that arm came free. Good—that was something.

Using her free right hand, she tried to leverage off whatever was pinning down her left arm. This one was heavier, but she writhed and pushed until she could slide that arm loose, too.

Her efforts were rewarded by another crash as the debris resettled. Ellie covered her head with her hands, and found that she could move them when all was still again.

Her legs were harder. They had something really heavy on top of them, and she was losing feeling in her feet. She tried to pull herself forward with her arms, but her legs wouldn't budge. The panic began to return. What good was it to be able to move her arms if she still couldn't get out?

Then she had an idea. Scrunching herself together, her nose pressed to the deck, she reached back with her hands. She groped until she found the edge of what felt like a crate, and pushed up as hard as she could. The pressure on her legs was relieved for a moment, and she scooted them forward before dropping the crate to rest. It banged into her calves, and she stifled a yelp.

It took her three more tries before her feet finally cleared the edge of the crate. She was free!

Hunched in a ball like a snail, Ellie pushed herself up, arching her back to clear whatever was on top of her. It was heavy, but not immovable. She pushed forcefully, her face red and sweaty, until at last something toppled off the top and light and air flooded her little world. She sat back on her heels, drinking in deep breaths. She was exhausted, from the fear as much as from exertion. But she was free.

The freedom, however, did not last. The first thing Ellie saw when she opened her eyes was a pair of urken coming around the captain's cabin. No, no! Why couldn't this confounded battle be over? She just wanted to go home and be safe. She reached for her slingshot, but couldn't find it. She must have lost it in the explosion. The ugly creatures spotted her and ambled toward her. Ellie's last fiber of courage snapped. She didn't have the energy to fight one more enemy. When one of the urken lunged at her, she rolled between its legs and began to run. Her eyes swept the decks and locked on the trap door. Losing sight of everything else, she jumped through the hatch and fell more than ran down the stairs. Where to go from here?

The library door stood open.

Ellie bolted for it and lunged inside. She slammed the door shut and threw her back against it. *Safe.* She closed her eyes, her chest heaving as she tried to catch her breath.

"Quiet in here, isn't it, Ellie?"

Ellie's eyes snapped open.

Chapter 20
The Illuminator

A beautiful woman sat in one of the library's comfortable chairs. She wore a fitted wine-purple velvet coat, the collar edged with diamond-shaped mirrors, and her booted feet were lazily crossed at the ankle. A black cloak was tossed over the back of her chair. She watched Ellie out of almond-shaped, half-lidded eyes.

"Who . . . who are you?" said Ellie. Her eyes darted around the room, looking for anything she could use to defend herself. "How do you know my name?"

"I can be anyone you want me to be," said the woman in a silky voice. "But I have heard a great deal about you. You may call me Nikira."

"What are you doing here?"

"I might ask you the same question," said Nikira. "There seems to be a battle going on upstairs. Don't you have a part in it?"

Ellie fumbled for words. "I'm . . . I couldn't . . . I needed to be away from there. Just for a while."

Nikira gasped softly. "So you ran away? Left your friends in the fight?"

"I . . . no, I didn't mean it like that! It was just . . . " Ellie faltered. "There were these creatures, and two of them were coming for me. One of them almost got my friend, and I was leading it away, but then it shoved me into a barrel and I couldn't get out. I almost suffocated." She took a deep breath, enjoying the abundance of air.

Nikira shivered sympathetically. "How terrifying."

Ellie nodded emphatically. "It was awful."

"Well, I don't think you ought to be ashamed, no matter what the others think. Fear masters us all at times."

Ellie looked into the woman's face gratefully. "Really?"

Nikira nodded. "Of course. Anyone in your place might have done just what you did. Unfortunately . . . " Nikira dropped her gaze uncomfortably.

"Unfortunately what?"

She sighed. "Unfortunately, I'm not so sure your friends will share my opinion. Look at it from their perspective. Why did you disappear when the battle was hardest? Why did you flee for your life, leaving them to fend for themselves?"

Ellie closed her eyes and swallowed. "I should go back up there."

Just then, there was a commotion outside the door. The urken! Ellie grabbed the wooden chair from Vivian's desk and jammed it under the doorknob, barricading herself and Nikira inside.

"They won't come in here," came Nikira's voice, so soft it was almost a purr. "You're safe with me. It's what your friends will think that worries me. What will your captain say when he finds out that you abandoned the crew during the battle? What about your red-haired friend?"

Ellie looked at the barricaded door. She ought to take away that chair and go help Jariel. But the sounds of battle roared outside, and her anxiety grew. She couldn't go back out there.

"What kind of a captain could keep you in his crew now? What could he call you except a coward and a deserter?"

Nikira's voice was gentle, without a hint of accusation, yet Ellie felt the words as sharply as the stings of the flying scorpions. "I'll explain it to him. I'll . . . I'll make him understand." Her voice sounded small and unconvincing in her own ears.

"Understand what? That you're too afraid to sail on a rescue ship? How can he keep you then?"

Ellie hung her head. *I'm just not the kind of kid people want to keep.* She remembered saying those words in Miss Sylvia's orphanage play yard, and Jariel had assured her that she just hadn't found the right family yet. When she'd come aboard the *Legend*, she had thought this would be her family forever—Jariel and Owen and Jude, Vivian and Captain Daevin and even Connor. But after this, she wouldn't belong with them anymore. She was too much of a coward. They'd discard her, just as the Beswicks, the Alstons, and the Cooleys had. She would be alone again.

"I have an idea," said Nikira, standing up. She was taller than Ellie had expected. "This crew may judge you for your actions, but I do not. Your crew may cast you out for a momentary lack of courage, but if you come with me, I will introduce you to my friends. They will not reject you. We all know what it is to make mistakes. You will belong." A glint flickered in her dark eyes.

Belong. That was all Ellie had wanted, all her life—a family who would keep her forever.

"Are you sure your friends will want me?"

Nikira's lips curled into an inviting smile. "I'm certain."

Just then, there was a blinding flash of light and an explosion. Ellie dropped to the floor, covering her head as one of the library's windows shattered into thousands of glass needles. She felt sharp stings of pain all over her. When she lifted her head, the floor was littered with glass and her arms were covered with tiny scratches. Through the gaping hole in the wall she caught a glimpse of a distant ship, its side lined with cannons. Was it the one Captain Daevin had signaled?

Bits of burning wood from the wall had scattered across the floor and were slowly kindling the floorboards. The flames began to creep toward a bookshelf.

"The Song Book!" Ellie scrambled to her feet. An invisible piece of glass pierced her finger, and climbing the bookshelf felt like holding a live coal in her hand. But she made it to the top and pulled the Song Book safely down.

Nikira stepped forward.

"You don't have authorization to handle that," she said. "Don't you think you've broken quite enough rules for one day? I'll take it."

Ellie hesitated. It was true; usually the captain or the highest-ranking person present handled the Song Book. She began to hand it over. She'd never meant to break any rules at all. Nikira eagerly extended her hand to take it. Suddenly Ellie stopped.

Nikira's fingers had webs between them.

Ellie gasped and clutched the Book to her chest. Nikira frowned.

"What's the matter? Just give it to me."

"No," said Ellie, stepping toward the door. "You're a creature of Draaken."

Nikira advanced on her. "You lying orphan! Give me the Book!"

"I'm the illuminator. And I say you can't have it!"

Ellie's back hit the door and the Book slipped from her hands. It fell to the floor and the cover fell open.

The first page shone forth, Ellie's illumination blazing with light and color. Nikira screeched and staggered back, her webbed fingers covering her face. "Stupid, worthless child!" Flames crept around her, but she kept backing up until she was flat against a bookshelf.

Ellie's heart stung as she heard echoes of Ewart's old insults, but she felt a strange courage well up in her. She picked up the fallen Book and held out the illumination, advancing on Nikira. At the same time, she began to sing.

The walls of the ship vanished away. Up on deck, she saw her friends still fighting, but they were grown tall, towering over the swarms of their enemies as if they were hordes of ants. Their bodies radiated light that shone in the dark sea all around them. They were pushed back on every side, but they were not yet destroyed.

And before her, Nikira's form had changed as well. Her smooth skin caved into a hag's labyrinth of wrinkles. Her silky, jet-black hair became oily strands of seaweed, and scales crawled up her body, fusing her legs together and deforming her face. Bits of carrion, remnants of past gorgings, clung to her. She was an unnatural sea monster, a revolting combination of hag and serpent.

The library doorknob rattled and Ellie lost the tune, her vision disappearing like a dream. The urken were getting through! There was a heavy pounding and the wood rattled, then splintered as a boot came through. Another kick and the door gave way. Ellie snapped the Song Book shut and pulled it toward her, ready to fight.

"Ellie?" said Vivian, lowering her drawn bow.

"Vivian!" Ellie cried in relief, running to Vivian's side.

Both of their eyes turned to Nikira, who was no longer flattened against the bookshelf. Her slitted eyes looked dangerous.

"She's evil!" Ellie cried, her vision of the hag-serpent still fresh in her mind. "Don't let her get close!"

"Get behind me," Vivian muttered, pulling her bowstring to her ear.

But before she could aim or even sight down the arrow, Nikira was on her. With surprising strength, she knocked the arrow away and twisted Vivian's arm, forcing her to drop the bow and pulling her into a chokehold.

"Let . . . me . . . go!" Vivian grunted, trying to wriggle out of Nikira's grip.

"I wouldn't struggle so much if I were you," Nikira purred, tightening her hold like a vise. "Now, Ellie. I have made you some generous offers. I renew them one last time: come with me, and bring the Song Book. I know about your gift of Sight, and my master greatly desires to know you better. Think carefully. You can have a better future, as well as redeeming your past cowardice by saving your friend here. But if you refuse . . . I can get what I want in other ways." Vivian squeezed her eyes shut as Nikira gripped her more tightly.

"Stop!" Ellie cried, clutching the book to her chest.

"It's up to you, Ellie," continued Nikira in her soothing tone. "You have the power to make it stop. Why are you making your friend suffer?"

Just then, Jude burst through the splintered library door, brandishing his quarterstaff. In one second, his eyes swept the whole scene. He took one step toward Vivian, but instantly Nikira's hand released Vivian's wrist and reappeared holding a sharp, slender dagger, its point at Vivian's ribs.

"Ah-ah-ah," Nikira chided gently. "Not so fast. Back away slowly."

His eyes fixed on Vivian, Jude backed toward Ellie.

"Why must you all be so stubborn?" Nikira sighed. "It's a simple trade: Ellie and the Book come with me, and no one else gets hurt. Wouldn't we all like to prevent more bloodshed?"

"Don't listen to her!" Vivian cried, her face reddening as Nikira's arm tightened around her throat. "She speaks . . . for the Enemy! Think of . . . the cost!"

"Yes, do," said Nikira, pulling the dagger closer to Vivian's ribs. Ellie looked at Jude, her mind blank with panic. Jude's face was white.

Just then, Nikira let out a bloodcurdling screech. Vivian had pulled an arrow from her quiver and stabbed Nikira in the leg. A slow black stain began to spread on her velvet coat. Vivian struggled, trying to take advantage of the distraction, but Nikira did not relax her hold.

"I tire of this banter," Nikira said, her voice suddenly flat and cold. "Make your choice, Ellie."

As if in answer, there was a groan from overhead. The fire had spread to the roof and weakened one of the rafter beams. With a loud *crack,* the beam fell.

Everyone scrambled to get out of the way. Ellie, still clutching the Book, dove for the doorframe. When she looked behind her, the burning rafter beam had fallen across the room, separating her and Jude from Nikira and Vivian.

"Look out!" cried Ellie. Vivian turned her face away as the other library window exploded inward, raining shards of glass over all of them. A rope snaked down past the gaping hole in the ship's side.

"Ellie," Nikira warned dangerously.

No, Vivian mouthed.

Jude's jaw was clenched so tightly that a muscle bulged below his ear.

All of Ellie's muscles were trembling, and her chest felt squeezed. For some reason, she began to remember images from her last dream. The lilies turning black. Ishua turning into a serpent, like the one Nikira had become a few minutes ago. What would happen if she went with Nikira? What would happen if she didn't? *Help me, Ishua!* she pleaded silently.

Jude looked at her. Vivian looked at her. Ellie looked at Nikira.

"I belong to Ishua," she said at last. "You cannot have the Book, and you cannot have me."

Nikira's slow smile sent a shudder down Ellie's back.

"Very well."

Swift as a striking snake, Nikira plunged the dagger into Vivian's side.

"No!" screamed Jude.

Vivian doubled over in pain and Nikira kicked her to the floor. She lunged toward Jude and Ellie, but Jude swung his quarterstaff around, cracking her on the side of the head. Nikira shrieked and reeled back, a black trail beginning to dribble from under her hair. Ellie crouched to the floor behind Jude.

"I'll get you . . . " Nikira panted. "If . . . you survive long enough." She met Ellie's eyes and spat. Then, before anyone could stop her, she leaped through the hole where the window had been. Ellie ran to the opening, but Nikira was already yards below them, sliding down the rope toward the tentacle platform.

She turned and saw Jude kneeling on the floor beside Vivian. Her face was contorted in pain. His hands hovered over her, unsure of what to do first. The bloodstain on her shirt was spreading fast. Flames licked the ceiling beams above them. At last Jude gently slid his arms under her and lifted her. Glass crunched under his boots as he carried her out of the ruined library.

Vivian's eyes fluttered open. "Put me . . . down. Fine. I'm . . . fine." A series of coughs twisted her convulsively. Blood came to her lips. "Don't talk," he ordered. He set her down under the stairs, where she lay back, her face drawn as she tried to hold in the pain.

"Get my herbs, Ellie," Jude said. "Quickly."

Footsteps thundered down the stairs. The urken had broken through! With a roar, Jude charged at them with his quarterstaff. Ellie dashed to the infirmary, where more flames had broken out. She grabbed the satchel by the door and ran back to Vivian, taking one of her hands. It was cool and pale.

"I'm . . . sorry, Vivian," Ellie whispered. "This is all my fault."

Vivian looked at her, her eyes strangely unfocused. "Did . . . right," she muttered.

Tears sprang to Ellie's eyes. She wished there were something she could do. There was a crash from the library, and suddenly she had an idea.

Inside the library, fire was everywhere. More beams had fallen from the ceiling, and flames were licking at the bookshelves. Ellie jumped over a burning log and grabbed any books she could reach. She made sure the illuminated Tehber book and her sketchbook were among them.

The ceiling groaned again, and Ellie ran from the library, a falling beam nearly catching her leg. It was only a small offering, but this was something she could do for her friend. She set the books down where Vivian could see them.

Vivian's eyes traveled over them slowly, her eyelids drooping. Her mouth moved, but Ellie couldn't hear what she said.

At last the noises of battle on the stairs stilled. Jude jumped down the remaining stairs and knelt down next to Ellie. Immediately he began to probe Vivian's wound with his fingers, his eyebrows furrowing.

"Still bleeding," he muttered. He rummaged in his satchel, chewed a dried leaf into a paste, and applied it to the wound. Unrolling a white bandage, he wrapped it tightly around her middle.

"There," he murmured soothingly. "You're going to be all right. Look, Ellie even brought you your books."

Vivian didn't open her eyes. Jude frowned, pressing his hand to the outside of her bandage. When he took his hand away, it was wet with blood.

He dove back into his satchel, selecting berries and mixing them with a few drops of liquid from a vial. He tipped it into Vivian's mouth, but she began to cough violently, causing the wound to bleed even more. She moaned softly. Her face was turning an ashy gray.

Jude turned his satchel upside-down, hunting madly through it for more leaves, more powders. He reapplied them under the bandage, but nothing seemed to help. He couldn't stop the bleeding.

Ellie looked at him worriedly and saw that his eyes were moist. Slowly he swept aside the mess of herbs, then pulled Vivian into his arms, cradling her like a baby.

Loud noises came from the hatch to the top deck. Jariel, Owen, Connor, and Captain Daevin tumbled down the stairs. They slammed the hatch shut.

"Quick! Get me some chairs! We need a barricade!" shouted the captain.

Jariel bolted down the stairs, but stopped when she saw Ellie, Jude, and Vivian huddled together.

"What's wrong?" Jariel asked. She had a scratch under her eye and a long cut running down her forearm, though her hand was no longer curled into a claw.

"Jariel!" yelled the captain.

Jariel grabbed one of the dining room chairs and dragged it up the stairs. A pounding sound began to come from outside the hatch.

"That won't hold them for long," came Connor's voice.

"And the ship is on fire," observed Owen.

"But none of that will matter if the urken get to the lumena," said the captain grimly. "That's our power source, what keeps us in the air. If it is destroyed . . . "

"What about that other ship out there?" asked Jariel. "Is it a friend?"

"It is," said Captain Daevin. "It's fired at the urken platform, though some stray shots have hit us, too. But it won't reach us in time to give us an escape route. Jude! Are you three all right?"

Jude didn't answer. Ellie watched him smooth fragments of glass out of Vivian's hair.

"Jude?" Captain Daevin appeared at the bottom of the stairs, followed by Connor, Owen, and Jariel.

"She looks bad," said Connor, gesturing to Vivian.

"What happened?" asked the captain.

"Can't you heal her?" said Jariel.

Jude answered none of them. He looked into Vivian's pale face. Her shallow breathing came with a dull rasping sound.

"There has to be some way!" said Ellie, her eyes swimming.

Jude blinked. "There might be . . . one way." He looked again into Vivian's face, smoothing her hair away from her closed eyes.

"Try! Please!" Ellie begged.

Jude gently lowered Vivian to the floor. He glanced around at the captain and the other children as if noticing their presence for the first time.

"Please . . . go away, everyone," he said softly. "Don't watch this."

Some of the others obeyed and turned away, but Ellie could not. Jude's tone gave her a tight feeling in her stomach. Jude leaned down to Vivian's ear.

"I love you," she heard him whisper.

Then he stretched himself out over Vivian, covering her completely. He pinched her nose shut with one hand and took a deep breath. Then he kissed her, slowly releasing his breath into her mouth.

For a moment, nothing happened. Both of them lay motionless. Ellie watched, frozen, as Jude's body relaxed and the color drained from his face.

Then Vivian stirred. She drew a sudden deep breath, and Jude's body rolled off of her. Ellie stared in horror and wonder.

Vivian opened her eyes. She sat up quickly, as if she'd overslept.

"Where is she? That woman—she wants the Song Book!"

Ellie swallowed around a painful lump in her throat. "She's gone, Vivian."

"Is the book safe?"

Ellie nodded.

Vivian sighed. "Good. But what are you all doing down here? Is the battle over?"

Ellie looked at Jude. Vivian followed her gaze.

"Jude?" Her voice rose with shock as she saw him lying beside her, a pool of blood soaking his shirt. "He's hurt!" She quickly tore a strip from the bottom of her shirt and pressed it to the wound. The blood on her own bandage was now dark and dry. "Jude, wake up!" She slapped his face gently and put an ear to his chest.

"His heartbeat is so . . . faint," she choked, tears springing to her eyes. "What happened to him?"

"I think . . . he gave you the Kiss of Life," Ellie said hoarsely.

"The what?"

"He . . . he told me about it once," Ellie said. "He said it was a gift every healer could give—their life for someone else's. You were . . . dying."

"No!" cried Vivian. She leaned down and kissed Jude.

Jude's eyes fluttered open, dim and cloudy. "That was nice," he mumbled.

"Take it back," Vivian pleaded. "The Kiss of Life."

"Can't," he whispered, his expression tightening with pain. "Only works . . . once."

"But I'd rather die than lose you!" It came out as a sob.

He smiled faintly. "So would I." His eyes drifted closed. Vivian rested his head on her lap and stroked his hair, her shoulders jerking as she wept.

The pounding at the hatch grew louder. "The urken are breaking through!" said Jariel.

"We can't let them get to the lumena," said the captain.

Connor stood silent, looking up at the hatch. "Maybe we can," he said quietly.

"What? Are you out of your mind?" said the captain, his voice so tense it could break.

"Well, how many urken are there out there? Thirty? Fifty? More?" said Connor. Ellie heard something new in his voice, a ring of authority. "We're overrun. We can't fight off that many. And what would happen if they take over the ship? They could attack that other Vestigian ship, or even ambush Rhynlyr. Wouldn't it be better to sacrifice one ship than to risk the safety of the whole fleet?"

The captain crossed his arms, his face grave. "None of us could survive a fall from such a height. There are three sets of wings left, but even those might not save anyone from the explosion."

Connor nodded. "I know. But the rest of the Vestigia Roi is in danger. We have to think of them."

There was a sharp *crack* as a beam from the hatch broke.

"*Captain,*" Connor warned. "We have to make a decision."

Captain Daevin's eyes swept over the crew. Ellie saw anguish written on his face.

"All right," he said at last. "Connor, you come with me. Jariel, Ellie, Owen, Vivian—cover us. Guard that hatch. Distract the urken and give us as much time as you can."

"Done," said Jariel, brandishing her knife. Ellie looked at her friend. She had the heart of a lion. The captain nodded, and he and Connor raced off in the direction of the Oratory.

"Right," said Jariel. "We're going to open the hatch. Ellie, Vivian, Owen—fire some missiles to open up a path. But get some hand weapons too, because then we're going to make a break for it."

"What about Jude?" asked Ellie, glancing at his motionless form.

"We'll come back for him later," said Jariel, her eyes fixed on the hatch. "Come on."

The four of them quietly ascended the stairs, loading their weapons. Vivian had an empty, hard look in her eyes. Jariel silently moved the chair away, unblocking the barricade.

"On my count," she whispered. "One—two—three!"

The hatch flew open, and Ellie, Vivian, and Owen wiped out the first line of urken with a spray of stones, arrows, and blowdarts. But before they could jump out on deck, they were nearly blinded by a flash of lightning, a bolt of fire and diamonds that seared their eyes. The urken screamed and howled, throwing themselves to their faces on the deck. There was a loud *boom* like thunder. Then the bow of the ship erupted in a blast of fire. The *Legend* shuddered violently, and Jude's greenhouse exploded in a shower of glass and timber. The defenders covered their heads.

The urken who were left alive and still able to move began to throw themselves overboard, wailing in terror and pain. Perhaps some of them landed back on the tentacle platform; others surely fell to their deaths in the ocean far below. The ship shuddered again, and the defenders, losing their balance, fell backward down the stairs, where they landed on Connor and Captain Daevin, their faces blackened and hair singed.

There were so many questions to ask, so many emotions to express. But there was no time for that now. Ellie's stomach lurched as the ship, its propellers stilled and wings broken, began to wobble and spin. The crew huddled around Jude and held tight to one another. Ellie scanned their faces, full of fear as the world drew to an end.

His voice low and husky, the captain began to sing from memory.

Listen, O heavens, and hear the Song.
The Good King's making-words,
Listen! They fall like the rain.
He sings from his throne,
The seat in the Great City
Where water meets sky,
And time is no more.

The falling ship picked up speed, and Owen cried out in fear. Ellie looked at him, looked at all of them. In her changed vision, they were tiny children, gray and ghostlike against the vague background of the broken ship. She knew what she had to do. She reached for the Book she had rescued, the Book for which Vivian and Jude had been willing to give their lives, and opened it.

Ellie knew the illumination she had drawn, but she had never seen it with her transformed vision. Now letters of gold rained down from a sky of rose and saffron and coral, the colors more vivid than any ink Ellie could make. A waterfall rose three-dimensionally off the page, drenching the words in its fine white-and-turquoise spray. Moving fish, all colors, swam and leaped in the sea beneath it. The ink began to flow off the page, absorbing into the faces of her battle-weary shipmates. The illumination spread until it covered the whole crew, the ghostlike children painted with color and light. And at last Ellie understood. In the midst of fire and fear and darkness, as they looked into the face of death, her drawing helped them to see what she saw. It gave them hope.

The *Legend* shuddered and listed to one side. The crew sang louder, drowning out the sound of their end.

From that glorious city
The home of the Song
His voice goes out to the islands,
His words to all the world.

The floor began to tip sideways and the crew stumbled as the table slid across the floor. Ellie grabbed Jariel's hand and held tight.

The wind outside changed from a moan to a roar. There was a loud crash as the mast broke and fell. Ellie squeezed her eyes shut.

Ishua!

Then there was silence.

Chapter 21
Amalpura

Ellie opened her eyes. Above her was a white canopy with soft light filtering through. Was she dead?

She stretched her arms and felt her sore muscles complain. No, she couldn't be dead. It hurt too much.

"Well, good morning," said a woman's voice from across the room. "Or perhaps I should say good afternoon?"

Ellie turned her head. A woman in a loose white robe stood in the room, a stack of folded linens in her arms. She had a round, cheerful face and a braid of dark hair.

"Where am I?" Ellie murmured. "And who are you?"

"You are in bed," said the woman with a cheery smile. "And that bed is on the island of Amalpura, the southernmost of the Vestigian Havens. I am Sister Kuta, and I have watched over you while you slept."

Ellie rubbed her eyes. She could see that her hand and arm were badly scratched up, but she no longer felt the sting of embedded glass. "How long have I been here?"

"You have been asleep here for nearly two days."

"Two days?" Ellie slowly raised herself to her elbows. "Where are the others? How did we get here?"

"So many questions," clucked Sister Kuta gently. "You will have plenty of time to ask them at the evening meal, and I have other duties to attend to before then. When you hear the gong, follow the sound. There is a basin here if you desire to wash."

Sister Kuta gave a slight bow and left the room. Ellie sat up and swung her legs over the side of the bed. Except for the scratches on her skin and the stiffness in her muscles, she felt well, even anxious to get up and move around. She went to the washbasin and splashed cool water on her face, drying it with a scratchy white towel.

Ellie slipped on a pair of sandals she found by the door. Outside was a small porch, screened by hanging curtains that fluttered in the light breeze. She crossed a trim green lawn and started down a path among wild, overgrown shrubs and flowers. The silence around her was tranquil, but she wondered where everyone else was.

Rounding a tall hedge, she almost smacked into Jariel.

"Ellie!" Jariel cried. Her hug was so tight that Ellie thought her ribs would crack. "I was worried about you. I was afraid . . . you were all dead and I was here alone." She laughed nervously. "It was so quiet, and I couldn't find anyone."

"I'm glad to see you too," said Ellie with a smile. "*I* thought I was dead for a while back there. When I woke up under that white canopy . . . " she pushed back her sleeve, revealing the scratches. "It was only these that convinced me I was still alive."

"I know, me too," said Jariel, pushing up her own sleeve. The healing gash on her arm had twelve stitches in it.

"Wow, are you all right? That looks bad."

Jariel shrugged. "I feel fine. It looks worse than it is. I hope it leaves a nice big scar, though." She grinned.

"Do you know where the others are?" said Ellie. "The woman in my room wouldn't tell me."

Jariel shook her head. "Truth is, though, I'm a little scared to find out. I just hope . . . everyone's still alive."

Ellie chewed on her bottom lip, thinking of Jude. "Let's go see if we can find them."

Jariel led the way back down the path. They passed a cluster of white-robed men and women working beside a pool, pulling plants with sparkling, fernlike leaves from the water. Ellie stopped to watch.

"What are those?" she whispered to Jariel.

"My caretaker—she's the one with the yellow braid over there—she said she had to go work in the lumenai pools," said Jariel. "Maybe that's what those are."

Ellie watched the plants coming out of the water, their delicate fronds dotted with tiny blue lights like stars. "Lumenai. Those are what powered our ship, right?"

Jariel nodded. "I think so. Come on! I think I see Owen."

Owen was coming across the lawn. He limped slightly, and there was a dark purple bruise around his eye.

"Hi, Owen," said Jariel. She paused. "You don't look so good."

"Nice to see you too," said Owen. "Hi, Ellie. How're you feeling?"

Ellie shrugged. "All right. Jariel and I have been exploring. How about you?"

Owen shrugged. "Okay."

Suddenly it dawned on Ellie. "Owen, your . . . your bugs . . . "

He looked at his feet. "They didn't make it. Well, except for . . . " He pulled a slender white coil, striped with blue rings, from the sleeve of his robe. Moby wriggled energetically. "He was around my neck during the whole battle. I still don't know how we were rescued, but he stayed with me." He stroked Moby's head, and the snake wound affectionately around his arm.

"Look!" Ellie pointed. Across the lawn, a tall figure and a short one were walking side by side.

Owen squinted. "What is it? I can't see anything without my glasses."

"It's Connor and the captain," said Ellie.

As the boy and man approached, Ellie saw that they had not escaped the battle unscathed, either. The captain had a bandage around his head, and Connor had one arm in a sling. Both had burns on their faces.

"Hello, children," said the captain. "I'm glad to see you're all right. I trust you're feeling tolerably well?"

They all nodded. Connor was quiet, but somehow it didn't seem like his old, sulky quietness. He seemed peaceful now, interested in what the others had to say.

"Where are we?" Jariel asked. "And how did we get here? I can't remember anything after the battle."

"Me neither," said Owen.

The captain sighed. "We were brought here by another Vestigian ship. It is a long and rather . . . peculiar story, most of which you will hear at supper. For now, it is enough for you to know that we are at a Haven—a flying island under the control of the Vestigia Roi. The Havens are safe harbors where Vestigian sailors can rest on their journeys. The brothers and sisters here have cared for us since we arrived."

"Was the Vestigian ship that rescued us the one we saw during the battle?" said Jariel.

The captain nodded. "I have spoken with their captain. You will hear the whole story from him later on."

"Did everyone . . . is everyone here?" Ellie asked hesitantly.

"Did they survive?" Captain Daevin nodded. "Yes. But I've seen neither Vivian nor Jude."

"I hope Jude is all right," said Ellie.

"So do I," said the captain with surprising earnestness. "Hopefully we will learn more at supper."

A strange sound, both natural and metallic, reached their ears. It was like wind trembling in brass trees.

"There's the gong," said the captain. "Come. Everyone is very punctual here."

They followed the sound to a low, circular building, its pointed roof thatched with reeds. They washed their hands in a basin outside, then entered.

It was surprisingly well lit inside. Many windows admitted the evening light, and even the walls were faintly translucent. Tall rush lanterns lined two low, parallel tables. White-robed brothers and sisters were already taking seats on cushions around them. There was no sign of Vivian or Jude.

Ellie found herself seated between Jariel and Connor. Across the table, she recognized Kuta, who smiled at her.

The gong sounded again, and everyone stood up. At the far end of the room stood an old man with a long silver beard. He folded his hands inside his wide sleeves. Then he began a low hum, which all the men in the room took up. The sound was eerie, primordial. Then it was broken as the female voices began the first notes of a melody. Ellie recognized the tune. It was the Song.

Ellie joined in softly, trying to both sing and listen to the brothers' and sisters' beautiful harmony. Her vision changed, but instead of seeing the human figures infused with light and grandeur, as she usually did, Ellie saw something entirely different: a still nighttime pool. The singing seemed to be coming from the stars reflected in the water. The music rose from the pool as a mist, swirling in many colors, and in the center she saw Ishua. He was standing, without crutches, on the surface of the water, and he was smiling.

Ellie was sorry when the singing ended and the vision disappeared. The silver-bearded man bowed to the group.

"We have guests with us tonight, my brothers and sisters. The crews of the Vestigian ships *Legend* and *Endeavor* are in our midst," he said, gesturing to Ellie's crew and to a group at the other table. Among them Ellie noticed a bearded man, an elderly couple, and a dark-skinned woman. "I am Elder Denparsi. Fellow Vestigians, you are welcome." He bowed again and sat down.

Immediately dishes and baskets began to circulate, each person holding plates for his or her neighbor. Ellie recognized very little of the food, but most of it looked as if it had been grown in a garden. The fruits were delicious but bizarre-looking: palm-sized round ones with bright orange flesh, long green ones with centers full of crunchy seeds, squiggly ones with leathery skin and juicy interiors. There were also flat discs of dark bread and at least four different varieties of cloud trout. It seemed like years since Ellie had had a square meal, but she enjoyed the lantern light and the cheerful conversation almost as much as the supper.

After the meal, Ellie followed a small group, including the crew of the *Endeavor,* out the back door of the hall. Embers glowed in a low fire pit on a large porch, which one of the brothers called a *lennai*. A sister offered her a mug of chilled pink tea that tasted like flowers. Ellie sat down in a corner away from the fire and looked out to the west. The sun was setting in rich hues of pink and orange, the clouds glowing as brightly as the fire's embers. Voices rose and fell in comfortable conversation around her until Elder Denparsi spoke.

"Are you recovering well, my friends?"

Captain Daevin looked around at the children and nodded. "Yes, Elder, we are, thanks to the good care of the people here. But two of us are missing. What has become of them?"

The Elder's forehead wrinkled. "The man—he is gravely wounded, and is being cared for by the brothers and sisters who are most skilled at healing. The woman is with him, as seemed fitting."

"Can we go see them?" asked Jariel.

"Jariel! Respect the Elder," chided Captain Daevin.

"You shall see them when the time is right," the old man said soberly. "Which may be quite soon."

"It is no small thing that any of you are here alive," said the bearded man from the *Endeavor*. He had quick eyes and a strong, square face. "We thought our rescue efforts would surely be in vain. In all my years with the fleet, I have never seen so many urken in one place."

"I assure you, we are deeply grateful for your efforts, Captain Gartz," said Captain Daevin.

"How did you do it?" asked Connor. "We were falling—we destroyed our lumena!"

"We were returning from the rescue mission to Suor," said Captain Gartz. "Alas, few were willing to return with us, but Zarifah was one of them."

Ellie followed his eyes to the dark-skinned woman wearing a white hood. Her eyes had a strange, glassy look to them. She looked off into the distance rather than at Captain Gartz's face, though she nodded periodically at his words. Suddenly Ellie realized—Zarifah was blind.

" . . . the ship was overrun," the other captain was saying. "We tried to reach you and fired a few shots at your attackers, but we feared to be more destructive than helpful. Then we saw a streak of lightning and knew your lumena must have been destroyed. We told Zarifah, and she produced a . . . most marvelous contraption, a huge net that could be fired from one of our cannons. As you fell, we fired the net, and it wrapped around your ship and bound you to us. The dead weight nearly sank us, and we knew we could not tow you all the way to Rhynlyr. Amalpura was the closest Haven, so we brought you here. On the way, a few of our sailors put out the fires on your ship and brought your crewmembers aboard the *Endeavor.* You were all unconscious, and none without wounds or burns. I still can't believe the Enemy deployed such a large, physical combat force. That has never been his way—not in our lifetime, at least."

"I fear we have not seen the last of such attacks," said Elder Denparsi gravely. "This may be only the beginning of something new, something larger and much more deadly. Who can predict the Enemy's schemes?"

There was a moment of grim silence.

"How did you come to be sailing these waters with such a small crew?" Captain Gartz resumed after a while.

"We were a transport ship, carrying orphan rescues to the Academy at Rhynlyr, when we were commissioned," said Captain Daevin. "Our ship was strategically positioned, and the crew voted unanimously to accept the mission to Suor. Though there were only seven of us aboard, these children fought like warriors and Vestigians." He smiled, and Ellie warmed with pride.

"Well, if you are ready, the *Endeavor* will be departing for Rhynlyr first thing in the morning and would gladly take you aboard," said Captain Gartz. "If you need more time, send a message to Rhynlyr and I will have a ship sent back for you. I'm afraid the *Legend* has sailed its last voyage."

Captain Daevin shook his head. "We cannot depart until all of our crew is well enough to travel. We will send word when we are ready for another ship."

The Elder smiled as if at a private joke. "We shall see," he said. "But now it is time to retire. All of you need rest."

Ellie rose with the others and, following their example, bowed to the Elder. He rose and slowly returned the bow. Then the two crews parted ways. Ellie glanced at Zarifah, who walked confidently, sweeping the ground with a slender, carved staff. Ellie wished she'd had a chance to talk with the mysterious woman and wondered if they'd ever meet again.

They walked the rest of the way in silence, taking in the peace of this garden island. Lanterns hanging from the trees lit their path, and softly chanted harmonies rose from the cottages they passed. Yet there was no peace in Ellie's heart. After surviving battle, fear, and fire, she had a strange foreboding that the worst was still to come.

Ellie awoke in the middle of the night to Kuta shaking her.

"You'd best come quickly," said Kuta, her face sharply illuminated by a lantern. "Your friend—he's taken a turn for the worse."

Ellie hurried after Kuta, rubbing sleep out of her eyes. She found her shipmates gathered in a room where a still figure lay in a white bed. Jude's face was pale, almost green, and Vivian sat on the edge of the bed, holding his hand. Her eyes were red-rimmed and dark with shadows.

"We've done all we can for him," one of the brothers said softly to Daevin. "The bleeding stopped yesterday and it looked as if he were recovering. But then it started again, and now it won't stop. His internal organs are damaged, and there may be an infection as well. He doesn't have long."

Tears stung Ellie's eyes. Jariel put an arm around her. Captain Daevin knelt down beside the bed. Jude's eyes were partially open, but they roved emptily over the room without recognizing anyone. His lips moved, mumbling incoherent words.

At that moment, a draft of cold air stirred the curtains around the bed. Kiaran stood just inside the doorway, his wings casting giant shadows on the wall. He extended one hand to the figure in the bed.

"Come, Jude. Ishua has seen your loyal service and your sacrifice. Because of this, I have been sent to personally escort you to the King's City. It is time to go."

"No!" cried Vivian, throwing herself over Jude. "Please—please spare him."

"The laws of life and death cannot be overthrown," said Kiaran sternly. "This man gave up his life, and now the debt must be paid."

"But . . . but he gave it for me," said Vivian, choking on a sob. "If you can't leave him here, then take me too. Don't leave me behind."

Jude gave a low moan, and Captain Daevin stood up.

"No, Vivian," he said softly. "That would waste Jude's sacrifice. He wanted you to live. *Wants* you to live."

Vivian's chin began to tremble. "But I don't want to. Not without him."

The captain looked at her, then at Jude. He took a slow breath.

"Kiaran, I know that the boundaries of eternity are fixed, and that the debt of a life must be paid. I envied Jude in life. I desired the love Vivian gave him, and when I could not take it away, I showed Jude cruelty and unkindness. But he has shown himself to be a better man than I am. He returned my anger with patience and loyalty. He has Vivian's love, and he has earned it." A muscle twitched in the captain's jaw. "I wish for him to enjoy the fruits of his sacrifice, and to redeem myself for the way I wronged my friend. Please accept an exchange: my life in place of his."

Captain Daevin knelt down before Kiaran, bowing his head. Ellie was so stunned she could hardly breathe.

Kiaran's brows knitted together. "Such a request is almost unprecedented," he said. "Why should yours be granted?"

"Because a sacrifice made for friendship is as great as one made for love," said Captain Daevin. "Jude's love for Vivian was stronger than his love of life or fear of death, and he chose to die in her place. Why should a sacrifice for a friend not be accepted for the same reasons?"

Kiaran frowned. "You realize that if I accept your petition, the exchange will be final?"

"I do."

Then Kiaran nodded. "Your request is rare, but I see that your sacrifice is sincere. I will escort you to the King's City in your friend's place. Brother," he said to the attendant standing there. "We need two drinking glasses."

Kiaran drew the two sharp sai sheathed at his back. The long, slim daggers gleamed in the candlelight. Ellie gasped and covered her eyes.

"Prick your finger," Kiaran said to the captain, and Ellie dared to look again. Captain Daevin pressed the tip of the sai to his finger until a bead of blood appeared. Kiaran held out one of the glasses to catch the drop, then pricked Jude's finger and let it bleed into the other glass. Finally, the winged man added a drop of his own blood, clear as dew, to both glasses.

"Water," he commanded, and a brother filled each of the glasses to the brim.

"Do you still wish to carry out this exchange?" Kiaran asked the captain one last time.

"Yes."

"Then drink," said Kiaran, holding out the glass containing the drop of Jude's blood to the captain. "Give this to Jude," he said as he handed Vivian the other glass.

"Thank you," Vivian whispered, looking at the captain with eyes full of gratitude and tears. Then she gave the drink to Jude, lifting his head to help him swallow. The captain downed his in one long draught. Then there was silence in the room.

"The drink requires a few minutes to take effect," said Kiaran. "When it has set in, we will depart."

The captain sat down heavily in a chair woven of rushes. His face was ghostly white. He looked at Vivian, then at Jude. Finally his eyes rested on the children.

"Farewell," he said. "I wish each of you the best on Rhynlyr. Serve Adona Roi well." His gaze lingered on Connor. Suddenly the boy rushed up and hugged the captain.

"You will do well, my boy," the captain murmured. "Jude will be captain after me, and you must help him. You know how to sail a ship. You are ready."

"And you will not be alone," Kiaran said to Connor. "You have your friends and your sister to help you."

"Sister?" Ellie, Owen, and Jariel said in unison.

Connor shook his head. "I don't have a sister."

"She's standing before you."

Connor's mouth dropped open. He scanned the room, looking from Jariel to Ellie to Vivian to the white-robed sisters. Kiaran frowned. "I suppose you did not know. Close your eyes." He put one hand on Connor's head and one on Ellie's. The winged man's hand sent a tingle through Ellie like a splash of cold water. She squeezed her eyes shut.

An image slowly came into focus: a dim, low-ceilinged room with a fire burning in the hearth. In a rocking chair sat a dark-haired woman with a book, reading aloud while a little girl in her lap looked at the pictures. The girl, perhaps two years old, looked relaxed and sleepy. On the floor, a man with a mop of sandy curls was lying on his stomach, feet in the air, building a tower of blocks with a little boy about the same age as the girl. The man would stack two or three blocks, then the little boy would swing out his fist and knocked them to the floor. No matter how many times it happened, they both roared with laughter. The mother hushed them, making the boy turn around, and Ellie saw his face. He smiled mischievously, creating a dimple in his left cheek.

The mother smoothed the little girl's wispy blonde curls and began to sing, making the girl yawn and snuggle closer. Ellie recognized the faint strains of the Song. The father chuckled, and the mother looked up with a smile. Her eyes were light blue, clear as a cloudless winter sky, with faint black rings around the irises.

Suddenly Ellie understood. She stared at Connor. "You . . . " Connor stared back, his pale, black-ringed eyes wide with disbelief. "We . . . "

"Those were your parents," said Kiaran gently.

"*Our* parents," said Connor. "Then we're . . . "

"Brother and sister," breathed Ellie.

"Twins, to be exact," said Kiaran. "Though Ellie is older by seven minutes."

"Twins?" gasped Ellie.

Connor frowned. "How did they . . . our *parents* . . . know the Song?"

"Your parents were part of the Vestigia Roi," said Kiaran. "Their names were Kiria and Gavin Reid. They settled on Freith as part of a long-term rescue mission, and you were both born there."

"What happened to them?" asked Ellie, her mind reeling.

Kiaran's colorless eyes softened.

"When you were three years old, an epidemic of sickness swept the island. You were both native-born and responded well to treatments. But your parents, who were foreigners, did not. Their bodies resisted the treatments, and they died within a week of each other. You were sent to an orphanage near Harwell."

An image fluttered dimly through Ellie's memory. A tall metal fence. The sickly sweet smell of rotting garbage. A disintegrating wooden structure in a muddy play yard.

"There was a . . . sled in the yard," Ellie remembered.

"I pretended it was a flying ship," Connor said slowly.

"*We* pretended." Ellie laughed. "I used to tell you not to put your feet on it 'cause you'd get mud on my skirt."

"And then . . . you got adopted," said Connor. "The people wouldn't take us both."

"I cried the day the Beswicks took me away."

"So did I."

"And when they returned me, they took me back to a different orphanage. Mr. Howditch gave me the last name Altess." Eight years of memories began to rush through the broken dam.

Suddenly a grin broke out over Connor's face. "I have a sister!" he whooped, picking Ellie up and spinning her around. Ellie laughed and held on tight. For the first time, she had a real family, a brother. *Her* brother.

Kiaran put his hands on their shoulders. "You will need each other to face what lies ahead of you."

"Vivian?"

Abruptly, everyone stopped talking and turned to face Jude. His eyes were fully open and no longer wandering about the room.

"I'm here," said Vivian. She touched his cheek, smiling through a screen of tears. "I'm not going anywhere."

"Jude!" Ellie rushed to the foot of his bed. "You're awake!"

Jude's eyes found her and he smiled. "Ellie." He rolled his head to the side. "You're all here."

There was a *thump* as Captain Daevin sagged in his chair, clutching at the armrest. His face was contorted with pain.

"Daevin?" said Jude, frowning. Testing his strength, he lifted his head.

"Hello, Jude," the captain ground out between clenched teeth. "An . . . odd . . . wedding present."

Jude looked from Daevin to Kiaran. "What . . . ?"

"He's going in your place," Vivian explained, a catch in her voice.

His face unreadable, Jude pushed himself up in bed. He leaned slowly over the edge and extended his hand. With all the strength he had left, Captain Daevin reached out and clasped it, and for a moment the two men looked at each other.

"Thank you—my captain—my friend," said Jude, his voice low and tight. Captain Daevin nodded weakly.

"It is time," said Kiaran. "Come, Daevin." Stepping forward, he lifted the captain as lightly as if he were a child. Captain Daevin's head sagged against his shoulder. He looked weary and in need of rest.

"Goodbye, Captain!" Connor choked out. Ellie put her arm around her brother.

As the night sky paled to dawn, the crew of the *Legend* watched as the Alirya's powerful wings carried their captain off to his waiting city. There was not a dry eye among them. The blue speck that was Kiaran faded along with the morning stars, and still the friends stared into the sky until the clouds turned to sunrise gold.

Chapter 22
Blank Pages

Captain Daevin had given Jude back his life, but it took the doctor several days to recover his full strength. Ellie watched from a distance as he and Vivian took slow walks along the garden paths or sat on his lennai and talked quietly together.

Meanwhile, Ellie explored Amalpura as much as she could. She watched the brothers and sisters care for the lumenai, cultivating them to power Vestigian islands and ships. They let her touch one, teaching her to handle it by its soft, fleshy root system to avoid being shocked by the electrical currents flowing through its fronds.

Ellie also discovered the Haven's scriptorium. She got turned around in the complex of thatch cottages and walked into one, thinking it was the refectory where they took their meals. But once she was inside, she knew better. Under each of the windows encircling the large round room was a sloping desk. At some of the stations, brothers and sisters were copying words in graceful calligraphy; at others, they were punching holes for binding or stitching pages together. Wandering to the far end of the room, Ellie found the illuminators: a cluster of artists dipping quill pens into every color of ink Ellie could imagine. Fascinated, she noticed the ways they used different angles of their pen nibs or used different pressures to create a myriad of effects.

"Beautiful, isn't it?" said the illuminator beside her, without looking up. He had white hair and a drooping mustache, and was drawing a shape like a graceful teardrop. "Have you seen illuminations before?"

"Yes," said Ellie. "Never so many in one place, though. Vivian—our ship's librarian—was teaching me how to do it. I don't know if any of our books survived, though."

"There were a few," said the old man, getting up from his stool as spryly as a youth. "We found a pile untouched in the center of your ship, though I fear all the others were destroyed by the fire." He ran his finger over a lineup of books on a shelf. "Here they are."

Ellie started. These were the books she'd saved from the library! Her sketchbook was there, and at the end of the row was the Song Book. She lovingly brushed the spines with her fingertips, then lifted down the Book and opened the cover for the illuminator.

"This is what I was last working on. See?"

The illuminator bent down with his hands on his knees. Ellie saw the colors reflected in his spectacles.

"Well!" he exclaimed, rumpling his white hair. "Well, why aren't you studying here? Bother the Academy at Rhynlyr. This is talent. Here you could have all the training you want, and plenty of peace and quiet."

"I . . . I have to think about it," Ellie stammered, caught off guard.

"All right, think about it, think about it. Go to Rhynlyr if you must. But send a message to let me know when you're coming back. I'm Brother Reinholdt, head illuminator." He lowered his spectacles, and his eyes twinkled.

"Thank you," said Ellie. "I really do want to learn to be an illuminator."

"That, you already are," said the elderly brother, tapping the illuminated page she still held open. "No training can 'make' you anything. It can only bring to light the gift you already have."

One week later, Ellie and Jariel were in Vivian's cottage, helping each other dress as they had for the ball on the *Legend* so long ago. Jariel tugged on the laces of Vivian's simple white dress, and Ellie held a wreath of wild roses in her hands.

"Too tight, Jariel," Vivian gasped, laughing. "I'm too excited to breathe as it is."

"Here," said Ellie, hopping up on the bed. "Hold still—right—there." She straightened the wreath on Vivian's head and arranged some curls around her face. "You're perfect."

"I know someone else who thinks that, too," teased Jariel, an impish grin stealing over her face.

"You mischievous little—" Vivian whirled around and tickled Jariel, who collapsed on the floor, shrieking with laughter.

"You'd better hurry and get dressed," said Vivian when she stopped laughing. "It's almost time!"

Ellie pulled the plain white Haven robe over her shift and fastened a chain of daisies around the waist. Smoothing her hair, she checked her reflection in the mirror.

Her same clear, winter-blue eyes stared back at her. But no one could call them puddle-eyes now. They had seen adventure and battle. They were the eyes she shared with her twin brother. They were the eyes of an illuminator.

Vivian kissed the girls' foreheads and they left the cottage, Ellie and Jariel carrying Vivian's train. All the brothers and sisters of Amalpura stood aside for them, forming a path for them to walk through. As they reached the end, they saw Jude, his face lit up like a lumena, with Connor and Owen standing beside him. Ellie smiled. This was her family. Where they were, she was home.

And so Jude and Vivian were married in the sight of their crew, save for the departed captain. Elder Denparsi sang a few lines from the Song Book, and Jude and Vivian repeated them. Finally, the entire assembly sang them together:

Sure as the spring that follows winter

Stronger than oceans' mighty waves

Seas and seasons both shall splinter;

Love alone remains.

Everyone tossed a handful of white rose petals in the air, and as they drifted down, Jude and Vivian kissed. Owen made a face.

Then there was feasting in the refectory. The brothers and sisters brought forth the best produce of their gardens in celebration. There were chilled fruit puddings, dozens of sweet breads, and huge melons carved to look like flowers, birds, and ships. Ellie bit into what looked like a large grape, and juice exploded onto her nose.

When the feast was over, the Elder stood and motioned everyone outdoors.

"We have one more gift for you," he said.

Curiously, they followed him down to the shoreline. At the edge of the flying island, to their great surprise, floated the *Legend.* Its wing sails were whole again, and the sides had been almost completely rebuilt with sturdy new planks. The propellers whirred lazily with the power of a new lumena.

"Certain builders took the liberty of making some—ahem—improvements," Elder Denparsi explained. "Brothers Cyrret and Zelfmir turned one of the old dormitories into a greenhouse. Sister Alkeena thought of a skylight for the dining room, and Brother Reinholdt oversaw the construction of larger shelves for the library. I hope you don't mind their boldness."

"Mind?" Jude ran a hand through his hair.

"And we've stocked the kitchen with provisions to last until you reach Rhynlyr," said Sister Kuta.

"How can we ever thank you?" said Vivian.

"You have risked much and lost much for the Commander we all serve," said the Elder, bowing. "We have done but a small thing for our fellow Vestigians."

Vivian, Jude, Ellie, Jariel, Connor, and Owen all returned his bow.

As the evening sky faded into quiet blue and lilac, Ellie curled up in a woven chair, her sketchbook in her lap. Connor lay on his back, looking up at the stars. Tiny glass lanterns winked in the willow tree above them. Jariel was watching from somewhere in the branches.

Across the lawn, Owen, wearing a new pair of glasses, played a slow tune on his panpipes while Jude and Vivian danced. A few of the brothers and sisters lingered to watch. The pair rocked back and forth as if there were no one else in the world. A faint radiance clung to them.

Tomorrow they would set sail for Rhynlyr. Jude would captain the *Legend*, and he'd already asked Connor to be first mate. Vivian would start organizing the new library, and Ellie planned to start illuminating another page of the Song Book. She wanted to dedicate the illumination to Captain Daevin, and she already had some ideas.

Suddenly Connor heaved a sigh. Ellie looked at him.

"What's the matter?"

He shook his head. "Seven minutes."

Ellie frowned. "What are you talking about?"

Connor sighed again. "Kiaran said you're seven minutes older than me. It's not fair."

Ellie smiled and leaned back in the chair. "Hm, that's something you'll just have to get used to."

A giggle came from above them, and Jariel swung down, hanging by her knees. "She's right. Older sisters are always right."

Connor grumbled, and the girls laughed. Jariel climbed down to sit by Ellie.

When the panpipes went silent, Owen strolled over to join them. Jude and Vivian kept dancing obliviously. Their music was in their heads and their hearts.

"Wait 'til you see what I found." Owen produced a woven grass box. Inside, an enormous black beetle with yellow spots sat on a pile of woodchips. "I caught it in the garden this afternoon. It's the beginning of my new collection. When I show it to the teachers on Rhynlyr, maybe they'll let *me* teach class!"

The beetle waved its feelers in the air.

"That's . . . wonderful, Owen," said Ellie. "Just . . . make sure it stays in that box, all right?"

"What does it eat?" asked Jariel.

As Owen began to rattle off the facts about his new pet, Ellie opened her sketchbook. She flipped through her drawings of their journey so far: the Oratory, the black hole from the fallen island, her sketch of the first words of the Song Book. The pages were warped, frayed at the corners, and scorched in a few places from the battle. But more than half of them were still blank. What adventures would fill the rest?

Taking up her pencil, Ellie watched the faces around her. Jariel laughed, the freckles on her nose scrunching together. Owen straightened the earpiece of his glasses. Connor's cheek dimpled.

Humming softly, Ellie began to draw.

Epilogue
Rhynlyr

"Land ho!" came the cry from the rigging.

The illuminator and the librarian looked at each other. Ellie's hands were covered with blue ink, and Vivian had her arms full of loose papers. They both dropped what they were doing and bolted for the deck.

The red-haired lookout repeated the cry: "Laaand ho!"

The first mate, spyglass to his eye, was already at the railing with the captain and the entomologist. Together the crew of the *Legend* peered toward the misty horizon, straining for a glimpse of the home they had waited so long to see. Ellie's palms were sweaty with excitement, and she wiped them on the railing, leaving blue handprints.

"There it is!" she cried.

Towering spires pierced the mist, structures as old as the Vestigia Roi itself. A bright river sparkled in the sun. Green forests and meadows circled the city.

The crew let out a whoop of joy. The lookout turned cartwheels on the deck, and the entomologist held up his snake for a look. The captain kissed the librarian. Ellie hugged her brother.

"We're home," she whispered. "We're home."

Glossary

A

Academy, the: A school on Rhynlyr that trains future members of the Vestigia Roi.

Adabel: An orphan girl at the Sketpoole Home for Boys and Girls.

Adona Roi (uh-DOE-nah roh-EE): "The Good King"; the immortal and supernatural ruler of The One Kingdom.

Aletheia (ah-LEE-thee-ah): The known world, home to the Four Archipelagos. Its surface is covered with ocean and dotted with islands.

Alirya (ull-EER-yah): Supernatural winged beings, servants and messengers of Ishua and Adona Roi.

Allarants, Father (AL-ah-raunts): Vestigian and village almsgiver on Twyrild. He sheltered Owen Mardel after his parents' death and sent him to the Academy.

Alston, Ma (ALL-stun): Mother of Ellie's second adoptive family.

Alston, Pa: Father of Ellie's second adoptive family.

Alston, Robert: Infant brother in Ellie's second adoptive family.

Alston, Samanta (Sam): Ellie's close friend and sister in her second adoptive family.

Altess, Ellie (ALL-tess): A twelve-year-old orphan with a talent for drawing and a history of rejection by adoptive families.

Amalpura (ah-mall-PUR-ah): Southernmost of the Vestigian Havens.

Anadyr (ANN-ah-deer): Newdonian island; Jude Sterlen's home island.

Antal, Master (ANN-tall): a long-deceased Master at the Mundarva Library.

Antoth (ANN-toth): a long-dead language of Aletheia.

Arbuck (ARR-buck): a town in the west of Freith.

Arjun Mador (ARR-jen mah-DORE): One of the Four Archipelagos.

Asthmenos (ASTH-men-ows): A poison deadly to island-supporting coral. Its only antidote is caris powder.

Aton (AH-tawn): Fever-reducing plant.

B

Basilean (bah-sill-AY-en): Term of contempt for a member of the Vestigia Roi, coined by Governor Dorethel Hirx of Freith.

Beswick, Darling (BEZ-wick): Mother of Ellie's first adoptive family.

Beswick, Nevin (NEH-vinn): Father of Ellie's first adoptive family.

Black borrage root (BLACK BORE-udge ROOT): Antidote for helkath poison.

Blenrudd, Daevin (BLEN-rudd, DAY-vinn): Vestigian sailor and captain of the *Legend*.

Blethea (bleth-AY-ah): A smooth-skinned yellow fruit with a seedy, purple interior.

Bramborough: A Newdonian island.

C

Caris (CARE-iss): Powder made from the leaves of the stellaria tree, used to feed and restore coral sickened by asthmenos poison.

Chinelle (shi-NELL): Maid at the Sketpoole Home for Boys and Girls.

Cilla (SILL-ah): Currency unit of Freith.

Cloud trout: A type of fish native to clouds; common food source for Vestigian ship crews.

Cobal (COE-ball): A guard at the Mundarva Library.

Cooley, Ewart Horaffe Theodemir (COO-lee, YOO-art HOR-aff thee-AWE-deh-meer): Brother in Ellie's third adoptive family.

Cooley, Horaffe (HOR-aff): Father of Ellie's third adoptive family.

Cooley, Loretha (lore-EE-thuh): Mother of Ellie's third adoptive family.

Cygnera (sig-NER-ah): Swan-like bird; figurehead of the *Legend.*

D

Denparsi (denn-PAR-see): Elder at the Vestigian Haven at Amalpura.

Draaken (DRAY-ken): "The Enemy," the supernatural being served by believers in Khum Lagor. Alleged to occasionally take physical form as a great sea serpent.

Drunyl (DROO-nill): A large bird with ostentatious feathers often used for millinery.

E

Edge, the: The boundary of Aletheia, where the waterfall at the rim of the world flows upward. The ultimate fate of islands that break free from their coral trees. None who go over it ever return.

Edrei, Vivian (ED-rye): Scholar at the Mundarva Library, specializing in Languages and Linguistics.

Elbarra Cluster (ell-BAR-ah): The lost Fifth Archipelago of Aletheia, destroyed by asthmenos.

***Endeavor*:** A Vestigian ship.

Eyret (EYE-ret): Heron-like messenger bird used by the Vestigia Roi.

Elgin, Master (ELL-jinn): Master at the Mundarva Library.

Freith (FREETH): Newdonian island; Ellie's home island.

G

Galen, Sylvia (GAY-len): A Vestigian agent and keeper of the Sketpoole Home for Boys and Girls.

Gartz (GARTZZ): Captain of the Vestigian ship *Endeavor.*

Guduk: A language of Aletheia.

H

Harwell (HAR-well): A city on the island of Freith.

Havens: Vestigian flying islands; outposts of refuge and sources of lumenai for the One Kingdom.

Helkath (HELL-kath): Creatures of Draaken whose bites cause a loss of hope in their victims.

Hirx, Dorethel (HURCKS, DORE-eth-ell): Governor of Freith, coiner of the term Basilean, and opponent of the Vestigian work on Freith.

Howditch (HOW-ditch): Keeper of the Liaflora County Orphanage.

I

Ishua (ISH-oo-ah): Son of Adona Roi, Commander of the Winged Armies, bringer of caris to the islands, and founder of the Vestigia Roi.

J

Jardon (JAR-dun): An orphan boy at the Sketpoole Home for Boys and Girls.

K

Kaspar (KASS-par): Early Lagorite, servant of Draaken, deceiver of Thelipsa, and first known source of asthmenos.

Khum Lagor (KOOM la-GORE): The ultimate goal of all Lagorites,: to subjugate or destroy all land-walkers until the whole world serves Draaken.

Kiaran (kee-ARR-un): One of the Alirya; winged messenger of Ishua and Adona Roi.

Kirke, Jariel (KIRK, jare-ee-ELL): Twelve-year-old orphan girl; Ellie's first friend at the Sketpoole Home for Boys and Girls.

Knerusse (neh-ROOS): A long-dead language of Aletheia.

Kuta (KOO-tah): Sister at the Vestigian Haven at Amalpura.

Kyuler (KYOO-lurr): Errand boy for the Sketpoole Home for Boys and Girls.

L

Lagorites (LAH-gore-ites): Followers of Draaken and believers in Khum Lagor.

Legend: a Vestigian transport ship captained by Daevin Blenrudd.

Lennai: Porch of an Amalpuran cottage.

Liaflora (lee-ah-FLORE-uh): A county of Freith.

Lumena (LOO-men-ah)(sing.)/**lumenai** (LOO-men-eye)(pl.): Water ferns whose fronds carry electrical current. Cultivated at the Havens, they are transported to Rhynlyr to power Vestigian flying ships and islands.

M

Manul (mah-NOOL): The Vestigian agent on Mundarva.

Mardel, Owen (MAR-dell): A nine-year-old orphan boy aboard the *Legend* with an interest in entomology.

Markos (MAR-kose): former lookout and navigator aboard the *Legend*.

Matshoff, Silas: Owner of a wool mill in Freith.

Meriaten (merry-AH-ten): A tree with large, distinctive leaves colored with gradations of yellow, orange, and red.

Moby: A Mundarvan bluestripe ribbon snake owned by Owen Mardel.

Mundarva (mun-DARR-vuh): An island from the south of Newdonia; a renowned center of learning and home of the Mundarva Library.

N

Newdonia (noo-DOE-nee-ah): One of the Four Archipelagos.

Niara (nee-ARR-ah): An orphan girl at the Sketpoole Home for Boys and Girls.

Nikira (ni-KEER-ah): A high-ranking Lagorite and servant of Draaken.

Numed Archipelago (NOO-med): One of the Four Archipelagos.

Nuthers, Miss: Ellie's schoolteacher in Liaflora.

O

One Kingdom, the: The original state of Aletheia; all the archipelagos unified under the governance of Adona Roi. Its restoration is the goal of the Vestigia Roi.

Orkent Isles (OR-kent): One of the Four Archipelagos.

R

Regents: Caretakers of the islands appointed by Adona Roi. Some, however, became hungry for more power, leading to revolts like Thelipsa's Rebellion.

Reid, Gavin: A Vestigian agent.

Reid, Kiria: A Vestigian agent.

Reinholdt (RINE-holt): Brother and head illuminator at the Vestigian Haven at Amalpura.

Rhynlyr (RINN-leer): Headquarters of the Vestigia Roi; the largest and most central flying island. Also home to the Academy.

Rilia (RILL-ee-ah): Plants commonly known as "falling stars." Its berries are used for relief of stomach pain.

S

Sai (SIGH): Long, slender daggers.

Saklos (SACK-lows): Largest village on the island of Mundarva.

Scorpionflies: Creatures of Draaken whose stings cause temporary, localized paralysis.

Sketpoole (SKET-pool): A coastal city on Freith.

Song, the: The powerful, never-ending melody used by Adona Roi to create life and sustain the universe. Also the anthem of the Vestigia Roi.

Stellaria (stell-AH-ree-ah): Tree native to the City of Adona Roi, transplanted to Rhynlyr by Ishua. Its leaves are used to make caris powder.

Sterlen, Jude (STIR-lenn, JOOD): Vestigian sailor and physician, gardener, and carpenter aboard the *Legend*.

Suor (soo-OR): An island in the south of Arjun Mador.

T

Tehber (teh-BARE): A dead language of Aletheia.

Tera: A prize tarantula owned by Owen Mardel.

Thelipsa (thell-IPS-uh): Regent and later queen of Vansuil, instigator of Thelipsa's Rebellion, and destroyer of the Elbarra Cluster.

Thelipsa's Rebellion: The first large-scale show of disloyalty to the One Kingdom. Thelipsa gave in to Lagorite advice and used asthmenos to break up the Elbarra Cluster.

Twyrild (TWEER-illd): A Newdonian island; Owen Mardel's home island.

U

Urken (URR-ken): Creatures of Draaken; souls plundered from falling islands and attached to unnatural bodies. Armies of them are not often seen, but are dangerous enemies.

V

Vahye (VA-yay): An island in Arjun Mador; Vivian's home island.

Vansuil (VAHN-soo-ill): Island governed by Thelipsa in the lost Elbarra Cluster.

Varian (VARE-ee-an): A guard at the Mundarva Library.

Vestigia Roi (ves-TI-jee-ah roh-EE): A secret organization whose goal is to restore the One Kingdom. They use land-based agents as well as flying ships and islands to undo the effects of asthmenos and rescue people from falling islands. Members are known as Vestigians or Basileans.

Vestigian (ves-TI-jee-an): A member of the Vestigia Roi.

W

Wark: a Scholar at the Mundarva Library.

Wynn, Connor: A twelve-year-old orphan boy aboard the *Legend* with an interest in navigation.

Y

Yrania (yur-AY-nee-ah): Hardy flowers that grow aboard the *Legend*.

Z

Zarifah (zarr-EE-fah): A passenger aboard the *Endeavor*, rescued from the island of Suor.

About The Author

Alina Sayre cut her teeth chewing on board books and has been in love with words ever since. Her favorite stories are the ones that blend adventure, faith, and big words. In addition to writing, she enjoys hiking, photography, crazy socks, and the smell of old books. She does not enjoy algebra or wasabi. When she grows up, she would like to live in a castle with a library.

Website: alinasayre.com

E-mail: alinasayreauthor@gmail.com

Facebook: www.facebook.com/alinasayreauthor

Twitter: @AlinaSayre

About the Illustrator

Amalia Hillmann isn't a brilliant writer, so her bio might sound dull. But her adventures in color, traveling, and dusty books are anything but boring! She can often be found with pencils in her hair, sketching or critiquing menus and posters. When she grows up, Amalia would like to be taller, please.

Website: theeclecticillustrator.com